JULIANA STONE

Cover design by John Kicksee/The July Group
Cover photography by Jon Zychowski
Cover models: Jillian Warmbir and Austin Zenere

Published by Sourcebooks Casablanca, an imprint of Sourcebooks, Inc.
P.O. Box 4410, Naperville, Illinois 60567-4410
(630) 961-3900
Fax: (630) 961-2168
www.sourcebooks.com

Printed and bound in the United States of America.
VP 10 9 8 7 6 5 4 3 2 1

To all those I call my family,
and you know who you are,
I love you…

Chapter 1

Mackenzie Draper woke up with a throbbing head, a dry mouth, and an ache in his neck that hurt like hell.

Vague memories of the Coach House, his buddies Cain and Jake, some loud, crazy band, and a bottle of tequila floated in his mind.

Or maybe it was two bottles of tequila.

Not that it mattered. Mac was sporting the worst hangover ever, and even though it had nothing to do with Crystal Lake—and everything to do with his weakness for tequila—his first thought was that he shouldn't have come home.

Things never went well when he came back to Crystal Lake, and after all this time—and with his bastard father in jail—it was still hard.

With a groan, Mac rolled out of bed and wondered why the hell he did it.

It was late morning, Friday of the Memorial Day long weekend, and Mac had arrived home the night before, hence the catching up with his buddies and the endless shots of tequila.

Damn. He knew better. Tequila always knocked him on his ass.

His nose wrinkled. He smelled like a brewery and was still in his clothes from the night before—he was pretty damn sure he looked like crap. Mac stumbled down the hall, wincing and cursing when he stubbed his toe on an uneven floorboard.

He ran fingers over the two-day-old stubble on his chin, rolled his shoulders, and groaned. The muscles were tight, but then again, everything was tight and sore.

With a scowl, he glanced back toward his room. Damn mattress. He was used to sleeping on the king-sized dream at his place in New York City, not the IKEA crap from his teen years.

"Shit," he murmured, wincing again as his neck creaked. There was a time when the floor between the Edwards twins' beds had been good enough for him. Hell, he'd spent many a night sleeping there when things got out of hand at home.

God, is this what it felt like to be old?

The family homestead was a modest bungalow with three bedrooms, a kitchen, a small dining room, and a TV room finishing off the main floor. The place hadn't seen a fresh coat of paint in years, and the wallpaper in the hall was curling in the corners. The roof needed done and if the windows weren't replaced soon, the frames would rot.

It was a mess, and he doubted the additional three bedrooms in the basement or the small recreational room was faring any better.

When he was a kid, he spent most of his time down there—anything to avoid his father, or rather, his father's fists. Back then, the house had seemed so damn small—so damn suffocating—it was hard to believe that anything could grow or thrive inside the four walls that made up the Draper residence.

No wonder he escaped as much as he could. Hanging

with the Edwards twins and Cain Black had been his salvation.

He glanced around the house, feeling as tired as it looked.

With only his mother puttering about, the place seemed empty and quiet. Too quiet. Mac needed noise, the hustle and bustle of the city, the sounds of people, music, and cabs.

He needed noise to shut out the quiet moments, because when it was quiet, it was way too easy to think and remember. And Mac didn't want to remember.

He wasn't alone in that sentiment. His five siblings were gone. They'd all left as soon as they could, and other than his younger sister, Becca, he was the only one who came home to visit. The long distance thing seemed to work for everyone else.

Mac paused and leaned against the door frame that led to the kitchen, watching his mother roll out dough. She wore simple clothes—a white cotton blouse, with faded blue and red roses, tucked into plain white shorts that fell exactly one inch above the knee. The colors had faded, but they were clean and pressed, with no creases.

Her long hair, as blond as Mac's and showing no sign of gray, was knotted loosely at her nape. She was petite—trim—and from this angle, she looked exactly like the mother he remembered from his youth. It wasn't until she glanced up and he caught sight of the sadness in her eyes, the wrinkles of worry etched into her brow, that he saw her age.

Age and heartache that had been put there by his father.

Just thinking of Ben Draper made Mac's gut clench, and it took some effort for him to ease out of the anger that ate at him. He breathed in and out, nice and easy-like, and managed a half-assed smile for his mother.

She smiled back, but it quickly faded when her eyes narrowed and she pursed her lips. She continued to roll her dough.

"Late night, Mackenzie?" There was disapproval in her voice and, dammit, even after all this time—he was thirty-five for Christ's sake—he felt like that kid who'd just got caught with his hand in the cookie jar.

Her husband was a mean drunk, and he got that she didn't like Mac overindulging, but still…it was kind of ironic that she would call him out for having a bit too much tequila when she never said a word to Ben.

Mind you, if she did, she'd see the back of Ben's hand, but there must have been a point in their relationship when she could have stopped him.

Heat swirled in his gut as a bunch of memories ran through him and none of them were good. Jesus, he needed to shut this shit down right now. There was no point in rehashing the past. He shoved it all aside and crossed to the fridge, grabbing a carton of juice.

"Is that for the Edwardses'?" he asked.

He poured himself a large glass and turned around to lean against the kitchen counter, his gaze on his mother as she methodically kneaded the dough.

"Yes. I'm making a raspberry pie for you to take when you go."

He waited a few seconds. He'd spent every Friday before Memorial Day at the Edwardses' for their annual friends and family barbecue. He always asked his mother to join him.

"So, you're not coming with me." It was a statement, because he already knew the answer.

She continued kneading the dough, her movements slow and precise. "No, honey. I've got more baking to do for the church bazaar, and I promised Mrs. Linden that I'd help her clean her house." She glanced up, though her smile didn't quite reach her eyes. "She's getting on and needs an extra set of hands. I've been helping her out ever since Maggie left town."

Mackenzie knew better than to press the issue. His mother wouldn't come.

Once, long before he was born, Lila McCann had run in the same social circles as the Edwardses. In fact, she'd dated Steven Edwards briefly…then Ben Draper had come into the picture and Lila's life took a turn.

A wrong turn. A wrong fucking *U-turn* away from anything good that she'd ever had.

Her parents had stood by her—even when she'd become pregnant with Mac's older brother, Benjamin Jr.—and had footed the bill for an extravagant wedding. His grandparents had died in a car accident about a month before Benjamin was born, and Mac had never met them.

His great-grandmother, however, was a bright light in an otherwise bleak childhood. It was only because of Grams that any of the kids went to college, and it was only because of Grams that the roof over their head stayed in their hands and not the bank's. His great-grandmother was nearing her ninetieth year and still right as rain.

He didn't want to consider what would have happened to the Draper kids if not for her.

Ben Draper used his looks and charm to get by, but he'd never quite managed to hold down a regular job. The booze always got in the way.

Like it had on a hot summer night when Mackenzie was about nine. That night, Mac had cowered in his room, afraid to go out and face his father but afraid that Ben was going to kill his mother. He'd called Jake Edwards, and less than twenty minutes later, the police and Steven had shown up.

That was Ben Draper's first trip to county lockup, and it signaled the end of his mother's relationship with her old crowd, including the Edwardses.

And now here he was, staring at a woman who could have had it all and yet she stood in the kitchen, dressed in secondhand clothes, kneading dough for a party that she would not attend.

"I ran into Raine Edwards the other day," she said quietly. "At the grocery store. She looks good. Happy."

"Yeah?" Mac drained his glass and rinsed it out. Raine was with one of his oldest buddies, Jake Edwards, and he was a lucky son of a bitch to have her. Even though Mac would never have what his friends did, that didn't make him any less happy that they'd finally found each other.

"I wouldn't be surprised if she turns up pregnant real soon."

Here we go.

"Nice, for Steven and Marnie to finally have a grandchild," his mother continued.

Mac nodded. "I'm sure it would make them real happy."

He waited for the questions that were headed his way. The usual ones.

Have you met someone?

When are you going to settle down and have a family?

I'd sure like to hold another grandchild before I get too old.

He hated disappointing his mother, but family—a wife, kids, and the white-picket fence—just wasn't in the cards for him. He and kids didn't mix, and besides, there was no need to pass along the family genetics.

He thought of his father and Ben's father before him. Nope. No need at all.

He was smart enough to know that it wouldn't take much for him to cross the line into Ben Draper territory.

Hell, it was only a matter of time. He knew that on occasion he drank too much, and he sure as shit wanted no responsibility other than his job, but he was willing to straddle the line. He had more control than Ben, and for now, it was enough.

But his mother surprised him. She bypassed talk of grandkids and a wife and hit him with something he wasn't expecting.

"Raine told me that Jake wants you to help him out with the new development across the lake."

Shit. He'd rather take her ribbing over his lack of commitment and family than talk about this. Did he want to get into it right now?

"It's been mentioned," he said slowly. No way was he spending the summer in Crystal Lake.

"I think it would be wonderful for the town if you and Jake worked together on this. A lot of folks aren't exactly keen on more construction, but Jake's promised it will benefit everyone." Lila turned over the dough. "How would that work with your job?"

Mac was at a point in his career where he could pretty much make anything work, but that didn't mean he wanted this particular situation to evolve into something solid. "I've got time in the bank, but…"

"But?"

"I don't think it's going to happen."

For a moment there was silence.

He watched her continue to knead the dough with her fingers and knuckles as he moved closer to her.

"It sure would be nice to have you home for the summer."

"Mom," he said gently. "Crystal Lake and I don't exactly mix." Weak excuse, but it was all he had.

"Your father won't be around."

There it was. The big old elephant in the room.

Mac didn't know any details about his father's incarceration other than the fact that he'd been caught stealing from his job—something he'd done before—and his ass had landed in jail.

Her bottom lip trembled for just a moment, but Mac saw it and his jaw clamped tight as that damn wave of emotion rolled over him again.

Her hands paused on top of the dough. "I miss you, Mackenzie. I know it's not your job to look after your mom, but I just…" She released a long, shuddering breath. "I hate being alone. Grams is getting on, and pretty soon there will be no one."

He slipped his arms around her shoulders and hugged her, the bottom of his chin resting on the top of her head. "I know," he said simply. "Though I'm pretty sure that Grams will outlive us all."

Except him.

His mother's bottom lip curved. "She's certainly is a strong old lady. I wish I'd gotten some of that backbone."

Mackenzie didn't know what to say to that—mostly because it was something he'd thought of a lot when he was younger.

"So...you'll think about it?" she whispered, her hands already working the dough again, his arms still on her shoulders.

Mac gazed out the window, his eyes resting on the fence that bordered their lot. A few sections were missing and though it had been light green at one time, the color had long since faded and the bits that remained were chipped and peeling.

It needed mending. Hell, the entire house needed a damn face-lift.

He felt the warmth from his mother, the frailty in her bones and spirit.

"Mac?" she asked softly, and though she tried to hide it, he heard the hope in her voice.

"I'll think about it," he answered, not knowing what he was going to do. He hated this place, not the town so much, but *this* place. This house. This situation. The toxic relationship between him and his father.

He hated the memories and the need he still felt for his mother to somehow make things right. She'd never stand up to his old man. Never.

A heartbeat passed.

"Okay," Lila Draper murmured. "Okay."

Chapter 2

ONE-NIGHT STANDS ARE NOTORIOUS FOR BITING A GIRL in the ass.

It's one of the first things a smart girl learns when she's younger. One of the first things that said smart girl vows never to do again.

But sometimes fate or stupidity intervenes and those life lessons are forgotten in the heat of the moment—life lessons that are there for a reason. And a smart girl is faced with the uncomfortable situation that arises when your one-night stand—the one-night stand you were hoping never to see again—suddenly pops up on your radar.

As of five minutes ago, Lily St. Clare's one-night stand was back in town, and as of five minutes ago, Lily St. Clare's ass was in danger of being bitten.

"You've got to be kidding me," she muttered, ducking behind a large fern tilted at an odd angle from the wind as it swung from the pergola overhead. She was on the back deck at Steven and Marnie Edwards's place, the one that overlooked Crystal Lake, and there were a few other ferns swinging in the wind if she needed them.

I knew this would happen.

Just not today. Not without warning. And definitely not with such an intimate crowd to witness the entire god-awful thing. Awkward situations were always worse in close quarters. And Lily hated awkward almost as much as she hated a scene—unless it was one that she orchestrated.

And Lord knows she'd orchestrated a few whoppers in her day, but this was different.

A quick glance over her shoulder told Lily that no one had witnessed her idiotic attempt to hide herself, but with Mac Draper making his way across the beach, that would soon change.

Her stomach rolled at the thought and the usually cool-as-a-cucumber blond let out a jagged breath. What the hell was she going to do?

It was Memorial Day weekend and everyone was home. All the Bad Boys. Cain Black had already hopped over the railing and was making his way down toward the beach where Mac stood chatting up Cain's wife, Maggie. Heavy with their first child, the redhead looked beautiful in a simple cream sundress, her long hair floating in the breeze.

Lily watched from behind her fern, a lump in her throat, as Cain's hand slid around Maggie's waist and settled on her stomach. Maggie leaned into her husband, their bodies melted together, and it was hard to see where one person ended and the other began. They looked content and happy and in love—three things Lily was pretty damn sure she'd never be.

She glanced to her right, over to her best friend Jake Edwards, who sat on a low-slung settee with the love of his life, Raine, across his lap. The two of them were talking quietly, intimately, Raine's hands in Jake's hair as she bent forward to kiss him. The knot in her throat tightened even more. If ever she felt like a third wheel, now was the time.

She should never have come. She didn't do family. She just didn't.

So why was she here?

Oh. Right.

She was that pathetic woman on the fringe who was invited to these sorts of things because she had no one else. No friends other than those gathered on this deck and no family close by—though that was by choice.

Lily had learned a long time ago that you couldn't pick your family. She knew that blood didn't always mean easy and happy, or even wanted—and it sure as hell didn't mean love.

In the St. Clare household, the mantra had always been sink or swim, and Lily had swum as far away as she could, as soon as she could.

Now here she was, settled in Crystal Lake since January, about to revisit the night she'd lost control, which was something she hadn't done in years.

"Shit," she muttered.

She was pretty sure Mac Draper never thought he would see her again. Hell, he hadn't asked for a name and she'd never provided one. That night hadn't been about getting to know each other. It had been strictly a physical reaction—a need to be with someone, to matter to someone even if only for a night.

She shook her head. Who was she kidding?

She'd been drunk and lonely, and the mysterious hot guy in the cab had scratched an itch that needed scratching. It was nothing more.

Lily hadn't found out his name until she moved into Raine's stone cottage—the same place Mac had taken her to New Year's Eve—and seen photos of the guy.

While she'd stared at the pictures of a younger-looking man with Cain, Jake, Raine, and the deceased Jesse, she'd listened to Jake ramble on about the Bad Boys.

Lily should have packed up then and left town. But she hadn't and now…

God, the thought of facing Mackenzie, here, with his friends… With Jake looking on? Steven and Marnie? Ugh, no.

It was time for this third wheel to roll the hell along.

Ignoring her hot cheeks, she turned quickly, her only thought to get as far away from Mac Draper as she could. She had a plan. She'd hide out at the cottage until he left town. From what little she knew about him, he wasn't close to his family and he had some fancy job in New York City. He was most likely only home for the holiday anyway.

Okay. This was good. This would work.

"Lily, are you alright?"

Her head snapped up and she attempted a smile as Marnie Edwards walked toward her, a cocktail in her hand, a gentle smile on her face. As always, her heart warmed when she saw the woman. It was then that she realized why she'd come. As much as she didn't do family, there was something about the Edwardses that made her feel wanted.

They were good people. Everything her family was not.

"I'm fine," Lily said quickly. "I just…I feel kind of sick to my stomach." She rubbed her belly for good measure.

"Oh my," Marnie said with concern. "I hope it wasn't the shrimp."

"The what?"

Damn. She heard Cain's voice, and it sounded a hell of a lot closer than it did a minute before. They were heading this way. She tried to sidestep Marnie, but the woman looked really worried and wouldn't budge.

"The shrimp cocktail? Did you have any of it?"

The shrimp.

"Oh." Lily cleared her throat. "I might have had one, but I'm sure that's not it. I wasn't feeling one hundred percent this morning, and I probably should have stayed home. I think I'm coming down with something."

She coughed for good measure, but only managed to draw looks from Jake and Raine—and from Steven as he walked outside from in the house.

"Christ, Lily. You sound like a damn cat with a hairball," Jake said.

"I think I'm going to have to leave," Lily stated, ignoring Jake. She couldn't look at him because he knew her well enough to know she was bullshitting. He'd know something was up.

Lily inched forward and then froze when she heard that voice. That deep, husky voice with a touch of sandpaper that sounded as if every word was soaked in sin.

That voice she hadn't forgotten.

She clenched her hands so tightly that her nails dug into her palms. Hard.

What. The. Hell.

"I've really got to go, Marnie."

Her stomach rolled so badly, she'd broken out in a sweat, and Lily thought she really was going to be sick.

Footsteps on the stairs below made her jump, and she gave Marnie a quick hug, still ignoring Jake as she quickly crossed the deck and tried to smile at Steven Edwards.

"I'm so sorry. I really need to get home. I just…I don't feel well." God, she was overdoing it. She gulped in some air. "I hope you understand." The words came out in a jumbled mess, but Steven nodded and moved aside so she could escape into the house.

"Hey! Lily! What's going on?" Jake's question hung in the air.

Cain and Maggie were on the deck now, and her panic was such that for a moment Lily couldn't breathe. She didn't glance back, and with her hand on the sliding glass doors, she spoke.

"I have to go home, Jake. I'll call you later."

She pushed her way into the house and ran across the smooth stone tiles until she reached the front door. She yanked it open, slammed it shut behind her, and then rested against it for a moment.

Her entire body shook and she let out a high-pitched giggle that wouldn't be out of place in the local loony bin. Feeling a bit light-headed, Lily smoothed the front of her pale-blue J. Mendel halter dress and pushed off from the door, her white Fendi flats making no sound as she crossed the porch and took the steps down.

Newly planted pink and purple petunias lined the walkway and followed the driveway down to the road. The lawn—thick and luxurious—had been freshly mown for the first time that morning and the smell of the grass clippings reminded her of summer. Normally she'd take a moment and enjoy it but not today. Nope.

The voices from out back echoed in her ear, and she picked up the pace, hurrying toward her car. Just before she reached her vehicle, she slid to a stop and swore—she swore like a trucker who'd just spent the last two weeks in confession.

Damn. Was nothing going to go right today?

"You've got to be kidding me."

Her BMW was parked behind Cain's truck, which in turn was parked behind his father's car. A car that normally would have been in the garage, but for some reason it wasn't, and there was no way for her to drive forward and turn around because of it.

She couldn't back out of the driveway either.

"Son of a bitch."

There was a sleek, sliver Mercedes behind her car and no room to maneuver around the damn thing. The idiot driver had pulled up much too close to her bumper.

She had a feeling she knew who the idiot driver was.

She stood there with her keys in her hand, chewing on her bottom lip as she glanced at the Edwardses' beautiful front lawn. The ground was still soft from the winter thaw and all the rain they'd had lately, so it was insane to even consider it, but dammit, she had no choice.

Lily gulped in a huge shaky breath, panicking when she heard Jake's voice from out back, and she shot forward, keys jangling in her fingers as she struggled to press the unlock button on the fob.

She would do it. She would drive across Steven's lovely grass and to hell with the consequence. She'd pay whatever it cost to fix the damage and hope they didn't think she was a nut bar, which she was kinda acting like.

Pushing her long, blond hair out of the way, Lily fingered her key fob and let rip another round of swearing as the damn thing slipped out of her hands and landed underneath her car.

"Oh. My. God."

She took a step back and peered beneath the vehicle. The fob was just out of reach and Lily knew she was going to have to get on her knees to grab it. On her knees. In this dress.

Her favorite J. Mendel dress.

Quickly she snuck a glance behind her and then got down to business—no, scratch that, she got down on all fours like a dog and had to lean way over in order to get to the stupid thing. By the time her fingers closed around the small black fob, she was out of breath, pissed off, and her knees hurt like hell because they dug into the concrete.

She inched her way backward and…

"Sorry, I didn't mean to box you in."

His voice came from nowhere. Well, actually that was wrong. He was right behind her and she was on all fours with her ass stuck in the air.

Jesus H. Christ.

Her eyes squeezed shut. She took a moment.

"Uh, are you okay?" he asked.

And then she took another moment.

"Jake said you needed to leave, so I'll just move my car onto the road and you can back out."

She nodded, lips tight, eyes still squeezed shut.

She heard his shoe scuff against the concrete, but then it stopped. Why did he stop? Why wasn't he moving away from her? Everything inside Lily was wound so tight she felt as if she was going to explode.

"Are you sure you're—"

"Will you just leave already?" she snapped. She sank

back onto her haunches, shoulders rigid, jaw clenched so tight it was painful. Hair blew across her face, and she yanked it away, tucked it behind her ear, and wished that she could just disappear.

"Sure thing, sweet cakes."

Sweet cakes? Really?

She let out a weak breath and waited.

And waited some more.

"I don't have all day," she muttered.

"What was that?"

He was playing with her. She heard it in his voice.

"I said I don't have all day, so if you could please move your car, I'd appreciate it."

Mackenzie Draper moved alright—he moved closer to her instead of toward his vehicle. He was so close that his scent drifted over her. In her. He was all kinds of sexy musk, clean soap, and something that was entirely unique to him. Some intangible secret ingredient that her body picked up on.

It was annoying as hell.

What the heck was he playing at? Flush with anger now, Lily slowly got to her feet, though she was careful not to turn toward him.

"Where are you from?" he asked, his voice dangerously low.

"Does it matter?"

"Not really."

"Then why do you care?"

"I don't."

"Then why are you still here?" She managed to say through gritted teeth. Her Boston accent was more pronounced when she was pissed, so Lily was willing to bet he'd have no problem figuring it out on his own.

"I'll go when you turn around so that I can see if the front of you is as hot as the back end. 'Cause the back end is smokin'."

"That's incredibly sexist."

"I know," he said softly.

For a heartbeat there was nothing but the warm breeze in her hair.

And then he spoke. "Boston."

She froze and blinked away an image of Mackenzie behind her, *inside her*, his hands on her hips, his breath at her neck. His strangled whisper, "Boston" as he came. That's what he had called her that night.

Boston.

Shit.

Slowly, Lily turned around and sucked in a breath at their close proximity. If ever a man was made in the image of a God, it was Mackenzie Draper.

He was dressed casually in a pair of worn jeans, bare feet shoved into Birkenstocks, and a plain white T-shirt stretched tight across his chest. His blond hair was brushed back off his face, waving almost to his shoulders, while his electric-green eyes bored into her with an intensity that made Lily a tad uncomfortable. There was something wholly alpha in that look.

He hadn't shaved in a few days, and the dark stubble on his jaw only made him look sexier. His mouth curved into a slow grin, and *Jesus*, her nipples went hard.

Lily crossed her arms over her chest and glared at him. She glared at him and didn't budge when he moved so close that she could count his eyelashes, when he moved so close that that damn secret ingredient of his—the one that made her weak—was all up in her business. Christ, if he could bottle it, he'd be a billionaire.

The pulse at the base of his neck moved rapidly and she knew he was as affected by their close proximity as she was.

"So," he said slowly, rolling out the word as if it was a secret. "That phone number you gave me was bogus."

She considered not answering him, but something about his attitude pissed her off.

"Oops." She thrust her chin forward. "Didn't think you'd actually call."

He bent forward and Lily held her breath as his mouth settled just below her ear, a whisper away from her skin.

"I called as soon as I woke up. I wasn't happy that you were gone."

She swallowed thickly, aware that the air was supercharged with something and it was that something that had her worried. She'd never been so physically affected by a man, and it scared her because it told her that she was close to losing control again. Just like she'd done New Year's Eve.

With him.

Over and over again.

And control was something she wasn't going to give up easily. She'd worked too hard for it. Come too far.

"Really," she managed to say, refusing to back down. "Why?"

His mouth grazed over her skin, and she shuddered as he blew hot air across her ear before tugging on her lobe. He didn't answer right away. He took a moment and let the tension drag out before he cupped her chin and forced her to look up at him. Forced her to look up into eyes that smoldered.

Eyes that make her weak, and weak wasn't something she was interested in. Yet that control thing was vanishing like water down the drain, and for the first time, Lily felt a stab of fear.

"Boston," he said, his voice low and intimate. "I wanted to talk because we weren't finished." He let that settle. "We were far from finished."

Chapter 3

Mac rolled out of bed at the crack of dawn tired, pissed off, and horny as hell.

He'd barely slept, which explained his grumpy mood, but there was nothing he could do about that. And as for the other situation—he glanced down at his aching dick—a hot shower and a handful of conditioner should just about do it.

Christ. What the hell was wrong with him? It was as if time rolled back and he was seventeen all over again.

He thought of Boston and scowled.

She'd blown him off like yesterday's news.

She'd politely asked him to take his hands off of her—which he did—and then she'd told him to move his "fucking" car or she was going to drive her BMW across Steven Edwards's lawn.

Something in her eyes told him that she would do it too.

What the hell? Everyone knew that Steven Edwards was anal about his grass, and the fact that she was willing to drive across it told Mac just how badly she wanted to get away from him.

That's what stuck in his craw this morning. He wasn't being an asshole, but shit, he'd never had a woman bail on him like that. He was the one who left. The one who made the rules. The one who didn't want a commitment.

Christ, even he'd never done an escape in the middle

of the night. There'd never been the need because he had always been clear on the rules. He was up-front about that shit.

Mackenzie stared at his reflection in the mirror as he turned on the shower. He was a good-looking guy, there was no way around it, but he was more than just a pretty face. In fact, his looks were the least interesting thing about him as far as he was concerned, mostly because he was the spitting image of his father.

He was so much more than the bastard had ever been. Mac was smart, graduated with honors, and was on track to become a partner at the architectural firm he worked for in New York City. He was driven, dedicated, and when it came to the ladies, he was candid and honest.

He showed them a good time between the sheets and out of them, but when it came to anything else, he wasn't signing up for it.

So what was it about this Lily that had his interest?

She was gorgeous, but she wasn't his usual cup of tea. He'd always been attracted to leggy, athletic, brunettes—Lily was curvy and blond. Which was why New Year's Eve had been such a surprise. She'd opened up that cab door and something in her eyes got to him.

It had been instant. Hot.

Their connection had been undeniable, and that night had been one he'd thought of a lot over the last few months. Never had he been with a woman who'd responded so…naturally to him, without any reservations at all. It had been as if she'd known what he was going to do before he did.

The hot water sprayed over his head and did nothing to temper the ache in his groin or the fantasies that played out in his head. He hadn't said a word to Jake the day before even though he'd been dying to know her story—he'd just listened to a few casual conversations. He knew that Lily was a St. Clare, of the Boston St. Clares, and that she was a close friend of Jake's.

But that's all he knew because he refused to dig deeper and ask the questions he wanted answers to. He had no idea why she was in Crystal Lake or what her deal was. He only knew that she wanted nothing to do with him and she was obviously embarrassed that they'd spent the night together.

Subsequently, Mac's mood didn't improve a bit, and he was still pissed off when he arrived back at the Edwardses' an hour after he'd rolled his ass out of bed.

It was Saturday of the long weekend, and they were taking the boat out to Pot-a-hock Island—Jake, Raine, Mac, Cain, and Maggie—another annual tradition, and with the sun shining high in the sky, it promised to be a great day. It was nothing more than a big party with hundreds of boats heading out to the island. There would be music and good times and fireworks.

Usually Mac looked forward to catching up with old friends—especially those of the female persuasion. Hell, he'd already had more than a dozen text messages from a few of them. But this year?

This year, things just didn't feel the same, and he couldn't put his finger on what exactly had changed.

Mac strode across the dock and spied Jake and Raine near the boat, anchored a few feet away. The two of them melted into each other as if they were one person, Jake's hand buried in Raine's hair as his other palm cupped her butt intimately. Mac glanced away, feeling as if he were witnessing something he had no right to see, a private moment between two of his best friends—two of his best friends who were now together.

Shit, was that it?

Sometimes he felt as if he was spinning his wheels when everyone else was moving forward. Cain had Maggie and a baby on the way. Raine and Jake had finally moved past all the bullshit and gotten together.

And Mac…

He shoved his hands through his hair and rolled his shoulders, clearing his throat so the two lovebirds knew they weren't alone.

Mac was fine just where he was, dammit.

"You stick your tongue down her throat again and I just may throw up," he said with a grin as he moved forward.

Jake snorted. "Whatever, Draper. You bring the beer and burgers?"

Mac set his cooler down and nodded. "You bring your mama's potato salad?"

Raine jumped into the boat, her slim figure barely covered by a deep-blue bikini top and cutoff jean shorts. "We've got it," she said. "Along with hot dogs and the portable grill."

Mac glanced around. "Where's Cain and Maggie?"

Raine shook her head and made an exaggerated sad face. "They're not coming. Maggie wasn't feeling well and Cain didn't want to leave her alone." She shrugged. "It's just the four of us."

That got Mac's attention.

"The four of us? Who else is joining?"

His heart began to beat faster as he pulled his aviators

down over his eyes and skimmed the beach behind him. He didn't see anyone.

"Lily," Jake answered.

Jake hopped off the boat and strode toward Mac, though he too was looking behind Mackenzie.

"You didn't get a chance to meet her yesterday," Jake said, "other than when you went to move your car."

"The blond."

Jake nodded, his eyes narrowed. "Yeah. The blond."

Mac didn't much care for the warning in his buddy's voice. "You trying to tell me something, Edwards?"

"No," Jake said, a slow grin creeping over his face. Funny, the grin didn't quite reach his eyes.

"She's a good friend is all and…"

"And?" Mac said, his eyebrows arched in question.

Raine stepped between the two of them, her hand on Jake as she planted a kiss on his lips. "Jake thinks that Lily is some fragile creature." Raine tweaked Jake's nose. "What he doesn't know is that she's a big girl and can look after herself. Besides…" She glanced at Mac. "It's not as if she'd go for someone like Mac anyway."

Okay, that pissed him off. What was with the tag-team thing the two of them had going on?

"And why would you say that?" he asked, trying his damnedest to not let his irritation show.

"Because you're a player and she's not."

He stared at his two friends for several moments, not really knowing what to say. Partly because it was true and partly because he was pissed off and didn't want them to know it.

"Whatever," he muttered and shoved past Jake and

Raine. He doubted Boston would come, not after the way she'd hightailed it out of the barbecue yesterday.

He'd just reached the boat when he heard Jake.

"Jesus, Lily. What did you do? Buy out the bakery?"

Mac glanced back and dammit if his heart rate didn't spike when he caught sight of her. Maybe he should have thought more about the impact she had on him, but he didn't. He drank her in, grateful that his glasses hid the covert moves his eyes were doing.

"Would you be surprised if I told you that I stayed up all night and baked this myself?"

"I'd be more than surprised," Jake shot back. "Domesticity isn't exactly your strong suit."

"Screw you, Edwards," she said with a smile, turning to Raine as she set down a large red, white, and blue beach bag brimming with containers. The two women nodded to each other but there were no girly hugs or anything like that. Lily smiled, said hello, and gazed down the dock at Mac.

Her long, blond hair was pulled back into a high ponytail and she sported large, black sunglasses that hid half of her face. Coupled with the short, yellow-and-white sundress that fell a few inches above her knees, plain white flip-flops on her feet, and the barest hint of gloss on her lips, she looked a hell of a lot younger than…Christ, he didn't even know her age, but he was guessing late twenties.

Though at the moment she looked like every teenage boy's dream.

She lifted her chin and gave a half nod toward him, a sort of *fuck you*, and heat pooled low in Mac's gut, burning up his skin until his jaw clenched tight. Her body language said "you don't scare me" and "you don't matter," but if that were true, she would remove those damn sunglasses.

A smile curved his lips and a jolt went through him when her chin inched up a little higher.

She was challenging him.

A fresh shot of adrenaline rushed through him, and Mackenzie pulled off his aviators as he walked toward the three of them.

Boston had no idea who she was wrangling with.

He stopped a few inches away, and his smile widened when he caught sight of the throbbing pulse at her neck.

She had no idea at all.

"This is a surprise," he said softly, his eyes piercing the dark glasses on her face. A smattering of small freckles danced across the bridge of her nose, so pale, you'd miss them if you weren't looking.

"Really?" she answered. "You don't look surprised."

"No?" Mac shoved his hands into the front pockets of his faded navy board shorts. "What exactly do I look like?"

"You really want me to answer that?" she shot back.

Mac shrugged, enjoying the color that slowly flushed up her cheeks.

"Only if you have something nice to say."

"That would be a stretch," she replied, not missing a beat.

"Am I missing something?" Jake said with a frown. "Do you guys know each other?"

Lily opened her mouth, but Mac beat her to the punch.

"Nope," he said with a grin. "At least not until yesterday. Isn't that right…Boston?"

Her mouth thinned a bit. Score one for Draper.

"Don't call me that," she said softly.

"I like it," Mac shot back.

"You would," she retorted.

For a moment there was silence, and then Raine let out a long, slow whistle. "Wow. This is gonna be fun."

Mac turned and headed back toward the boat. "Got that right."

Suddenly it was as if the clouds parted and the sun shone on everything in his sight. The tension across his shoulders dissipated and not one single muscle or bone ached. All was right with his world.

He saw the way Boston's pulse still ran…the way she let her tongue glide across those pouty, full lips—a nervous gesture, no doubt about it.

She wanted him to think that he didn't matter. That New Year's Eve didn't matter. That the way she'd responded to his touch *didn't matter*.

Mac hopped into the boat. It mattered.

It mattered a lot.

He knew when a woman wanted him.

He pulled his aviators down over his eyes and turned back to the dock, a grin on his face, legs crossed casually as he leaned against the wheel. The grin faded when he spied a tall man just behind Lily. A tall man who had his hands on her as if they belonged there.

His eyes narrowed on the dark-haired newcomer. A guy he recognized. What the hell was Blair Hubber doing here?

Jake strode toward the boat and shrugged when Mac raised his eyebrows.

"What's he doing here?" Mac asked carefully. The

guy was doorknob. Or at least he used to be, though Mackenzie hadn't seen him in years.

Jake shrugged. "Apparently Lily asked him to come along. They've been hanging out a bit."

Mac stood a little straighter. Boston was involved with Hubber?

"What the hell does she see in a guy like him?" he said without thinking.

Jake rounded on him sharply. "Why do you care, Draper?"

"I don't." But he did. "It's Hubber though. He's the guy who ratted us out on the whole Ronald McDonald thing. Or did you forget that?" His jaw tightened. His father had kicked Mac's ass but good over the stolen statue.

"Come on, Mac. That was what? Fifteen years ago? We were kids."

"I still think he's a doorknob."

"Yeah, well, the doorknob is now our mayor."

"Really?" Mac murmured as he watched Raine, Lily, and Blair make their way down the dock. Lily's chin was still up and those damn glasses were still in place.

Mac stood back and shook the hand offered to him by Blair. It was true that Hubber no longer wore his jeans halfway down his ass and his metalhead hair was long gone, but still…

"Mackenzie," Blair exclaimed. "Good to see you."

"Same," Mac replied, his eyes on Lily as she walked past him without a word. The woman's silence said something. It said that either the she was truly embarrassed about their hot night together, or it said that Mac pushed her buttons.

He was guessing she didn't like her buttons pushed,

and judging from the heat in her cheeks and the way her chest rose and fell, he was willing to bet that it was door number two.

For the first time in forever, it seemed Mackenzie Draper had found a woman who challenged him.

A woman he wanted to get to know—he glanced toward Hubber—regardless of the fact she'd dragged the mayor along for the day.

And the thing of it was, Boston thought she had the upper hand. She thought that she could hide behind those glasses and Blair Hubber. She thought that she could hide behind that cool persona and the cold front that came with it. But he knew it was nothing but a mask.

Mackenzie was used to masks because he wore one every single day. He was used to hiding. Hell, he was the king of that shit.

But more importantly, Mackenzie Draper was used to winning.

Chapter 4

LILY WATCHED MAC FROM BENEATH LOWERED LASHES as she leaned back in her seat near the front of the boat. They'd just arrived at Pot-a-hock Island, one of at least fifty boats scattered around the immediate area. Most people lounged in their boats for the day, enjoying the water and sun, but there were several couples and families on shore, setting up their gear for the day—coolers, towels, and beach stuff.

She breathed out a long, slow breath, adjusting her dress so that the top wasn't pressing in on her chest.

Last night she'd convinced herself that Mackenzie wasn't anything more than the result of a bad decision and too much cheap champagne—there was a reason God had invented Dom Pérignon. For all she knew that hot, passionate night was nothing more than a fantasy. A big, inflated version of something ordinary.

But she was wrong. Holy hell was she wrong.

The physical reaction going on inside her was crazy. She had come here today, armed with Blair Hubber as an extra buffer, confident that her overreaction the day before was just a fluke. Why else would she run away from him like a teenager?

Lily St. Clare didn't run. Lily met things head on. She dealt with things in a no-nonsense manner with a heavy dose of cool detachment thrown in for good measure.

But with just one look, he'd made her gut clench, and right now, her freaking nipples were standing on end.

She blew out a long, hot breath.

Again.

What the hell? Sure he was all male and gorgeous to boot, but she was used to the pretty people. They populated her old life on a regular basis, yet Mackenzie Draper transcended that.

With his longish blond hair, golden skin, and wicked green eyes set beneath the aristocratic arch of his eyebrows, he made her heart beat like an out-of-control drum. His even, white teeth, chiseled jaw, and square chin were enough to pull any girl into his orbit, and Lord knows, Lily was spinning crazily. Christ, if she didn't hold on, she was going to float away and never come back.

Never had she reacted to a man this way, and she might not know much, but she was pretty darn sure that Mackenzie Draper wasn't the kind of guy to get hung up on.

"Are you going to tell me what's going on?" Jake slid into the seat beside her, his eyes on Raine, who was at the wheel of the boat. Mac had already jumped into the water, the shallow water at mid-thigh as he chatted up the couple in the boat anchored beside them.

Blair stood, his hands shoved into the front pockets of his shorts, a smile on his face as he turned to acknowledge a shout from someone else.

That was the thing about small towns. It was hard to be incognito, especially when everyone knew your name and your business. It was the only aspect of living in Crystal Lake that she wasn't yet used to.

"Lily?" Jake prompted.

For the moment, Lily and Jake had some privacy. She considered lying, but Jake knew her too well, and besides, lying wasn't her thing.

She glanced behind them. A boat cut through the water, churning up spray in its wake. Overhead, the sun shone, and she knew it was going to be a hot one, especially considering it was only the end of May. It didn't bode well for what was coming this summer. Already her dress clung to her body, the bathing suit underneath damp from the heat. She waited a few more seconds, gathering her thoughts.

"I slept with your friend on New Year's Eve."

For one brief second, pure shock filled Jake's eyes. "You slept with Mac?" he sputtered.

She nodded but didn't answer.

"Mackenzie Draper," Jake said.

"The one and only."

"You've got to be kidding. You and Mac?"

Lily leaned closer. "Get it together, Edwards. I don't want this broadcast all over the place. Lori the hairdresser is in the boat next to us, so unless you wipe that stupid look off your face, she's going to smell gossip, and it will be all over Crystal Lake before I make it home."

Jake's eyes narrowed, and he leaned back, exhaling loudly. "You and Mac…you guys… I don't get it. How the hell did you two get together and I didn't know about it?"

"It just happened, okay? Call it a moment of insanity. I was leaving the Coach House and he arrived in a taxi." She shrugged nonchalantly, though she was feeling anything but. In fact, heat ran through her like wildfire as images of the two of them danced in her mind.

"I got in," she continued as she turned around to face the water. "He didn't get out. End of story."

Jake settled his elbows on the edge of the boat as he too looked out over the water. In the distance, several boats dotted the pristine, blue lake. All of them headed for Pot-a-hock Island.

"You never said anything," Jake said quietly.

"It wasn't any of your business," she answered abruptly.

"Huh."

Lily glanced at Jake and knew she'd offended him. Tugging a few loose strands of hair from her eyes, she tucked them behind her ear and leaned into Jake. "Don't take it personally, sweetie, but I don't tell you everything."

"Yeah," Jake said. "You do."

Okay, he had her there.

"Look, I had no idea he was your friend, and he didn't know who I was until yesterday."

"You guys spent the night together but didn't bother to exchange names?"

"Honey, we were busy doing other things, and I left before he woke up."

"Jesus."

She glanced at him sharply. "Don't get all judgmental on me, Jake. Guys pick up women all the time. They get a pat on the back and a wink, wink from their buddies, and the girls think he must be great in the sack, so they flock to him, wanting to be the next in line. Just because a woman chooses to have sex with someone she just met doesn't make her a slut. As long as she's careful and in control, there's no difference."

"I didn't say anything."

"Good. Because that's all it was. Sex. I wanted sex, and he was there, and it was just...sex."

"Wow."

"What?"

Jake shrugged. "I just...you've never really been interested in anyone before and, Lily, you barely tolerate a hug."

"Jake," she said carefully, "I'm not interested in Mackenzie, not in that way. I might not be the most physically affectionate person you know, but sometimes that itch needs scratching." She shrugged. "He was there. He was convenient. And he scratched it. End of story."

Keep telling yourself that, she thought.

Jake's eyes narrowed again, and his lips thinned when he glanced over to where Mackenzie was chatting up Lori the hairdresser. Lily had to work hard to keep the distaste off her face as she watched the two of them.

She didn't know Lori all that well, but she knew the type—newly single, with a nice figure and a need for validation. The woman had dated her way through a hefty number of Crystal Lake's eligible guys. From the looks of it, she had her sights set on Mackenzie.

She was preening like goddamn peacock, her crimson and black hair tousled, her trim body barely covered by a super-hot, pink bikini. The man with Lori looked impatient as his "date" flirted outrageously with Mackenzie.

Something curled in Lily's gut. Something hard and hot. Something maybe a little ugly and green.

"I love Mac like a brother, Lily, but I have to tell you,

he's got some hard-core issues." Jake shook his head. "He's not a forever kind of guy. I'd hate to see you get hurt."

"Hurt?" She turned to Jake in surprise. "Hurt would imply that I care for him. I don't know Mackenzie at all, and I have no plans on getting to know him." She bristled. "I'm not looking for a forever kind of guy. New Year's Eve was a one time thing, and I'm sure he feels the same." She frowned and bit her bottom lip, eyebrows pulled tight. "He didn't say anything to you did he?"

"Say anything?"

Lily nodded. "About New Year's Eve. About meeting someone."

Jake shook his head. "No. This is the first I heard."

"Oh." Somehow she thought Mac would have shared the fact that he'd scored New Year's Eve. Lily wasn't sure if she should feel relieved or annoyed. Or both.

"So that's why you practically ran from my parents yesterday."

Lily tore her gaze away from Mackenzie and glared at Jake. "I didn't run."

"Bullshit. You ran as fast as those pretty legs of yours could carry you."

She stared at him for a few seconds and then shrugged. "I was surprised to see him and didn't want an awkward scene. You never told me he was coming, or I would have stayed home."

"Uh-huh."

"What?" Irritated, Lily stood and wiped her damp palms over her hips.

Jake followed suit. "I just think there's more to it, is all."

"Maybe you should try not thinking," she retorted.

A slow grin crept over Jake's face when he leaned close and tweaked her nose. "Maybe I should. But what would be the fun in that?"

"You two done flirting?"

Raine's voice cut between the two of them, and Lily's head shot up.

"Seriously," Raine said with a soft laugh. "Half the town already thinks something is going on between the three of us."

"Three of us?" Jake's head whipped around.

"Yep," Raine answered and held up three fingers. "I heard about it when I was in the hardware store the other day. I was in aisle six looking for barbecue utensils, and Mrs. Lester was in the garden-tool section. She was telling old man Lawrence that"—Raine made quotation marks with her fingers—"'the Edwards boy was having his cake and eating it too, carrying on with those two women.'"

"Seriously?" Jake's mouth hung open in shock.

Raine giggled. "She seemed quite scandalized at the thought, so I had to assure her that Lily and I traded off on a weekly basis."

Lily bit her lip at the expression on Jake's face.

"You know," Raine continued, "so that she could sleep at night because technically the Edwards boy wasn't having his cake and eating it *at the same time*."

Jake moved toward Raine, his hands reaching for her. "You did not say that to Mrs. Lester."

"I did," Raine managed to squeak out before Jake's lips silenced her.

Lily moved past them, a lump in her throat and an ache in her heart that she was getting more than a little tired of feeling. There was no point to it because when had she ever wanted *that* for herself?

When had she ever wanted love? Love was too complicated. Too painful and, besides, only in rare cases did it ever last. She hoped it worked out for Jake and Raine. She really did.

Lily took two more steps and halted when Mackenzie jumped back into the boat, his eyes on her, the look intense. He edged his way past Blair, whose ear was still tuned to the boat beside them and the guy who was complaining about garbage pickup.

"So, Boston," Mackenzie said softly, *dangerously*, "looks like we'll be spending the day together."

"I don't think so," she managed to say. "I'm here with Blair."

A slow smile swept over his face. It was the kind of smile that a girl had to beware of, because it was the kind of smile meant for one thing only—seduction.

Heat curled in her gut, pulling tight, and it took a lot to hold his gaze when everything inside her screamed, *run*!

"Sure you are," he said. "But..."

"But?" She arched an eyebrow.

Mackenzie took the few steps needed to bring him within an inch of Lily. He'd already doffed his T-shirt, and his bare chest gleamed from the sunlight. The tattoo she'd noticed New Year's Eve drew her eye—only for a moment—before she tore her gaze away from his left bicep and exhaled. Jesus, did the man have to smell as good as he looked?

He leaned forward, his breath caressing the side of her neck, sending a pack of goose bumps crawling down her flesh. Again, everything tightened inside her, and an ache began to pulse between her legs.

"Do you really think it matters who you came with?"

Her heart took off again, and she ground her teeth together, trying to remain calm as he continued.

"Because I'm thinking the real question is..." He paused, and she stopped breathing, shivering, as his eyes bored into hers. "The real question is who are you going home with."

"It won't be you," she said in a clipped tone.

Mackenzie laughed, a soft, throaty kind of thing, and moved back, though his hand caught her chin, forcing her eyes upward.

Wrong thing to do.

His eyes were dark, filled with heat and something else...a promise of things to come.

"Is that a challenge, Boston?"

"No," she said. "It's a fact." She was all bravado on the outside, but inside, Lily was a mess.

Get it together, Lily.

His hand dropped from her face, and with a rakish grin, Mackenzie gave her a cocky salute. "We'll see."

Lily had no comeback. Hell, all she could think about were the zigs and zags running through her—hot, cold, and intense. All that just from the touch of his hand.

Holy. Hell.

Lily St. Clare was in trouble, and she had no idea what she was going to do about it.

Chapter 5

"So, you made a decision yet?"

Mac glanced up and shifted a bit as Jake eased into the sand beside him. The sun was setting, the music was thumping, and there were still at least a hundred boats surrounding the small island.

It had been a hot one, and considering it was only the end of May, Mac figured it was going to be the kind of summer he missed the most. He loved the heat, and he loved the water. He loved boating and fishing. If he could take all of this and transplant it somewhere in New York City, he'd be one happy guy.

Ignoring Jake's question, Mac tossed his buddy a cold beer and settled back on his elbows. "What's her story?"

Jake followed his gaze. "Lily?"

Mac nodded. "Yeah. Lily." He was curious. Hell, he was more than curious but didn't see the need to share that info with Edwards.

Jake took a swig of beer before answering.

"She's…she's like family, Mac."

There was that warning note in Jake's voice again, but instead of getting Mac's hackles up, it made him more curious. What was it about this woman that made Jake so protective? She wasn't some simpering female and seemed to be in control of her shit from what he'd seen.

"Family, huh?" he prodded. "You never mentioned

her when I was in Texas, so I know you haven't known her that long."

The shadows across Jake's face made him look fierce, and for a second Mac was pissed that he'd ever brought up Texas. Texas equated Fort Hood, and those wounds were still fresh. Hell, Mac felt them cutting into his heart and soul—he couldn't imagine what Jake felt. To lose Jesse, his twin, wasn't something that anyone should have to deal with.

"Her brother, Blake, served with us," Jake said quietly. "He was hurt in the attack that killed Jess."

Shit. Mac let that settle a bit. "How's her brother doing?"

Jake shook his head, his lips tight, and words weren't necessary.

"Wow," Mac said quietly, his gaze on Lily. "Were they close?"

Mac had grown up in a loud, busy house filled with siblings who were always wary of an attack at the hands of their father. In some families, he was pretty sure that kind of environment would foster a tight-knit group. In the Draper house? Not so much. It was every man for himself, and other than Becca, he wasn't real close to any of his brothers or sisters.

The Bad Boys had been his family—Cain, Jake, and Jesse.

"They were tight. Real tight," Jake acknowledged. "After Jesse died, I headed back to base and went to see Blake, who'd been brought back and was in a hospital there. He'd been in a coma for weeks, and that's where I met Lily. She was..." A ghost of a smile lit up Jake's face. "She was fierce and broken and crazy."

Jake glanced at Mac. "You think your family is

fucked up? Hers would give yours a run for the money. I think Blake was her anchor, and she went a little bit crazy when he decided to enlist, and when he was hurt…" Shadows crept into his eyes and Jake shuddered. "We were both in a bad place and we got each other through."

Mac watched his friend closely. "Were you guys… did you and Lily…" What the hell? He couldn't even vocalize his thoughts because the idea of Jake and Lily together rubbed him the wrong way, and he had no right to even go there.

"Nah," Jake answered quietly, with a shrug. "One night things got a little out of hand, but we shut it down before it went too far. It was nothing more than a combination of tequila, the fact that Blake had taken a turn for the worse, and well, I was convinced that I had screwed things up with Raine for good. I hadn't been home in months, and I tried like hell to forget her but…"

"Glad you worked things out."

"Yeah," Jake said with a slow smile. "We fit. I don't know how, but it's all good."

Mac took a sip of his beer, eyes narrowed as Hubber moved in closer to Lily. They stood around a bonfire near the water. She'd doffed her sundress hours ago, and even though dusk was settling, it was still hot as hell. God, the woman filled out a bikini like nobody's business.

His eyes got hung up somewhere between the toned, flat expanse of skin above the waistband of her bottoms and the way her top cupped those amazing breasts. Her ponytail was long gone, and wild waves tumbled down her shoulders. Her skin was golden, and he had the urge to pull down that damn waistband, just to see if there was a tan line or not.

"Why is she here?" he asked abruptly. Hubber's hands were still on her shoulders, and he didn't like the fact that she seemed really comfortable with them there. Had he read everything wrong?

Jake shrugged. "She had no place else to be."

Mac finally dragged his eyes from Lily and looked at his friend. "She's obviously single, but why would she want to settle in Crystal Lake? I'd think New York or LA would be more her speed."

"I guess you'd have to ask her that," Jake said.

Hubber leaned closer to Lily, his mouth next to her ear—she didn't move away, and Mac was damn sure anyone looking at them would think they were a couple.

Mac didn't like it one bit because he knew he wasn't wrong—there was a lot of heat between him and the lady. Heat and attraction and the scorching memory of what had to be one of the best nights of his life.

Mac nodded. "Yeah. I think I will."

He'd been a good boy—he'd given her space for the day—but he was done being good. Hell, he'd passed good about two hours ago and wanted to be bad.

He wanted to be bad with Boston.

Mac got up and rolled his shoulders, smiling automatically at a squealing Shelli Gouthro as she stumbled toward him, though his eyes never wavered from his goal.

"Mackenzie Draper," Shelli said, obviously drunk. "You never texted me back."

With an inward groan, he kept the smile on his face. Christ, he didn't want to deal with Shelli. She was sweet—easy but sweet—and he usually made time for her when he was home. Why wouldn't he? The girl was up for anything, but tonight she was the last thing on his mind.

"Sorry, Shells, I was busy."

She pouted, pushing her tits up as she stretched her arms above her head.

"But we always get together when you're home." Shelli tried to grab him, but Mackenzie was quick and sidestepped her, eyes locking on to Lily's as she turned toward him.

For a moment, something passed between the two of them, something hot and electric, and his gut clenched in response.

"Not this time," he said, pushing past Shelli, his eyes still on Lily. Blair glanced up and said something to her, his mouth close to her ear, and a shot of anger rifled through Mac. He glowered at the man as he strode toward them.

"Mac!" someone shouted, but he ignored it.

Raine was a few feet away, chatting with Tammy George, and she stepped in front of him just before he reached the bonfire.

"What's got you so riled?" she asked lightly.

"What?" He tore his eyes from Lily and looked down at Raine.

"You look pissed off."

"I am."

Raine looked surprised at his answer and glanced over her shoulder toward the fire. She studied it for a few seconds, and when she turned back to him, a soft smile lit up her face.

"You're jealous of Blair Hubber?"

Mac didn't hesitate. "Damn right I am."

"Really?"

"Yep."

"Wow."

"Yep."

Raine's eyebrows shot up. "Because he's here with Lily?"

Again, no hesitation. "Yep."

"Why?"

He ran his hands through his hair and let out a long, hard breath.

"Because she belongs with me." An arrogant comment for sure, but it was the truth, or at least it's what he felt.

Jesus, he wanted to march his ass over there and physically remove Blair Hubber from Lily's space. He'd watched the two of them all day, an easy smile on his face as if he didn't care that Hubber had been all over her.

But he cared. He cared a lot. And maybe that should surprise him, but for now, he wasn't going to think about the reasons behind it. It just was.

Raine's eyes widened slightly. "Okay, if you're going for the Tarzan thing, I gotta tell you, Draper, you've got it down pat." She paused, obviously curious. "If I didn't know better, I'd say that the two of you had already met."

"We have," Mac said tightly, his eyes once more on Lily. Blair's arm was around her shoulders now, and Mac fisted his hands, even as he envisioned plowing them into the guy's face. A broken nose on Hubber looked pretty damn good right about now.

"Oh," Raine whispered.

Mac glanced down, immediately regretting his admission. Since New Year's Eve, his night with Lily had been for him and him alone. He'd never said a word to anyone about it because it had just seemed wrong.

"No one knows, alright? I..." He shrugged, not really knowing how to express what was inside him. The only thing he knew was, if Hubber's hands wandered anymore, Mac was going to remove them himself, and he sure as hell wouldn't be nice about it.

"She's not as tough as she seems," Raine said quietly as she stepped closer and wrapped her arms around Mac's waist. Rising up on her tiptoes, Raine kissed his cheek and grabbed his face, forcing his eyes back to her. "But then again, neither are you."

He stared down at one of his oldest friends, not really knowing what to say and feeling like a bit of an idiot.

"So, the Tarzan thing doesn't really work?" he joked.

"No. I'd suggest something a little more subtle. You need to tone it down."

"Gotcha."

Mac reached the edge of the bonfire and didn't waste any time. Ignoring Blair, he squared his shoulders and gazed down into Lily's eyes. There were a few more people around the fire, but he didn't care.

"Can I talk to you?" he asked softly.

"We're enjoying the fire," Blair said.

"I wasn't speaking to you," Mac replied. The heat curling in his gut was something fierce, and he was pretty damn sure she knew it. His eyes dropped to the base of her neck and—bingo—her pulse was beating erratically.

Good to know.

"Boston?" Mac said carefully.

Her tongue darted out to moisten her lips, and damn if he didn't feel his dick harden. Christ, there wasn't a lot of room in his shorts for that kind of shit, and it took a lot of mental strength to put that sucker down.

"Draper, can't it wait?" Hubber said.

Mac took one more step closer. "No," he said carefully. "It can't."

Blair opened his mouth to respond, and Mac's fists were at the ready. His temper began to boil, and if Hubber knew what was good for him, he'd just back the hell off. But before Blair could get a word out, Lily spoke.

"You've got five minutes."

She extracted herself from Blair's hands and moved away from the fire, shadows dancing across her skin, hair wild as the wind picked up.

Mac stared at her hungrily, his mind going places that he should stay away from, because his goddamn shorts were tightening up so badly, he was pretty sure Mrs. Lancaster, the pastor's wife, could see wood from the other side of the damn fire.

"Are you coming?" she said sharply as she headed into the dark.

Mac turned on his heel.

Boston didn't have to ask twice.

Chapter 6

MAYBE LILY ST. CLARE WAS GOING CRAZY. THERE WAS no other explanation for it. She'd been drooling over Mackenzie Draper all day.

All freaking day.

Like a thirteen-year-old with a first crush, she'd studied him covertly for hours. Every. Single. Inch.

Things that she'd not noticed the night they'd spent together were suddenly in focus. Mackenzie didn't sport a six pack. Hell no. His abs were rock hard and more in the eight-pack range. He obviously hit the gym hard, and his butt…

Good Lord, the man's butt was made to be admired and touched and…

She wasn't even going to dwell on how good he looked shirtless, with all those tanned muscles and that indent just above his shorts.

God, she'd licked that indent.

More than once.

She didn't want to think about the tattoo on his bicep or the thin line of hair below his navel that made her eyes wander lower than they should. Or how his easy smile made every woman feel special when he looked her way. Heck, even Mrs. Lancaster, the pastor's wife, had giggled like a little girl when Mac whispered something in her ear. He'd given the woman a quick hug, and she'd blushed so deeply, Lily had noticed it from several feet away.

The woman was pushing seventy for Christ's sake.

Lily didn't *want* to think about any of those things, except she couldn't *stop* thinking about them.

Mackenzie Draper was trouble with a capital *T*. He could break a girl's heart—maybe even when that girl's heart was frozen. In fact, he could smash what little bits of it were still left intact.

So why the hell was she heading off into the shadows with him? What good could come out of this?

Lily's feet dug into the sand as she headed down the beach, out of range of the fire and most of the people on shore. Overhead, stars were just starting to twinkle, and out over the lake, the sun had set, shooting vibrant beams of red and gold over the horizon.

It was beautiful. Peaceful.

And nothing like what she was feeling inside.

She kept walking, aware that he was only steps behind, and as she approached a pile of brush that had swept up onto shore, she paused, welcoming the cool wind off the lake as it rolled over her body.

God, she was hot. And bothered. And confused.

He stopped inches from her back and was so close that she felt the heat from his body. So close that his earthy, fresh scent filled the air around her.

The guy had been out in the sun all day. He'd played a hard-fought game of touch football and didn't have any business smelling as good as he did.

And even though it was childish, the first thought to enter her mind was that it wasn't fair. And somehow wrong.

Suddenly irritated, Lily exhaled a deep breath and turned around.

Don't look into his eyes.

But of course, it was the first thing she did, and *boom*, there went that damn horde of butterflies in her stomach. They flew and dove, and man, did they make her feel woozy. Mouth dry, she held on.

Get a grip, St. Clare.

Luckily, years of hiding behind a mask of indifference saved her, and she crossed her arms over her chest, arched an eyebrow, and was able to manage a sentence without sounding like an idiot.

"Five minutes is all I got, so what's so important?"

"Mac," he said without skipping a beat, his eyes smoldering.

"What?"

"My name is Mac. I want to hear you say it."

Surprised, Lily took a moment. "That's it? You want to hear me say your name?"

He nodded and leaned closer. It took everything in Lily for her not to shrink away. For her to remain still as his warm breath slid across her heated skin. Goose bumps followed in his wake, and she couldn't hide the shudder that rolled across her shoulders.

"Are you going to make me beg?" His mouth hovered near her ear, and she felt the imprint of his lips even though he hadn't touched her. "'Cause I don't mind begging. I don't mind doing a lot of things."

"Mackenzie," she managed to say, her hands now on his chest as if she wanted to push him away. Except she didn't push him away. She did nothing. Hell, she didn't even breathe.

"Mac," he said, his voice a little rougher. A little sexier. "Mackenzie is what my mother calls me. Mac is what my friends call me."

She swallowed the lump in her throat, her eyes daring to travel up to his again.

"And you think we're friends?"

"I don't know, Boston. Are we?"

Unnerved at the look in his eyes, she finally managed to push against his chest and took a step back. She needed some distance.

"Mac," she said, drawing out the one syllable. "What do you want?"

He smiled, a full on smile that made her heart lurch and her breath quicken. "Nice," he murmured. "That sounds real nice, darlin'."

Lily said nothing, mostly because she didn't know what to say.

A few moments passed, and she found her voice. "So that's it? We're playing name games?"

"Are you and Hubber involved?" Mac asked abruptly.

Something in the air changed, an electric shot that was hot and dangerous, and hot and… Lily exhaled and shook her head. She considered lying, but what was the point? Mackenzie would see right through her. "No."

"Then why is he here?"

"Because I asked him to come."

"Why would you ask him to come if you're not into him?"

"I never said I wasn't into him. I just said that we weren't involved."

It was a lie. Blair was just a friend—a good friend, mind you, but nothing more.

Mac inched forward, and the shadows that played across his face emphasized the sharp angles and full lips. His eyes, always so light, were now dark, and for the first time, she noticed how fast his pulse raced at the base of his neck.

"Yet," she continued, strangely exhilarated.

Mac studied her for a few moments—a few moments that felt as if she were going to crawl out of her skin.

"Interesting," he said, a slow grin creeping over his face.

Something about his attitude pissed her off. "How is that interesting?" she snapped.

Mackenzie shrugged. "He doesn't seem to be your type is all."

"I don't have a type."

"Yeah," he said. "You do."

"And I suppose you think that you're my type?"

Oh God, Lily. Shut your damn mouth.

His smile widened, and for a few moments, there was nothing but silence between them.

"Have you kissed him?" he asked, his voice low and hitting a timbre that no man had a right to hit.

Chin jutted out, Lily dropped her arms from her chest, totally aware that her nipples were saluting him and not caring one damn bit. She was unnerved, pissed off, frustrated, and…horny as hell.

"That's none of your business."

His head dipped and Lily's toes curled into the sand. She was pretty sure it was the only thing anchoring her and preventing her from falling into him. Considering it was sand, she was going to face-plant into Mackenzie if she didn't get her shit together.

"What if I want to make it my business?"

Lips parted, she stared up at him. The ache that had lingered inside her for hours was now front and center. Her chest rose and fell, and when his dark gaze dropped to her breasts, she thought she might have gasped. Or groaned.

Or both.

"Do you remember the way I kissed you on New Year's Eve? Do you remember how good it felt?"

Again, she had nothing and stared up at him in silence. It didn't matter though, because Mackenzie seemed to have no trouble doing all the talking.

"Because I do, Boston, and I've thought about it a lot," he murmured, lashes lowered. "I've thought about how sweet you tasted, how soft your mouth was, and I…"

She waited for him to continue, fighting the need to cross her legs and somehow alleviate the ache between them.

"I think it would be a shame if we didn't at least try and see if it was fluke." His breath was hot on her cheek. "Maybe that night wasn't as hot as I remember." His hands slid up her shoulders. "Maybe when I kissed you…maybe when I slid inside you…maybe all of that was just a fantasy and not real."

"Why are you doing this?" she whispered, not aware that she'd spoken aloud until his eyes snapped back to hers. Her breath caught in her chest at the look inside them.

Waves from the lake lapped up onto shore, and in the distance, she heard voices echoing from those gathered around the bonfire. The breeze was still cool but her flesh was so hot that a film of sweat coated her skin.

"Do you want me to kiss you, Boston?" he asked, dipping his head to her shoulder.

Yes!

No.

She held her breath.

And then closed her eyes when his warm mouth slid along her collarbone, lingering over her pulse point. All kinds of things were going off inside her. She was hot, yet she shivered. She wanted to pull away, yet her feet wouldn't move. She was alive, yet she was terrified of being alive. How screwed up was that?

Opening herself up to someone left so much room for pain, something she knew intimately. If Lily were smart, she'd run as far away from Mackenzie Draper as she could.

And yet she didn't.

His mouth opened on her skin, there where her pulse beat. His touch was wet. Hot. So incredibly hot. His heat seeped into her skin, invaded her cells, and left her quivering beneath his touch.

His tongue slowly licked up the side of her neck until he suckled just below her earlobe, and she couldn't help the groan that slid out of her mouth.

"I'm going to kiss you," he whispered into her ear before his tongue delved inside, and then his hands crept up to her face, forcing her to look at him as he pulled back. "Do you want that?" he murmured.

Lily's hands dug into his hair, and she brought him down to her, her mouth open as she welcomed him into her.

Tongues slid against each other—each taking and giving. It was a hard, fast coming together—a hungry taste that left her wanting more. His hands roved down her back and settled on her butt, pulling her against him so that every inch of her was pressed into his hard body.

"Jesus, you taste better than I remember," Mac said

roughly, finally pulling his mouth from hers, but only long enough to trace the contours of her jaw.

God, what his tongue did to her.

She arched into him and, when his mouth traveled lower, groaned her disappointment because he only skimmed the tops of her breasts before making his way back to her mouth.

His hands were still on her butt and the thrill that shot through her when she felt his erection against her was fierce. It was fierce and hot and made her feel incredibly powerful. Mackenzie nipped at her bottom lip, and then slid his right hand into her hair, holding her in place while he tasted, suckled, and nipped at her lips. His tongue slid inside once more, this time aggressively, and with each pass, the ache between her legs curled harder, pressed harder.

So hard that she whimpered.

It was the most incredible kiss of her life.

When he pulled away and rested his forehead on hers, she wanted to cry because she wanted so much more. She wanted his heat and his hardness. She wanted the kiss to go on forever, and she wanted him inside her.

They were both breathing heavily, and for a few seconds, neither one said a thing. Slowly, the sounds from down the beach invaded their space, and Lily jumped when the first firecracker shot up into the night sky.

Mackenzie slowly let his hands drop and stepped away, his eyes still dark and full of sinful promise. He ran his hands through the disheveled mess of blond hair at his nape, as a slow smile swept over him.

Lily's heart might have stopped.

"I think my five minutes are up."

She swallowed and exhaled. "I think so."

His grin widened. "What are we going to do about this, Boston?"

Trying to get her bearings, she took a moment, eyeing him warily. "This?"

He nodded. "You and I. Us. That kiss. What are we gonna do about it?"

Lily moistened her swollen and still-tingling mouth. Right. That kiss.

Suddenly, every fear and neurosis and painful memory inside her shot to the surface and Lily shrugged, that cool mask she so desperately needed back in place as she stared into his eyes.

"It was just a kiss, Macken—"

"Mac," he interrupted.

She paused. "*Mac*. It was a nice kiss."

His brow furrowed. "Nice? Come on, Boston. You can do better than that."

"Can you not call me that?"

"Why?" His voice dipped again. "Does it remind you of New Year's Eve?"

God, yes.

"It just…" She blew out a hot breath. "It just makes it seem that we're a lot more than—"

"Friends?" he said silkily.

Lily nodded.

"Trust me." He winked. "We're more than just friends. And that kiss was a hell of a lot more than just nice."

Why was he doing this to her? Irritated, she frowned.

"Whatever it was, it doesn't matter. You're going back to New York, and besides, neither one of us is exactly the relationship type."

Oh. God. Had she just pulled out the *R* word?

"Bull," Mackenzie said.

"Excuse me?"

"Sounds like bullshit to me."

A sliver of warning rushed through her and she eyed him warily.

"The thing of it is, Boston, what just happened between us does matter. It matters a whole lot." His grin faded as his intense, dark eyes studied her. "I'm thinking that maybe now is a good time for some changes." He spoke, more to himself than anything, and then nodded. "Yeah, change is good."

"Change?" Something stirred in her gut. Something that might have been anticipation or adrenaline or plain old fear.

"Summer in New York City isn't looking all that interesting to me."

"It's not." Mouth dry, she watched him closely.

"Nope."

Her heart lurched.

"What do you think about that?" he asked.

"I think that you can do whatever you want to do."

"Bullshit," he said softly.

The lump in her throat swelled, and Lily couldn't have spoken if she wanted to.

"I'll be honest. That relationship thing?" He shrugged. "I think we're on the same page there. Relationships are overrated for people like us." He leaned forward and brushed his mouth across her lips. "But that kiss that we shared is sure as hell worth exploring, don't you think?"

Mackenzie stepped back. "I've leaving for New York

City on Monday, but trust me…I'll be back, Boston." And then he disappeared into the shadows.

Lily's fingers crept across her tingling lips as she stared into the dark. She stood there for so long that eventually the fireworks ended.

And she still wasn't sure what the hell had happened.

Chapter 7

June flew by and Mackenzie spent most of it tying up loose ends in the city. He finished up a big project, met with a few clients scheduled for the fall, and ended a casual thing he had going with a wannabe model. The woman, Dru, had kicked up a fuss, and he'd felt bad at the sight of her tears, but hell, he hadn't promised her anything more than a good time.

He closed up his brownstone, made arrangements for his cleaning lady to check in every few weeks, and had managed to rent the Booker cottage for the entire summer. It was a rustic place, heavy with that Michigan charm, and it boasted a private beach and dock.

The cottage was a large A-frame building made entirely of logs. Open concept, the front was all glass and gave him an unfettered view of the lake, with a massive fireplace tucked into the corner. It wasn't exactly roughing it, considering the flat-screen mounted above the fireplace, but it had the charm and feel of an old pair of jeans. Not exactly fashion forward, but comfortable.

Mac might be Mr. Armani in New York City, but back here, he was that old pair of jeans, and the Booker cottage was more than enough for him.

At the moment, he was all about worn and comfortable, having pulled on a pair of khaki shorts this morning and an old BlackRock T-shirt that had seen better days. It was the second Saturday in July, a week or so after all the Independence Day shenanigans, and he'd arrived in Crystal Lake the night before.

"Is that all you need, Mackenzie?"

Mac tossed a couple sheets of sandpaper onto the counter along with a scraping tool and frowned at Mr. Daley, owner of Crystal Lake's one and only hardware store. "I've got a lot of fence to cover, but I'm thinking two cans will be enough."

"Okay, son. I tossed in the brushes you wanted and a few extra stir sticks." The large, balding man grinned as he peeked over the top of his glasses. "If you need anything else, just give me a call and I'll get it ready for you. If the timing is right, I can even drop it off at your mother's on my way home to the missus."

Mac had to smile. Now that was customer service.

Mr. Daley set about ringing through his order. No barcode scanner here. "I hear you've rented the Booker place for the summer."

"I did."

"I also hear that you're working with Jake Edwards on the new development across the lake."

Mac smiled. There were things about Crystal Lake that would never change—like the gossip wheel that constantly turned. "That's right. Jake hired me to help with the design, so I'll be starting on Monday."

"And you're staying for the summer?"

Mac thought of Lily. "Planning on it."

He was planning on a lot of things with the blond, starting tonight.

"Hmmm." Mr. Daley shoved the sandpaper and tools into a bag. "And how's your mother these days?"

"She seems good." Mac hadn't actually seen her yet, but she was always the same—apathetic, a little sad, and weighed down by the choices she'd made. All of the shit he never ever wanted to feel.

Mr. Daley paused, his face serious. "And Ben?"

Mac ground his teeth together and shrugged. "Still inside as far as I know. I don't ask and I don't care."

Mr. Daley nodded but said no more. Everyone knew that Ben and Mac didn't mix. Heck, most of the town thought that Ben Draper was a no-good son of a bitch… and they'd be right.

After Mac signed his receipt, he scooped up his tools, grabbed his cans, and stowed them in his truck. He'd stored his Mercedes in New York and bought a used, red Ford F150 for the trip out. He sure liked his slick silver car, but there was something about a truck that made him feel like a kid again.

He smiled at a sudden memory of riding in the back of Jake Edwards's beat-up Chevy when he was about seventeen, heading out to the lake with a couple of girls for a day of fishing and whatever else they could fit in. Him, Cain, and the Edwards boys had been inseparable, and even though his younger years were filled with its fair share of brutality and darkness, there were still a hell of a lot of good times that had gotten him through. The Bad Boys were the main reason for that.

Mac cranked the radio and blasted some old Led Zeppelin as he pulled out of the hardware store, waving to Mrs. Avery, the flower lady, and grinning like an idiot when she winked at him.

He was still in a good mood by the time he reached his mother's house, and he eyed up the fence, thinking it would take more than the weekend to get it looking half-decent. He'd just set the cans onto the front porch when the door swung open and a kid peeked out at him.

Mac straightened, brows furled as he studied the boy.

The kid was blond, with longish wavy hair, big blue eyes, a skinny frame, and knees that were dirty and scraped. He was tall for such a young-looking boy, with wide shoulders that he'd need to grow into, and his T-shirt, an ode to Superman, hung off him. His jean shorts were on the short side, and his feet were bare.

"Are you Uncle Mac?" The kid didn't sound insolent…not really, but there was something about his tone that got Mac's attention.

Surprised, Mac took a moment. He had more than one nephew, so whose kid was this?

"You don't look rich," he said.

"You've got some serious attitude, kid."

The boy shrugged and Mac thought he muttered, "whatever" under his breath. The little shit.

"I'm Liam."

Ah. Liam. Becca's kid.

Maybe. Or was he Dara's?

"I didn't know you were visiting. Where's your grandmother?"

Liam shrugged. "She left an hour ago. I think she went to church or something."

Figures. His mom had more time for church than any lady he knew besides Mrs. Lancaster, and since her husband was the pastor, she didn't count. He's always thought she used to go there to escape the house, but maybe it was more for her soul after all.

"We came in the middle of the night."

That surprised Mac, and he glanced toward the door.

Liam nodded. "I think we scared the shit out of Grandma."

"Your mom know that you curse?"

From the looks of it, Liam didn't care. Huh. He was going to take a wild guess that this was Becca's kid. Had to be. The eyes were uncanny. Mac wasn't sure what was going on. He hadn't seen Becca in a few years, though they kept in touch via email.

He tried to remember the last time he'd seen Liam, and the only thing he came up with was the kid's baptism. Had it really been that long since he'd seen his sister? He'd been out to visit her in Iowa—once—but for the life of him, he didn't remember much about his nephew.

God, he was a sorry excuse for an uncle. He didn't even know how old Liam was, though if he had to guess, he'd say around ten…maybe?

"Liam, is that Mackenzie?"

His sister Becca appeared behind her son.

Becca was a cute little thing except that at the moment she had a black eye and her left arm was in a sling.

They'd come in the middle of the night.

Mac's jaw tightened, and his hands fisted as all the good vibes he'd had going on evaporated like raindrops on hot pavement.

Becca whispered something into her son's ear, and Liam rolled his eyes at Mac before disappearing into the house, leaving Mac alone on the porch with his sister.

"What the hell happened to you?" he asked as soon as the door closed behind his nephew.

Becca's eyes shimmered, and he felt like an asshole as a tear slowly made its way down her cheek. She shuddered and opened her mouth to say something but then closed it without saying a word. There was no need really. Her face pretty much said everything.

Along with the black eye, her bottom lip was split, and there was bruising along the top of one of her cheekbones.

Becca's eyes fell to his fists, and he forced himself to relax them, running his hands through his hair instead as he stared at his sister.

Jesus. Fuck.

Rebecca was two years younger than Mac, but she looked worn, sad, and—it hit him like a punch to the gut—Christ, she looked just like their mother.

"Did David do this to you?" he asked, trying to keep his voice neutral because he wasn't good with tears and emotion. He didn't need a shrink to tell him it was a direct result of his screwed-up childhood.

Becca wiped at her eyes with her good hand and dropped onto the lone chair on the small porch.

"It's a long story," she said softly.

"Story?" Mac snorted. "It looks more like a fucking nightmare."

"Keep your voice down, Mackenzie, and please watch your language. I don't need Liam to hear any of it."

Mac stared down at his sister. He had no words. He wasn't close with her husband, but he had thought that David was one of the good guys. But then, growing up, he wondered how many neighbors had thought that the Drapers were a picture-postcard American family. They sure as hell had looked the part, all those blue eyes, blond heads, and perfect features.

It wasn't until Lila started showing bruises that

people began to whisper, and when the kids started showing up to school with obvious signs of violence, word had quickly spread.

Mac knew firsthand that what you saw on the outside didn't mean shit. What happened behind closed doors mattered.

"Are you going to tell me what happened?"

His sister's light brown hair was pulled back into a ponytail and her skin was so pale that she looked sick. She'd always been a golden, tanned, outdoors kind of girl. All the Draper kids had loved the outdoors. Being outside meant they weren't in the vicinity of their father's toxicity—or flying fists. To see her like this made him sick.

His hands clenched again at the thought.

"David's always been a little…" She paused and sighed. "Physical." She glanced up at him, her expression fierce. "But it was nothing I couldn't handle, and sometimes I pushed him. It wasn't always him."

Mac didn't say a word. He'd heard that line of bull before—hell, he'd lived it.

"It got worse last year when he lost his job. David's a proud man, and it ate at him that he couldn't find anything, you know? He hated that I had to go back to work, and then he started drinking."

"Jesus Christ, Becs. He's a carbon copy of Ben."

She winced at that but didn't offer up anything more.

"So, you're here because he put you in the hospital?"

"I was only in emergency for a few hours, and I left…" A sob escaped. "I didn't want the police involved, so I left."

"Oh." Mac threw out his hands. "Because the police are such a bad thing when someone beats the shit out of you."

"Don't," she whispered harshly. "Just don't, Mac."

He studied her closely, watching how she twisted her hands nervously in her lap. "What did you tell Liam?"

She took a few moments, and when she spoke, her voice was tremulous. "I told him that I slipped and fell."

"Classic."

She whipped her head up. "What do you expect me to tell him?"

"I don't know," Mac shouted. "Maybe try the fucking truth? Do you really think that your kid believed you fell down the goddamn stairs? Did you believe every lie that Mom fed us? Hell, by the time I was five years old, I knew that it was only a matter of time before he came after us, and I was right."

"David didn't…" She swallowed and shook her head, and a fresh batch of tears slipped down her face. "David wouldn't hurt Liam."

"I'm sure Mom told herself the same thing. Didn't stop Ben, did it?"

The siblings stared at each other for a long time before Becca broke the silence. "I can't take your judgmental attitude, Mac. I just can't."

She broke down, and Mac knelt in front of her, gathering her into his arms and feeling like a jerk for making his sister cry. He awkwardly patted her back, not really knowing what to do but feeling the need to do something.

It was a miracle that he was able to keep it together, because inside, the blackness swirled, feeding his anger, and if David were in front of him right now, he'd put the bastard in the hospital himself.

Or he'd kill him.

Eventually the sobbing subsided and Mac leaned back, arms still around his sister's shoulders. "So what are your plans? What are you going to do?"

She sniffled. "I'm staying with Mom for the next little while. She seems happy about it."

"That's because she's lonely as hell. She let Ben Draper take her away from everything and everyone that she knew years ago, and now he's gone, locked up where he should be, and she's left with nothing."

Becca blew out a long breath. "God, I never thought I'd be home again. Not at thirty-three. I just…I had nowhere else to go." She looked at him. "I'm glad you're back in Crystal Lake for the summer. Maybe we can—I mean, Liam could maybe spend some time with you. I've told him so much about his Uncle Mackenzie. We're all so proud of everything you've accomplished, but he was starting to think you were a ghost."

His mouth tightened, and he stepped away. No way was he going there.

"I'm not here for a vacation, Becca. I'm here to work. A lot of stuff needs to be done around this place, and I'm working on a project for Jake. I don't think I'll have much time for your kid."

"His name is Liam, and he's your nephew."

"Yeah, well. I'm not real good with kids."

"Or family," she shot back.

Mac shrugged. "Or family."

Becca got up from the chair and reached for the door. "You want everyone to think you're this guy who doesn't care much or that you're incapable of getting attached to anyone, but…" She turned the handle. "We both know that's a load of crap. You're still the brother who brought home that bird with the broken wing, the one that we tried to heal. You're still the brother who cried with me when it died and then buried him in the woods with the little cross we made from twigs. I just saw that same compassion inside you, Mackenzie. Just now. You feel as much as anyone else, but you've just gotten a lot better at hiding it."

Becca opened the door. "Liam will help with the fence and anything else that needs to be done around here. It will be good for him, so when are you starting?"

Mac had planned on starting today, but he was no longer in the mood. Hell, he could barely contain the heat and anger inside him. He needed to expel all of it, and he thought a hard run should do it.

"Tomorrow," he answered. "I'll be here early though." He paused. "Tell Mom I'll be back."

"Okay," Becca said softly. "It really is good to see you, Mac. I just wish..."

"Yeah," he said eventually.

Becca's lower lip began to tremble again, and with a quick nod, she disappeared inside.

Mac swore all the way back to his truck, and by the time he reached the Booker cottage, he'd worked himself up into a state. He changed into his running shoes and shorts, grabbed his iPod, and headed out for a run.

The direction? Hell, he didn't know. He just put one foot in front of the other and tried to forget all the shit that seeing Becca brought up.

Yet more than an hour later, he paused at the edge of a clearing, his sides heaving and his head soaked from sweat. He'd removed his T-shirt about halfway through the run, though it was stuck in the back of his shorts. He reached for it and used it to wipe the sweat from his brow as he looked across the clearing at a plain, stone cottage.

Flowers surrounded the pathway, pink, purple, and white petunias. Two large baskets hung from the wide porch, filled with red geraniums. A BMW was parked in the driveway and though the grass needed to be mowed, the place looked quaint. Lived in.

Raine's place.

Seemed as if his feet had known where they were going after all.

He'd run straight to Boston.

Chapter 8

LILY'S BREATH HITCHED IN HER CHEST WHEN SHE SPIED a half-naked man on the edge of the property. The golden head, damp with sweat, the large expanse of naked skin, and those long, muscular legs were unmistakable.

Mackenzie.

She'd heard he was due back in Crystal Lake the day before. She'd swung by Jake's office for lunch—he was out—but she'd overheard his office staff gossiping about the fact that Mac Draper, hottest bachelor in Crystal Lake, was coming home and was going to work with Jake on the developing the new site.

And here he was.

Lily had set up her studio in the large back room of the cottage because of the abundance of windows on both the back wall and the side wall that faced the surrounding forest. She took a step back and nearly tripped over her easel as she watched him wipe his forehead and then take a long drink from a water bottle. He paused, looked straight at the house, and she froze, like a deer poised in the wild, glad that she was inside where he couldn't see her.

She'd thought a lot about Mackenzie Draper over the past month. A lot.

Some nights she'd lain in bed and his whispered words, "I'll be back, Boston," had played in her ear over and over again.

Along with the memory of that kiss.

A kiss that was a promise of so much more, but it was that so much more that made Lily nervous. Mac had been right. She wasn't a relationship kind of girl, and he obviously wasn't into long-term commitments, and yet here she was wondering…

Wondering about things that she shouldn't be wondering about. Things that might hurt her if she wasn't careful. Lily had already been down heartbreak road, and she'd promised herself that she would never travel it again.

But what if… She bit her lip, mouth dry and heart beating fast as Mackenzie shook out his long, wet hair and began to walk toward the house.

God, what if she embarked on something that wasn't defined by the boundaries of a relationship? Something that would fulfill the need she'd felt ever since New Year's Eve, a need to connect and to matter on a physical level without the emotional? Was it so wrong to want that? Especially when she'd pretty much come to the conclusion that love and family weren't in the cards for her?

The night she'd spent with Mackenzie had been a gift. It had shown Lily that she wasn't some frozen wasteland—that there was still flesh and blood and heat beneath her invisible scars.

Could she do it?

Could she grow a set of balls and do what guys did all the time? Could she enjoy a purely physical relationship? Could she have her cake and eat it too?

Did she dare?

Before she could change her mind, Lily whirled

around and rushed toward the front door, pausing for a second to get her shit together before she opened it. Her hand trembled a bit, and she wiped a damp palm against the top of her skirt before stepping out into the hot summer afternoon.

The smell of lilac drifted up her nostrils—the entire right side of the property was filled with purple lilac bushes—and she exhaled slowly as she leaned against the railing and watched Mackenzie.

Acutely aware that she was braless beneath the light pink halter top, Lily bit her bottom lip as her sensitive nipples poked against the fabric. She'd pulled on a simple cotton skirt that morning—one that was on the short side—and her feet were bare. She didn't have to glance down to know that her toenails were chipped, that the pale pink polish was nearly gone, and that she was in desperate need of a pedicure.

Her hair hung in wild tangles down her back because she'd not bothered to brush it this morning, and her face was free of makeup. For a moment she hesitated, panicked at the thought of what she must look like. But then Mackenzie started walking toward her, and his long legs ate up the distance between them in no time.

He stopped at the bottom of the porch, one foot propped on the steps, head lifted as he gazed at her. Damn, but his eyes were electric, and a hint of white showed as he offered a light smile. With several days' worth of stubble gracing his chin and his long hair hanging in damp waves against his neck, he looked exactly as a man should—hot, sweaty, muscular, and…

Hot.

For several seconds, there were no words. There was

only the sound of blood rushing through her veins, a heartbeat gone crazy, and the swoosh of air in her lungs as she struggled to remain calm and collected.

She was really going to have to work on her physical reaction to him if she was seriously going to consider the plan settling in the back of her mind.

"Looking good, Boston." His voice was low and seductive, and it instantly had all sorts of warning bells going off inside her. With a toss of her head, she pushed back those warning bells. "I like the natural look on you."

"You look hot and sweaty."

"I am," he said casually, taking a step up. "Hot." He took another step until his head was level with her chest. A chest that he stared at wickedly. A chest that was once again saluting him.

"And sweaty," he added, a touch of rasp in his voice.

She swallowed slowly, and her heart picked up again as his eyes moved to her throat.

"If you were a nice lady, you'd invite me in for a drink."

"I'm not," she managed to say cheekily. "A nice lady. Besides, I just watched you drain an entire water bottle." The words popped out before she could stop them, and Lily's cheeks heated as a slow grin touched his mouth.

"You're a watcher." He cocked his head and winked. "Good to know."

One more step, and his head was level with hers.

"Did you miss me?" he asked, his direct gaze never wavering.

"I've been busy."

"I can see that." He reached for her, and Lily froze, muscles pulled so tight that they ached.

She held her breath, afraid to breathe when his fingers

brushed across her forehead. The touch was light—like a feather—yet it rocked into her, touching parts of her that it had no right to touch.

He glanced down at his fingers, and she followed his gaze, licking her lips at the sight of a dark, black smudge. It was from her heavy sketching pencil and she knew that she must look a mess.

"What is this?" he asked.

"Lead." Simple. To the point.

"Are you an artist, Lily? Do you like to draw?"

She nodded.

"That's nice."

Mac took that last step, and she inched back.

"I'd like to see your work."

"I don't show my stuff to just anyone," she retorted, finding a bit of that fire she so desperately needed.

Mac grinned down at her. "Well now," he said like it was a secret. "I'm not just anyone, Boston."

"No?" she replied, hiding the smile she felt inside. "Who exactly are you, Mackenzie Draper?"

He winked. "I'm the guy you're going to invite inside."

A shot of heat sat low in Lily's gut. "Really?"

"And you're going to feed me because I'm starved."

"Huh."

"And maybe find me something cold to drink." He paused. "I'll even let you watch…if you want to."

Lily shook her head, but she couldn't quite hide the smile tugging at her lips. "What if I'm done watching, and what if I'm not in the mood for company?"

Mac bent forward, and Lily's eyes fell to his gorgeous mouth. A mouth that was made for kissing and licking, and suckling.

The ache in her gut intensified, spreading lower and settling between her legs.

He was so close that only a whisper separated them. "Trust me, darlin'. I'll make it worth your while."

He was unbelievable. And arrogant. And confident. And hot.

And so damn sexy that if she didn't move, Lily was afraid she'd melt into a puddle right there in front of him.

Jesus! Get it together.

"One drink," she said as she turned and opened the door.

Mackenzie followed her into the house, and she waited for him to doff his running shoes, which left him barefoot as well. She wasn't petite by any means, standing just over five feet six inches, but he had to be at least six three or four, and his frame towered over hers.

She proceeded down the hall and took a left into the kitchen, not realizing he hadn't followed her until she turned around. Stepping through the dining area, she leaned against the door frame that faced the large family room she'd made into a studio and watched him as he stopped in front of her easel. She had several sketches strewn around the room, but he'd homed in on her current piece.

It was a stark, simplistic winter landscape of Crystal Lake, with bare trees, angry skies, and footprints in the snow that led nowhere.

Palms damp once more, her heart skipped when he looked up and caught her watching.

Her work was so personal. And truthfully, the only person she'd shared this stuff with had been her brother, Blake. Her father had scoffed at her idea of being an artist, and though he'd paid for her education, not once had he expressed interest in her work. Not even Jake had seen the stuff she was working on.

Mackenzie ran his hands through his still-damp hair and leaned down to get a better look at a large sketch leaning against the fireplace. The muscles along his back moved as he bent forward, and she found herself mesmerized by the play of shadows across him.

He was beautiful.

There was no other word to describe him. Everything perfectly balanced and in proportion. She'd love to sketch him.

Suddenly embarrassed and unsure, Lily escaped back into the kitchen. What the hell was she doing? Mackenzie Draper wasn't a young boy that she could control. He was a grown man with appetites and desires and, contrary to her reputation, a hell of a lot more experience than she had.

Lily had always been a great actor, able to hide behind walls so thick she could be anybody. But she had a feeling that he'd smash through those walls pretty quickly if she wasn't careful.

"You've got a lot of talent."

She froze when she heard his voice.

"Thanks," she said softly, cocking her head to the side. "What do you want to drink? I've got wine or beer or…tequila."

Mackenzie moved beside her and leaned against the kitchen counter.

"So you're a tequila girl."

A faint smile touched her lips. Tequila reminded her of Jake and Texas.

"You could say that. But I only drink it on certain occasions."

His eyebrow shot up. "Such as?"

She shrugged and opened the fridge. "Tequila is for forgetting, and it usually involves some backward Honky-Tonk, Texas, and Jake Edwards."

Lily grabbed two cold beers and tossed one to Mackenzie. He grabbed it, popped open the lid, and raised the can in toast. "So, this is good then."

"Good?" Lily took a sip, watching him warily.

"Sure," he said. "I don't want to be the guy you forget." He winked. "Trust me, you don't want me to be that guy."

"How do you know I've not forgotten everything about you except the fact that you're incredibly arrogant and full of yourself?"

Mackenzie set his beer down on the countertop and rolled his shoulders before glancing back at her. "When I look into your eyes, I see New Year's Eve. I see every moment of that night, and you remember every single bit of it as much as I do."

Damn, there went her heart again, speeding ahead and making her feel more than a little dizzy. Lily gripped the chair in front of her, glad that she had something to lean on for support.

Mackenzie trailed his hands across the dark granite counter, his forearms glistening with golden skin. "I look at this counter and I see you bent over it."

Okay, her knees were going to give way if she didn't get a hold of herself. Flashes of naked skin, of masculine shoulders, and of her fingers gripping the edge of the granite—of Mackenzie behind her, his hot, sweaty, and naked body sliding into her—made her weak, and she took a step back.

She felt as if they were dancing around the entire New Year's Eve thing, and frustrated, she shook her head, her voice not as controlled as she would like.

"I'm not having sex with you tonight, Mackenzie."

He thrummed his fingers on the granite, a devilish glint in his eye, a wicked smile on his mouth. "Maybe not," he said casually. "But, Boston, we've got all summer. And though I'm not real big on the whole being patient thing, when it's something I want, I'm willing to do whatever it takes."

I can't do this with him.

"So why don't we take our time and see where this goes? No strings. No expectations. Let's just roll with it."

Lily considered his words carefully, her pulse beating a rhythm she hadn't felt since the last time she'd laid eyes on him. She *wanted* to pursue this. Whatever the hell this was.

"No strings?" she asked.

He shook his head and took a step closer. "Nope."

"I call the shots?"

"I don't mind a woman being in control. That's kind of sexy."

He bent his head and her lips parted, waiting for his mouth—wanting to feel him on her. Against her. In her.

Lily closed her eyes. She felt his heat invade every pore on her skin and just when she couldn't stand the anticipation anymore…

Just when her hands started to creep upward, intent on burying themselves deep in hair at the back of his head…

He whispered against her ear and a whole new set of shivers rushed across her skin.

"Do you have any meat in the freezer?"

It took a moment for her to process his words, and she yanked her head back, annoyed at the grin on his face.

"Meat?"

"Steak maybe?" he asked with a nod toward the fridge. "I'm starving. Thought I'd barbecue us up something."

Slowly she moved away from him. Already he thought he had the upper hand.

A thrill shot through Lily, and she let her eyes move down his bare torso until she rested them on the nice package between his legs. "I've got some meat."

"Good. Do you want to get started?"

Hell, yes.

Lily nodded and moved aside. "After you, *Mac*."

Now if she'd been thinking clearly, the grin on her face would have faded immediately, and she would have run away as far and as fast as she could. Because Lily St. Clare wasn't in control.

She was so far from control that she wouldn't know what control was if it bit her in the ass.

As it was, Lily pointed Mackenzie toward the fridge and headed outside, toward the deck and the grill. She missed the wicked smile on his face and the way he eyed her up, as if *she* was the tasty piece of meat he'd be having for dinner.

Lily St. Clare should have treaded lightly…

Because from the looks of it, Mackenzie Draper was hungry.

Chapter 9

"YOU DO HAVE A SHIRT, RIGHT?"

Mac glanced across the table at Lily. She looked annoyed. Maybe more than a little annoyed. Maybe kind of hot and bothered and annoyed. The thought made Mac smile, though he was careful to keep it hidden. He didn't want to piss her off, but he sure as hell liked getting under her collar.

The sexual buzz between them had grown steadily over the past few hours. It was thick and meaty and like an adrenaline rush—he was high on the effects of it, and it was a high he'd take any day. It had been a long time since a woman had gotten under his skin like this—a long time since he'd been so caught up in all of it.

The seduction and the romance. He wasn't an asshole. He knew what women wanted, and he was more than willing to give it to them—as long as they didn't go getting any ideas about anything permanent.

It was nearly nine, and they'd shared a great meal. The steaks had been grilled to perfection, something Mac had picked up working his way through college at a steak house in the city. The salad Lily had thrown together was simple but tasty—the caramelized walnuts had been a great touch—and the company? His eyes settled on Lily.

The company was outstanding. Lily was smart, witty, and engaging. They'd danced around each other all night, and the sexual undercurrents were something else. Damn, when he finally got her back into his bed, it was gonna be explosive. The fun part was getting there.

Mac took a sip of his red wine and settled back in the chair as he gazed at her over the rim of his glass.

"Something bothering you, Boston?"

Irritation flickered in the depths of her eyes, and Mac leaned back even more, totally enjoying himself.

"Can we dispense with the Boston thing? Please? I get it, Mac. The accent. Ha. Ha. But it's getting a little old, don't you think? I do have a name."

Mac shook his head and answered without hesitating. "Nah."

Her eyebrow shot up. "Excuse me?"

He couldn't hold back his grin any longer, and her eyes narrowed dangerously as she gazed back at him. "I like calling you Boston."

"What if I don't like you calling me that?"

"You know you do."

She opened her mouth to say something but then snapped it shut. She took a good long sip from her wineglass and set it down carefully in front of her. She stared at the glass for a bit, her long, delicate fingers twirling around the edge. Damn, but she had beautiful hands. Mac thought of her artwork.

Talented hands.

He thought of New Year's Eve, his mind wandering to a moment when her hands had been all over him. Caressing. Stroking. Holding and massaging.

Lily St. Clare had really talented hands and her mouth…those lips…

He moved a bit, trying to ease the ache between his

legs, but it was no use. He'd been sitting across from Lily for the last hour and most of it had been spent with a raging hard-on. Watching her mouth, the way she swallowed, slow and sure, was enough to get the fantasies going. It was a good thing that she couldn't see the situation between his legs because it would totally blow away his plan to be in control, or at the very least, his plan to *appear* to be in control.

She looked up suddenly. "Tell me about your family."

Mac's smile didn't waver even though something cold and nasty stirred inside him. "Not much to tell. I've got three sisters and a brother."

"That's it? That's all you got?"

When cornered, always deflect. It was a life lesson he'd learned before he even knew what it was. The easiest way to avoid fists coming your way was to place blame somewhere else. Didn't exactly inspire sibling devotion, but it sure as hell saved his ass on more than one occasion.

Lily wanted to know about his family? Hell, there was no way this Boston princess could even begin to comprehend the tragedy that was his childhood.

"I'm not much for details." He eyed her carefully. "What about you?"

"Please," she said, heavy on the sarcasm. "Do you seriously expect me to believe that you didn't Google me?"

Sure he had. It was the first thing he'd done when he'd gotten back to New York City. He knew all about Lily St. Clare, or rather, he knew what everyone else on the planet could find online. But that shit wasn't real. It didn't tell the entire story.

"What's up with your sister?" he asked.

A slight tightening around her mouth told him that there was a lot there. Her sister was a few years older than Lily and she'd posed for *Playboy*, more than once, had been involved in an infamous sex tape scandal with some senator's son, and had appeared in a reality show on MTV. There were numerous other half siblings, due to the fact that her father had remarried four times.

The St. Clares as a whole were famous for being rich and beautiful, much like the Hilton girls, and from what Mac gathered, Lily's sister was a mess.

"Maddison and I aren't close. Haven't been for a long time." Lily took another sip of wine and paused. "I had a brother. Blake. He was…he was an amazing man, and I miss him a lot."

"He served with Jake and Jesse," Mac said, eyes on her lower lip as it trembled slightly.

Lily nodded. "Yes. After the incident…after the ambush that killed Jake's brother and injured Blake, they brought him back here, to the States. Back to Texas. He hung on for a long time you know…he was so strong, but in the end he didn't make it."

"I'm sorry."

She quickly changed focus. "What about you? Are you close to your siblings?"

He thought of his older brother, Ben Jr., a guy he hadn't seen in nearly five years—Mac had no idea where he was. Last he'd heard, Ben Jr. was in Hawaii, working as a pilot flying tourists around the islands, but who knew if he was still out there. His two older sisters, Lisa and Dara, had fled Crystal Lake when Mac was still in high school. They'd married guys they met in college, had kids of their own, and both lived on the West Coast, just outside of San Francisco.

He hadn't spoken to either of them since the Christmas before last, though he knew his mother kept in touch because she made it a point to let him know how well they were doing, how successful and happy they were. He wondered if it was bullshit. He wondered if they'd managed to break the cycle of violence or if they too hid bruises and broken arms behind closed doors. He thought of Becca, and his mood immediately darkened.

"Mackenzie?"

"Ah, not particularly. My younger sister is in town for the summer with her kid. She's staying with my mother."

"Oh, how old is your…niece? Nephew?"

"Nephew. Liam. And I think he's…he's ten."

"Ah," Lily replied, her eyes thoughtful. "Just visiting?"

Mac's fingers tightened around the stem of his wine-glass as an image of her black eye floated in front of him. "I have no idea. Her prick of a husband beat the shit out of her and put her in the hospital. But I wouldn't be surprised if she heads back home before the week is out."

What the hell? Mac exhaled as he clamped down on the surge of emotion inside him. Why would he open his mouth like that?

"Sorry," Lily said. "I didn't know…"

"Don't worry about it. It is what it is." He spoke abruptly, pissed off at himself. He never shared that kind of shit—not even with Jake or Cain. Christ, how many times had he showed up at the Edwardses' place, his lip split open or his arm in a sling and he never once said a word? It was the elephant in the room—his friends knew it was there, but they never talked about it.

"Is she…is she alright?" Lily asked hesitantly.

Is she alright?

"No," he replied. "She's not alright."

She'll never be alright. None of us will.

Silence enveloped the two of them, but it was a silence filled with heavy and dark things. It permeated the air around them and the light, easy, flirtatious meal had suddenly changed into something entirely different.

It had become something dark, and he hadn't seen it coming.

Suddenly all thoughts of seduction fled as the ever-present anger inside him, the one that was never far from the surface, had the muscles across his shoulders tightening. He knew his mood would turn black. There was no stopping it. He downed his wine and pushed back from the table.

He needed to run or punch something—preferably the punching bag he'd had installed at the cottage.

"I should go."

"What?" Surprise widened Lily's eyes and a sliver of regret rippled through him. But he knew that the ugliness of Becca's situation—the restless anger inside him—would ruin any chance at a normal evening for the two of them.

It was his own damn fault for opening his mouth.

Mac nodded at the table. "I'll help you clear this stuff, but it's getting late, and I…"

He had a bottle of whiskey at the cottage, and he was thinking that some alone time with Jack was what he needed right now. Already, his mind was filled with things he didn't want to think about, things he wanted to forget.

He could always count on Mr. Daniels to get him through. Lately, he'd been trying to curb the need to disappear into the bottom of a bottle of vodka, but sometimes the need was too strong. Like right now.

The difference between him and his father was that if he was gonna go on a bender, he would do it alone. Less chance for someone to get hurt that way.

"Late? It's barely nine o'clock."

He didn't know what to say, so he said nothing.

"You're really going to go?" Disbelief colored her words—disbelief underlined by a healthy dose of pissed off.

Mac got to his feet and tossed his napkin on the table. They were outside, sitting on the deck, and a slight breeze had picked up, throwing long strands of Lily's blond hair into the air.

"Lily, trust me. I'm not great company right now."

"Unbelievable." Lily tossed her napkin and got to her feet as well. "Are you kidding me?"

"I—"

"You are not walking away right now."

Mac felt the walls closing in. He didn't like to have his actions dictated. "Yeah. I am."

"Wow," Lily said, shaking her head. "You're something else. You show up here, half-naked, sweaty, and ready to jump into my bed. You've said all the right things, flirted like a pro, and you've been mind-fucking me from across the table all night." She leaned her hands onto the table and bent toward him. "And now you think that you can just leave?"

"Christ," he muttered under his breath. He was used to women who pouted when they didn't get their way, women who used their bodies to try and change his mind. That he could handle. But a confrontation? He didn't do confrontations—he tried to avoid them—because his temper always got the best of him and shit happened.

"Don't mumble. Mumbling is for babies. Say what's on your mind."

Mac stared at Lily in surprise. She was a lot more of a firecracker than he'd imagined. Kind of made him wonder what else she was hiding.

"Look, Lily." He blew out a hot breath and tried to think of something to say…something that wouldn't make him look like such an asshole. It was kinda hard because he *was* being an asshole.

"Don't, 'look, Lily,' me. What are you so afraid of anyway?"

Afraid? He scrubbed at his eyes. This was really going downhill fast.

"Boston, can we not try to label shit? I'm not afraid of anything. I'm just not in the mood for"—he gestured toward the table—"I'm not in the mood for this."

"You're lying," she shot back. "Ten minutes ago you weren't able to sit still because your cock was so hard that you couldn't get comfortable."

His eyebrows shot up. Man, there was something insanely hot about a woman who looked like Lily St. Clare and spoke with a trucker mouth.

"What? You think only guys can say that word? *Cock?*" Her chest heaved and he was very aware of her nipples pressing up against her top. Hell, he even felt a twinge down there and, considering he was pissed off, that was saying something.

"I can call it a dick if that makes you feel any better."

"No," he said. "Cock is good."

"Or the *P* word."

"*P* word?"

"Peiner, you know instead of—"

"Yeah, I get it."

Mackenzie felt a chunk of that darkness leave him as he stared across the table at the hottest woman he'd ever met. And it wasn't just the physical. It was so much more than that. She had a fire inside her…a state of being that he wanted to immerse himself in.

Lily St. Clare could quickly become his drug of choice.

"Peiner sounds kind of juvenile," he said, after a few moments had passed.

Lily shrugged. "If the shoe fits…"

She drained her wineglass and set it on the table carefully, her delicate fingers crinkling the edge of her napkin. Her forehead was furrowed, and she bit on her lower lip as she stared at the table. When she suddenly looked up and caught his gaze, Mackenzie felt like he was falling.

Falling into her.

Her lips were parted, her hair still riding the wind, and damn but his cock, or dick or whatever the hell she wanted to call it, was suddenly roaring to life.

"You want me," she said softly.

Mackenzie didn't say a word because there was no point.

Her eyes dropped down to the bulge in his shorts and damn if he didn't twitch. "That's good," she whispered, eyes still on the prize. "I want you too, Mackenzie, and I don't think I realized how much until right now. You're different from any man I've met before, and maybe it's because I see something inside you that I recognize..." Her voice trailed off and he wondered what she meant. "Or maybe it's because I like looking at you. I like talking to you and I like touching you." She paused and licked her lips. "I want to be with you again, Mackenzie. I want New Year's Eve in the summer. I want you inside me."

Jesus.

"I want it hard and fast."

Holy. Hell. Okay, he was going to explode if she didn't stop.

"And then I want you to make love to me, slowly, touching every inch of me with your hands, your fingers, and your mouth. I want to ride you. I want you behind me... I want you in me for as long as we want to do this." She gestured with her hands. "Whatever it is that we want to call it. But I want us to be honest with each other. I know that you're not a commitment guy, and I'm pretty sure you know I feel the same way. But this has to be an exclusive thing. I don't share."

He nodded. He could do that.

"If you meet someone and want to break it off, just tell me, or if I meet someone—"

"You won't."

"What?"

A heartbeat passed.

"You won't meet anyone else," he repeated.

And then another.

Lily took a moment. "Okay. Seems as if we want the same thing, but..."

Mackenzie was so hot for her, he barely registered her words. To finally meet a woman who was more than willing to explore an explosive physical relationship without the emotional crap was unbelievable. Sure, he'd met a few women who walked the walk in the past, but none of them had his interest the way Lily did.

"But?" he repeated when the fog cleared.

"You need to get your shit together because I don't want to be with a guy who likes to run away when things get heated. You're either all in or you're not. I get that you've got some issues with your family—"

"How the hell would you know anything about my family?"

She didn't say anything for a few seconds. "Jake is my best friend. He's said some things…nothing specific, but enough for me to know there's stuff there."

Mac was going to kick Jake in the ass the next time he saw him.

"You need to get over it. When you see me, you need to leave the baggage behind. We all have scars. We all have regrets. But there's a time and a place, and it sure as hell isn't in the bedroom."

Lily moved past him and reached the patio doors. She glanced over her shoulder, her hands on her breasts, those damn, delicate fingers slowly rotating over her nipples.

"Think about it, Mac. I don't want to be a punching bag for all your emotional shit. I've got too much of my own to deal with, but if you can get past all that stuff, well…"

She pushed the door open and disappeared.

A few seconds later, his brain registered her parting shot.

"It's gonna be one hell of a summer."

Mac stared after her, his pulse quickening at the thought. It certainly was.

Chapter 10

Mac's mother had a fresh pot of coffee brewing when he arrived just before seven the next morning. Always an early riser, Lila was dressed for church in a pale pink dress, with biscuits cooling on the counter and her blond hair in curlers. She handed Mac a mug as soon as he walked through the door, and he accepted it, kissing her cheek before settling down to the kitchen table.

"Do you want something to eat, Mackenzie? I can whip you up some eggs if you like."

He shook his head. "Nah. I'm good. Had a bowl of cereal before I left the cottage."

His mother took a sip from her mug, a slight frown on her face. "I don't know why you're spending money renting a cottage when there's plenty of room right here."

"I'm a big boy, Mom. Been looking after myself for years now. I need my space."

"But the cost…it's a waste if you ask me."

Mackenzie didn't have to pinch pennies—his job paid him very well—but he knew his mother was used to watching every dime. There wasn't a time that he didn't remember when she wasn't questioning the cost of something.

Do you really need that?

Was it on sale?

Or his favorite.

It might be a little big on you, Mackenzie, but you'll grow into it.

Mac took a swig of coffee. "Don't worry about it. Technically I'm here working, so I can write some of it off. Besides, looks as if you're going to have a full house for the summer."

His mother nodded but didn't answer. Mac let a few moments pass before he pressed her.

"How long have you known?"

"Known?" She looked at him in surprise.

"How long have you known that Dave's been using Becca as a punching bag?"

His mother looked horrified. "What are you talking about? Becca told me that she fell down the stairs."

Holy. Christ. Was his mother that much in denial?

"Fell down the stairs," he repeated.

When she didn't say anything, his voice rose. "Becca fell down the stairs and broke her arm."

"Her arm's not broken. It's just sprained, and don't you dare raise your voice to me, Mackenzie Draper."

Mac shook his head but lowered his voice. "She split her lip and somehow managed to end up with a black eye. All of that from a fall down the stairs."

Again, his mother said nothing.

"Huh, those stairs must have had grabby arms."

Mac set his coffee mug on the table and rolled his shoulders. He didn't get this. He didn't get this one bit. How could his mother be so goddamn blind?

"She came to you in the middle of the night without her husband," he continued.

His mother's mouth pursed in that way that she had—that way that told him it didn't matter what he said, she was looking down a tunnel, and it wasn't one that he could see. It was a tunnel that led straight to denial.

"Becca told me that she was restless and couldn't sleep. Said she missed me. Nothing more. David's busy trying to find a job, so she decided to come for a visit."

"For the entire summer?" he said, pushing back from the table. "Let me get this straight. You think that Becca would rather be back here because she doesn't have a life in Iowa? That Liam is jumping up and down to be in Crystal Lake because he has no friends back home in Iowa?"

Mac thought of his buddies and how they had got him through the toughest, darkest times in his life. Liam must be pissed. No wonder the kid seemed so insolent.

His mother slowly got out of her seat and grabbed both of their mugs. She rinsed them in the kitchen sink and then placed them on the drying rack on the counter.

"Becca's marriage is none of my business, Mackenzie, and it's certainly none of yours."

Unbelievable.

His mother would never allow herself to see what was right in front of her because if she did, she'd have to confront her own demons. Her own weaknesses.

And her sins.

Not protecting a child from a maniac like Ben Draper was a sin that he didn't think he would ever be able to forgive, no matter how much he loved his mother. Loving that bastard more than she loved her own kids was something he would never be able to wrap his head around.

He glanced up at the clock—7:10 and already his mood was black. This had to be some kind of record, even for him. Mac didn't have time for any of this shit.

He scraped his chair back and headed out of the kitchen. "I'm going to start on the fence."

Mac spent a few hours sanding and scraping the fence boards so that it was ready for paint and by the time he rolled out the cans and grabbed his brush, the sun was burning hot. He inserted his earbuds and got busy, listening to some old classics from U2 and The Stones as he lost himself in the therapy known as good old-fashioned labor.

He managed to get three sections finished before his sister stepped in front of him, and Mac withdrew the buds, tossing his brush into a can as he turned to Becca.

Her bad eye was now a great shade of puke green, with yellow and purple along for the ride, though on a positive note, the swelling had gone down. She'd pulled her hair up into a clip, and without makeup, she looked young. And sad.

And kind of broken.

"Liam's changing into some old clothes. I told him to come and help you."

Mac wiped sweat from his brow. "I'm sure he was real happy to hear that."

Becca attempted a smile. "It was that or church with Mom."

"Well now, I guess Uncle Mac beats the gospel on a hot summer day."

She handed him a bottle of water, and Mac accepted it, taking a long drink and then whipping off his sweat-soaked T-shirt.

"Wow," Becca said. "When did you get that?" She pointed to his tattoo.

"The week I graduated from college."

Her brow furrowed. "I didn't know. What does it mean?"

Mac glanced at the Sanskrit that graced his bicep and was quiet for a few seconds. "It means…don't look back."

"Oh," Becca said softly.

And then, "Oh my God! Is that Cain Black?" She moved so that she was half-hidden behind Mackenzie, her hand tugging on his arm crazily. "Holy shit, I didn't know he was back in Crystal Lake. Why didn't you tell me he was here?"

"Maybe because he's married and so are you." Christ, some things never changed. All of his sisters had gone kooky over the rocker, and they used to fall all over themselves trying to get Cain to notice them whenever he was around.

Mac turned toward the driveway. Big black SUV. Yep. It was Cain.

"Jesus, Becs, you're going to yank my damn arm out of its socket. He's a guy. Flesh and blood like the rest of us."

She let go, and Mac strode over to Cain as he exited his truck, grabbing him up in a guy hug, which basically meant they kinda sorta slapped shoulders and head butted each other. A small head popped up beside him, and Mac messed up the curls of Maggie's boy, Michael. Last he'd heard, Cain had adopted him. They were one big, happy family now with another on the way. Cain had moved his family back to Crystal Lake a few months ago and, from what Mac understood, planned on recording his band's next record in his basement.

Cain's hair was a lot longer these days, but the look was good, and judging from the reaction of his sister, it worked. Dressed in jeans and a plain black T-shirt, the guy seemed relaxed considering he was gonna be a daddy in a few months.

Or weeks? Hell, Mac wasn't up on all that stuff.

"Jake told me I could find you here," Cain said.

"This a social call or do you need something?" Mac grinned.

"No. I…" Cain's wide, easy smile moved past Mac, and Mac had to hand it to him, Cain managed to hide his shock at the sight of his sister.

"Wow! Little Becca?" he said.

"Hi, Cain."

Mac watched as his sister played with the loose strands of hair that fell out of the clip, drawing them forward as if that was going to hide the damage to her face. Cain didn't say a word, but Mac caught the question in his eyes.

"You're all grown up." Cain cocked his head and grinned. "It's nice to see you again."

"Becca's here for the summer with her kid, Liam."

"Really?" Cain replied. "How old is your boy?"

"Uh, he's ten." Becca moved closer to Mac.

"Shit, Becca. You look like you're barely out of college. How the hell can you have a ten-year-old?"

His sister blushed and glanced away, suddenly embarrassed, and there were a few awkward moments until Cain cleared his throat and tugged on Michael's arm.

"Well, Becca. This here is my son, Michael, and he will be ten in a week."

Michael's smile lit up, and he shoved his hand toward Becca. "Hi," he said, although he wasn't as good at hiding his thoughts as Cain was. His face puckered up as he studied Becca, and he opened his mouth to say something, but Cain beat him to the punch.

"Is that your son?"

They all glanced back at the house as Liam hopped down the steps and paused, surprised to find a crowd in the driveway. He got his bearings and sauntered over to them as if he had all the time in the world. Mac watched the kid closely. He saw the attitude. The swagger. And he knew that if he looked closer, he'd probably find the pain.

Damn kid reminded Mackenzie of himself.

"Liam," Mac said when the boy reached them. "This is one of my oldest buddies, Cain, and his son, Michael."

"Hey," Liam said, lifting his chin. He didn't sound real friendly, but he didn't exactly sound disinterested either. He was caught somewhere between wanting to know more and not being willing to ask.

"Hey," Michael answered, shuffling his feet in the dirt.

Mac lifted an eyebrow and tried not to laugh at all the male posturing.

"Liam," Becca said excitedly, "Cain is the guitarist and singer from BlackRock. Remember I told you? He's been on the cover of *Rolling Stone* and he's played with Bruce Springsteen, and—"

"I don't know those guys," Liam said. "But I might have heard of BlackRock."

"He's not really a big deal," Mac said, grinning at the look of horror on his sister's face.

"That's exactly what my wife would say," Cain replied.

"So, what did you need?" Mac asked, glancing back at the fence that wasn't going to get done unless he got his ass in gear.

"I've got a favor to ask," Cain said.

"Anything."

Cain laughed. "Don't you want to hear it first?"

"As long as it's not illegal, I'm good."

"Nah. Those days are behind us. I need an assistant coach, and since you're here for the summer, I thought you could help me out."

"Coach?"

Cain grinned and ruffled Michael's russet curls. "Yeah. Baseball coach. Brad Kitchen was helping me out, but he's got stuff going on and quit last week. Seems as if he's trying to get back with his wife, but after stepping out all over town with Lori Jonesberg, Cindy is really giving him the gears. Jake suggested you."

"Did he now?"

Cain nodded. "We have a practice tomorrow night and a game on Friday. So what do you say?"

Mac rubbed the back of his neck. He didn't really have a reason to say no even though the thought of coaching a bunch of ten-year-old boys wasn't exactly at the top of his list. God, he remembered what ten-year-old boys were like. The maturity gene was still a long way off.

"Um, can Liam..." They both glanced at his sister and she froze. Becca cleared her throat. "Liam loves baseball. Is it too late to add him to the team? He's Michael's age."

Cain shook his head. "We can make it work. What position do you play?" The question was directed at Liam.

The kid shrugged as if he didn't give a crap, but Mac saw the interest. "I pitch."

"No way!" Michael said. "My buddy Timmy broke his arm jumping from the dam into the river, and he was our number one pitcher."

"Dam?" Liam asked.

"No way, mister." Becca looked stern as she gazed at her son. "The dam is off-limits."

"You in?" Cain asked.

Mac glanced from his nephew to his sister. The hope in her eyes and the I-don't-give-a-crap-even-though-I-really-do in Liam's made up his mind.

"I'll warn you boys: I mean business when it comes to sports. I'm not a pussy like Mr. Black here."

Michael laughed and moved past Mackenzie, Liam following him until they stopped a few feet away. He heard Liam ask Michael if the guy with the long hair was really Cain Black, from BlackRock.

Michael nodded, hands shoved into the front pockets of his jeans. "Yeah. He is."

"Wow," Liam replied, sneaking a look back.

Michael shrugged. "He's just like any other dad though. My mom says he pees standing up like the rest of 'em and usually forgets to put the seat down."

"Nice," Mackenzie murmured with a smirk.

"Talk to me when you start living with a woman," Cain said.

"Yeah. That will never happen. Who the hell wants to worry about whether the toilet seat is up or down?"

Cain shot a smile toward Mac's sister. "Nice to see you again, Becca. I think the boys are going to have a fun summer." He turned to Mac. "Practice is at six thirty, tomorrow night. See you at the park."

"Sure," Mac replied. It wasn't as if he had anything else to do. Like get busy with a certain blond who'd pretty much starred in his pornographic dreams the night before.

"Hey," he said quietly, following Cain to the truck. "You wouldn't happen to have Lily St. Clare's number, would you?"

Cain's eyebrows rose. "You're really going to go there? Jake will have you by the balls if you screw with that woman."

"Don't worry about my balls."

Cain shrugged. "Don't say I didn't warn you." He opened the driver's door. "I don't have her on speed dial or anything, but she's renting Raine's cottage."

"Yeah, I know."

Cain stared at him for a few seconds. "Doesn't she have something going with on with Blair Hubber?"

"Not anymore."

"Shit," Cain murmured. "I hope you know what you're doing."

Michael ran to the truck, and Mac took a step back as Cain maneuvered the large SUV out of the small driveway. With a wave, the rocker pulled onto the street and disappeared from view.

"Who's Lily?" his sister asked.

"A friend of Jake's," he answered absently, his eyes still on the road.

"Sounds like she could be trouble if you ask me."

He moved past his sister toward the fence and grinned, glancing back at her just before inserting his earbuds.

"I sure as hell hope so."

Chapter 11

Monday morning came way too early for Lily. God, it felt as if she had just gone to bed and already sunlight was poking through her window and hitting her square on the face.

With a groan, she rolled over, slid out from beneath the duvet, and stepped on something furry.

She let out a shriek just as a yelp split the air.

And then nearly landed on her ass.

"What the—?"

Large, brown eyes looked up at her, and a long, fluffy tail thumped the floor excitedly. Oh. Right. She was dog-sitting for Raine.

Raine had brought her golden lab, Gibson, over the night before because she was heading out of town for a few days, shopping with her girlfriend Maggie. With Jake busy at the development across the lake, Raine didn't want to leave the dog alone, because the last time they'd done that, the dog had eaten several pairs of shoes as well as Jake's favorite football.

"Come on, Gibson. I'll let you out."

With a yawn, Lily glanced at the clock on the table beside her bed, surprised to note that it was later than she thought. She was usually up at seven, but it was half past.

Padding on bare feet, she moved through the silent house, stretching her arms over her head in an effort to get the blood moving. She opened the front door, let the dog out, and then headed into the kitchen, coffee the only thing on her mind.

She grabbed the can and measured out enough grinds for two cups before adding the water and turning the machine on. After grabbing a cup from the cupboard, she reached for the sugar and then headed to the fridge for the—

Crap.

With a groan, she stared into fridge. Into the fridge that had no cream.

Her fingers rested on the milk container, but she made a face because milk and coffee just didn't make sense. She needed two generous scoops of sugar and a healthy dose of cream—and not that diet cream either. Hell no, she wanted ten percent not five.

Slamming the door shut, she glared at the coffee machine as it brewed a pot she would never use.

Gibson barked.

She ignored him. If she was gonna spend the morning in a pissy mood, the dog was going to have to wait.

The dog barked again and still she ignored him, her eyes on the brewing pot of useless coffee.

When Gibson barked for the third time, she whirled around and stomped toward the door, swearing and using every nasty-ass word she'd ever learned. She yanked open the door.

And then froze as she stared up into clear green eyes.

Clear green eyes that were staring at her in amusement.

Clear green eyes that were attached to the sexiest man alive.

Mackenzie's hair was combed back, the ends damp

at his collar as if he was just fresh out of the shower. Judging from the clean, fresh scent that drifted in the air, that was a pretty good bet. He hadn't bothered to shave, but then the stubble on his chin and jaw added a sexy, dangerous edge to him.

He was dressed casually, although no jeans today. A crisp, white button-down shirt open enough to show off a bit of skin and rolled up his forearms. Paired with green cargo pants that fit his long legs very nicely and heavy boots, he was incredibly male.

Incredibly hot.

"Like what you see?"

Her eyes flew back to his and she scowled.

Incredibly arrogant.

"Someone got up on the wrong side of the bed."

Lily opened her mouth, a biting retort on her lips, when she spied the bag in one hand and the tray of—

"Is that coffee?"

Mackenzie nodded. "Are you going to invite me in?"

"Is that the only way I get my coffee?"

"Sadly, it is."

"I take double cream and sugar."

A slow grin curled his mouth. "I know."

Lily hesitated—but only for a second—and then she moved out of the way, holding her breath as he walked into the house. He was so…vibrant.

It felt as if the house itself had shrunk.

She walked ahead of him into the kitchen and felt the heat of his gaze on her back. It was like a physical touch, and every hair on the back of her head felt as it was standing on end. Electrified. Alive.

"Tinker Bell?"

She whirled around, the countertop between them. "What?"

Mac's eyes crinkled. "Your pajama top."

Lily's eyes flew to her chest, and she bit her lip in an effort to eat the groan that sat at the back of her throat.

"I didn't take you for a Disney princess kind of girl. Kind of pictured you as more of a Wonder Woman fan."

"Technically, Tinker Bell isn't a princess," she mumbled.

"Boston, I don't give a rat's ass whether Tinker Bell is a princess or not. She looks hot flying across your chest."

Lily's nipples hardened and she fought the urge to cover them up. When Mac's grin widened even more, she plunked her butt into a chair and pointed to the tray in his hand.

"Can I have my coffee now?"

He handed it to her and settled himself across from her. Then he opened the bag and brought out two mouth-watering hot biscuits.

"Jean's café?" she asked.

"Is there anyplace else?"

He offered her one, and she accepted it, tearing off a piece and popping it into her mouth.

The two of them sat together like that for a few minutes, no words between them, though their eyes did a lot of talking.

Lily had been in a sexual haze of lust ever since she'd left him on her deck Saturday night, and it irritated her that he hadn't stopped by the day before. She'd kinda sorta expected him to. Heck, she'd even run to town and bought a lasagna and a couple bottles of red wine.

But he hadn't shown, and then she'd started to think that she'd misread everything. Maybe Mackenzie wasn't looking for what she needed.

And yet, here he was.

Her stomach clenched.

And there was that hot spear of lust still sitting low in her belly, and the reason she'd tossed and turned all night.

"So, Boston," he said slowly, wiping away a crumb from the corner of his mouth.

She took a moment, tried to clear her throat in a way that didn't tell him she was nervous as hell.

"Are you ever going to call me by my name?"

He shook his head. "I like Boston."

"Why are you here?" she asked. It was time to cut through the bullshit because her poor body couldn't take much more of it.

"I thought about what you said the other night."

"Apparently. And it took all day yesterday?" Lily wanted to kick herself. She sounded like a petulant ten-year-old.

He slowly nodded, though the grin that had been there was long gone. "Yeah. I thought about it all day yesterday and most of last night."

Mouth dry, Lily took a sip of coffee and played with the corner of her biscuit. She was too nervous to eat. Hell, she didn't know what she was, but it was a lot more than nervous. Throw a little bit of anxious and fear into the mix and that came a bit closer to describing what it was she was feeling.

Her body flushed hot and she felt the burn of it on her cheeks.

There was also that…the lingering, burning desire that she couldn't quite seem to shake.

"And?" she managed to ask, as if they were chatting about the weather or the fact that the New York Yankees were sucking huge this season.

Mac's eyes glittered. He leaned forward and she held her breath.

"I think it's going to be one hell of a summer."

Lily exhaled, her body tingling, her heart racing.

He got up from his chair and walked around the counter until he was inches from her. Lily had to crank her head back in order to see him, and her heart took off like a rocket when their eyes met.

He didn't say anything. He didn't need to. The man wanted her. It was there in his eyes, and God help her, but something primal went off inside Lily. Primal and hot and sensual.

She was wet. With just that look, she was already wet and ready for him.

Mackenzie took another step until he was between her legs. He bent over, his hand slipping into the hair at the back of her head, fingers massaging, warm breath on her cheek.

"You look so beautiful in the morning," he murmured, swiping his mouth across her lips before settling near her ear.

Delicious sensations rolled over her skin and she shivered, breath held in anticipation.

His nose nuzzled just below her earlobe, and she groaned, wriggling her butt in the seat in an effort to alleviate the exquisite torture between her legs.

Mackenzie kissed her neck. He breathed hot breath

onto her skin. He trailed soft butterfly kisses along her jaw, teasing the corner of her mouth, as he sank his other hand into her hair, pulling her up a bit.

Lily's hands crept to his shoulders and she made a sound—an impatient groan—and she felt him smile against her.

Which kind of pissed her off. Since when did Mackenzie think he was in control?

She opened her legs and settled them around his hips, moving her butt slightly so she could get as close to him as she could. And then she grabbed the back of his head, holding him in place as she sought out his mouth. Her tongue darted between his lips and she opened wide, her mouth seeking, tongue thrusting, hips moving in tandem.

She kissed him, long and hard, loving the hot wetness of his mouth. The taste of his coffee, the feel of his tongue.

With a growl, his hands slid to her hips, and in one move, he lifted her onto the counter, his mouth sliding from hers in a hot trail of sensation as he made his way down her neck, to the top of her breasts.

One hand held her in place while the other was already under her pajama top, his thumb against her hard nipple. He glanced up at her, hooded eyes filled with desire, and slowly pushed her top up exposing both breasts, eyes never leaving hers even when his mouth closed over one turgid nipple.

With a groan, Lily buckled. She arched her back and moaned as his hot, wet tongue slid over her breast and when he closed his mouth over her nipple once more, when he began to circle it with his tongue and then suckle her hard, she felt the tension between her legs begin to build.

"Oh my God," she muttered, writhing in his hands.

Mackenzie moved to her other breast, his eyes still on her. "God has nothing to do with this," he whispered wickedly before claiming the other nipple.

As he tongued and suckled her breast, his free hand slid down her stomach.

Lily's eyes widened, and she opened her legs, giving him room. When his fingers made their way over her sex, when he slid a rough pad over her clitoris, she jerked so hard that she had to rest her hands on the counter in order not to fall over.

"You feel so fucking nice, Boston." His hot breath was near her ear again and she was glad that he wasn't looking at her. She didn't want him to see how turned on she was and how close she was to losing control.

He slipped a finger inside her. "So fucking nice."

And then another finger.

When he began to stroke her, she couldn't help herself, and she began to rotate her hips, rising and falling as he massaged her clit with his thumb. The pressure that coiled inside her was fierce. It clawed at her insides, *hard*, with steel fingers that wouldn't let go.

"Mackenzie," she whispered. But there was nothing else. No more words to describe the sensations racing through her.

"Are you going to come for me, Boston?"

She nodded in wonder. Holy shit. She was going to come for him. Right here in her kitchen.

Her eyes stayed on him as he moved a bit so that he could see her face clearly. Gone was the fear of exposure, the fear of baring herself to him. All that existed was his fingers. His hands. His eyes and his mouth.

He bent forward, brushed his lips against hers,

eyes open as he continued to finger and love her with his hands.

When she couldn't stand it anymore, she gripped his shoulder and cried out, shattering against his him, her body convulsing, her mind blown.

It took a few moments for her breathing to calm down, for her body to stop shuddering, and for her mind to settle.

Mac let her top fall back into place. He kissed the top of her head and pulled her in close, his arms around her, his heat invading her.

"Well," he said, his voice a little rough, "that was a good start, don't you think?"

Lily could only nod because she didn't have control of her vocal chords just yet.

"I have to go out to the site and meet Jake."

"Okay," she managed to reply, eyes on the floor, cheeks burning beneath his gaze.

"Hey," he said gently, forcing her chin up. "I didn't come here for this. I want you to know that. I really only wanted to bring your coffee." He grinned, an infectious kind of thing that gave Lily a glimpse into what he must have looked like as a young boy.

It made her heart turn over.

And maybe she should have paid attention to that reaction, but she didn't. How could she? Mackenzie Draper was utterly charming and totally engaging.

"But there's something insanely hot about you, and I'm sorry if I got carried away."

She cleared her throat. "It's alright," she said softly. "Breakfast is the most important meal of the day." She licked her lips. "I really enjoyed mine this morning."

"Glad I could be of service." He grinned and swooped in for one last kiss before stepping back. "What are you doing tonight?"

Tonight. Crap. There was something tonight, but for the life of her, Lily couldn't remember what it was.

"I think I have something…I—"

"Cancel whatever it is. I'll call you later."

With one more brush of his lips across hers, Mackenzie left, and it wasn't more than a minute later that Lily remembered what it was she had on for her Monday evening.

Unfortunately, she couldn't cancel.

And she had a feeling Mackenzie wasn't going to like the fact that her Monday evening involved dinner with Blair Hubber.

Chapter 12

"OKAY, BOYS. LET'S PACK IT UP."

Mac tossed his old, worn, falling-apart ball glove onto the bench and directed the four kids fooling around in the dugout to head back onto the field and retrieve the bases. He watched as the tallest one, Finn Bigelow, put Maggie's boy into a headlock instead.

He glared at the boy, but he was too busy trying to overpower Michael and his grunts only grew louder. The other two boys took one look at Coach Draper and didn't have to be told twice. They hightailed it out of the dugout, glancing over their shoulders at Finn.

"Bigelow!" Mac's voice was sharp, and since he'd been a bit of a bastard for the entire practice, he wasn't surprised when Finn dropped Michael like a hot potato and turned to Mac, shoulders hunched, a wary look in his eyes.

"Ah, sorry, Mac—" He gulped. "I mean, Mr. Draper. I didn't…" The kid tossed a furtive look toward Michael. "We were just fooling around."

"I can see that," Mac replied. "Now get your butt out there and stow those bases in the shed."

"Yes, sir."

"And when you're done, I want twenty laps around the diamond."

Finn looked taken aback and glanced at his cohorts, but they were already heading out to the field.

"Okay," the kid said weakly and followed Michael and the other two out onto the field.

"Jesus," Cain said. "This isn't football."

Mac shrugged and drained his water bottle before tossing it into the bin beside the bench. "That kid bugs me."

"No shit. Seems as if everyone was bugging you tonight."

Mac glanced at Cain and scowled. It's not like he could deny it. He'd been in a pissed-off mood since noon. He'd snagged Lily's cell number from Jake's and gave her a call, thinking a nice boat ride and maybe a late dinner at his cottage sounded really good.

That's when he'd found out Lily wouldn't be around this evening because she had dinner plans with Blair Hubber. Apparently, she'd made her plans a week earlier and they couldn't be changed.

He called bullshit. If Hubber meant nothing to her, then why the hell didn't she tell him to stuff it?

He'd been pissed. Hell, he'd been more than pissed.

But Mac had played it cool—what else was he going to do? She told him that the dinner was a "nothing kind of thing" and he needed to respect that. But the knowledge that she would be with Hubber tonight worked on him all afternoon. It was the reason for his current state of—

"You're being a dick. You mind telling me why?"

Mac ran his hands through his hair and exhaled loudly. "I'm fine. Everything is fine."

Cain gave him a questioning look before he glanced out at the field where the boys were stowing the bases.

"Does it have anything to do your sister?"

"No." His answer was curt, and most people would

have heeded the warning and backed off. But this was Cain. And Cain Black had been in Mackenzie's business since they were younger than the boys they'd been coaching.

"Then it must be Lily."

Mac shot Cain a warning glance, which only managed to make his friend chuckle.

"Holy shit. She actually turned you down?"

"Who turned who down?"

Both men turned to the end of the dugout as Jake Edwards jumped inside.

"What's going on?" Jake asked.

Christ. Jake was going to love this.

"Can we just get out of here?" Mac said roughly. "I need a drink."

Jake shrugged. "Raine's out of town with Maggie for a few days, so I'm good."

Cain grinned. "Yes, our Mr. Edwards is rocking the single life."

"I don't know about rocking, but a night out with the boys sounds good to me," Jake replied.

"Okay." Cain grinned. "I'll meet you guys at the Coach House. Michael's spending the night at Timmy's, so I'll drop him and then swing by for a drink. But I'm not staying out all night."

"Don't be a pussy," Mac grumbled.

Mac grabbed his gear and jumped out of the dugout, following Jake back to the parking lot. He tossed his stuff onto the seat and watched Jake pull away. Some loud rap shit blasted from the radio, and with his ever-present scowl deepening, Mac changed the station to alternative rock.

He put the truck into gear and pulled out of the parking lot. He drove a few yards when he skidded to a halt, his eyes on his rearview mirror. Staring back at him, from the dugout, stood a kid.

"Shit," he whispered to himself.

Liam.

Great. Just fucking great. The kid was going to tell his sister that he'd almost forgotten him at the damn ballpark, and he'd have to listen to her barking in his ear for God knows how long.

Reversing back into the parking lot, he honked the horn and waited for his nephew to make his way over. By the time Liam reached the truck, Mac's temper was starting to flare because the kid was walking slower than Mrs. Lambert from the Market—and that woman had a bum knee and used a goddamn walker.

"I don't have all night," Mac said tersely as Liam climbed into the cab and stowed his gear on the floor.

Liam shrugged but didn't say anything. He pulled his seat belt into the clip and turned toward the window.

Mac was quiet for a few moments as he navigated his way back out of the parking lot. They pulled onto the street and cruised along until they hit their first traffic light. He stopped behind a shiny red Corvette and cleared his throat.

"You did good out there. Who taught you to throw a breaking ball like that?"

"My dad."

Mac glanced at the kid. Liam's voice was soft, with a bit of a tremble.

"He knows his stuff."

"Yeah."

Everything about Liam's posture screamed "leave me alone," and not knowing how to break through, Mac remained quiet.

He pulled up to his mother's house, and he saw Becca on the porch. She leaned against the railing and something about the way she looked, there in the shadows, hit him in the chest.

Liam hadn't made a move to open the door—he hadn't reached for his bag either. He stared out the window at his mother, his left fist clenching and unclenching.

"You okay?" Mac asked.

Liam shrugged but didn't answer.

Becca took a step down from the porch, and Liam reached for his bag.

"Good," Mac said. He didn't want to kick the kid out, but he sure as hell didn't know what to do or say. "I'll see you Friday night for the first game."

Liam slung his bag over his shoulder and opened the door. He slid outside, slamming it shut behind him, and started up the driveway, his thin frame hunched forward as he trudged toward the house. He walked past his mother without a word, disappearing inside without a backward glance.

Becca watched her son for a few seconds and then gave Mac a small wave before following Liam inside. Mac waited until the door closed, disturbed by the quiet sadness he'd just witnessed.

It was a quiet sadness he knew too well, but that didn't make it any better—made it worse actually because he knew that the kid was probably scared, confused, and more than likely angry as hell.

He gave a bit to the gas pedal and five minutes later

found a parking spot near the entrance to the Coach House. Most of the slots were full, which kind of surprised him. It was a Monday night after all, and sure it was summer, and things were always busier this time of the year, but it was the Coach House. No offense to the owner, Sal, but the guy hadn't spent a dime on the place in years.

It was dark, filled with old tables and rickety chairs. The floors were perpetually sticky, there was always an odor of stale beer and greasy fries—but the music was always good and the memories, well, the memories, they were abundant.

Mackenzie strode inside the bar, a grin on his face when he spied Tiny, the big, bald bouncer. The guy wore a leather vest that was two sizes too small, and paired with a massive beer gut that hung about five inches over his belt, he looked about three Big Macs away from a heart attack.

Sweat poured down Tiny's neck, and Mac winced when Tiny slapped him on the shoulders.

"Draper! Heard you were back in town!"

"You heard right," Mac answered. "Jake or Cain here yet?"

"Jake walked in a few minutes ago, but I haven't seen Cain."

Mac nodded and slid through the crowd as he headed for the back, where he knew he'd find Jake. A quick nod here and a slap on the back there, and Mac felt as if everyone he knew was in the place.

"There you are! I've been looking for you."

A soft, feminine hand on his forearm brought him up short, and Mac paused as Shelli Gouthro sidled up beside him. The blond looked good. Hell, her pipes were almost as cut as his, and judging from the amount of skin showing above her low slung jeans, he was guessing the rest of her was just as hard and trim.

He used to like that look.

She cocked her head, slick mouth open in a grin, and shoved her hands in the back pockets of her jeans, which thrust her girls damn near up in his face. He couldn't help it—Mac was a guy, and what guy wouldn't at least take a peek?

But…nothing. He had nothing going on as he gazed down at what had to be a set of double Ds. They were too large for Shelli's frame, too round, and he knew from memory that they were as hard as a goddamn basketball.

He thought of Lily and how sweet she'd felt in his hands, how soft and feminine she'd felt in his mouth—the accompanying pull in his groin woke him the hell up.

He shook his head, squared his shoulders, and gave Shelli a polite smile.

"What's going on, Shelli?"

He looked over the top of her head, toward the back corner where he knew Jake was.

"I texted you, like, five times." She moved closer and the hand on his forearm crept higher.

"Yeah. I've been busy."

She pouted—what was with women and pouts? Did they honestly think they worked?

"Why don't you buy me a drink and then maybe we can get out of here?"

A flash of silky blond hair caught his attention, and

everything inside Mac kind of froze. His heart sped up a bit, and he cranked his neck in an effort to see around Shelli, but she was in the way.

"Can you ah…move a bit?" he said, taking a step to the side as his irritated meter began to rise.

"Sure, babe." Shelli's fingers slid to his chest, and she pressed her hard body up against him, grinding her hip into him suggestively. "Anything."

"What?" He looked down at her with a frown.

Surprise flickered across her face. "Do you want to leave now? 'Cause I'm fine with that. I just kinda wanted a shot of tequila first."

"Look, Shells. Maybe some other time, but I'm seeing someone right now, and well, I'm not looking to hook up with anyone else."

The surprise in Shelli's eyes turned dark. "Seeing someone?"

He nodded, still trying to catch a glimpse of that blond head.

"Since when does the fact that you're dating someone else matter to you?"

Okay. He didn't like the tone Gouthro was taking. He opened his mouth, intending to tell her that exactly, but she beat him to the punch.

"Last fall when you were home for a few days, we got together, and I know for a fact that you were seeing some stuck-up bitch from the city because she called when you were in the shower, and she and I had a nice chat."

"Huh," Mac said with a frown. So that's why Christy had been in such a pissy mood and had canceled their plans to have Thanksgiving dinner together.

"It's okay, Mac. I know what you're all about. Every

woman in Crystal Lake does. I know you're not into relationships or anything."

His frown deepened.

"I get that about you, and I'm totally fine with it. So why can't we have some fun?" Her arm was on him again. "Honestly, you're the best fu—"

"It's not gonna happen," he snapped.

Mackenzie pushed his way past Shelli and strode through the crowd, head turning in all directions. Where the hell was Lily?

He reached the booth, the one in the corner that he and the guys always sat in, and spied Jake pouring out three glasses of cold draft from the large jug in the middle of the table.

"Hey," Jake said glancing up. "Cain's not here yet."

"I know."

But Mac's eyes were no longer on the table. He turned in a circle, his gaze moving over the entire bar. "Why the hell is it so goddamn busy in here? I can't see shit."

"Half-priced wings."

"Whatever," he muttered.

"Who you looking for?"

"No one," Mac replied. Maybe he was seeing things, because the Coach House didn't exactly look like the kind of place that Lily St. Clare would frequent. And if Hubber was stupid enough to bring her here, well, that said a lot about the guy.

"You're looking in the wrong direction."

"What?" he snapped back to Jake.

His buddy leaned back in the booth, took a good, long sip of his beer, and nodded toward the bar.

"She's over there."

Mac slowly turned and followed Jake's gaze. He caught sight of Sal, his round, chubby face grinning from ear to ear as he leaned over the bar toward a sexy blond perched on the edge of a barstool. Her back was to him, but as she rose up a bit and bent forward to whisper something into Sal's ear, there was no mistaking who that sweet, round ass belonged to.

Or the fact that nearly every male at the bar was taking a good, long look.

Mac took a step forward but paused when Blair Hubber walked up to her and placed his hands low on her back. Sal was nodding at whatever the hell they were talking about, and then she twirled around in her seat, a smile on her face.

A smile that slowly slipped away when she caught sight of Mackenzie. She moistened her lips, nodding absently to whatever the hell Hubber was saying.

Mac felt like everything was stretched thin and tight. He might have fisted his hands. Or maybe growled like an animal.

Because something hot and electric passed between the two of them as they stared at each other—something that traveled across the bar like a conduit. It hit him hard and he saw the exact same reaction in her eyes. So why the hell was she here with Blair Hubber when she could be with him?

"Have a seat, Mac. You're making me nervous."

Mackenzie ground his teeth together but managed to calm himself the hell down. He slid into the booth across from Jake.

"And Jesus, reign in the alpha crap, will ya? Sal will kick our asses out of here if you get into it with Hubber, and Raine will have my ass if we get into fight. From what I can see, you're looking for trouble, but Blair is not the kind of trouble you want to look for. He's the goddamn mayor."

Mac didn't give a crap if Hubber was the president of the United States, the guy was homing in on his woman, and damned if he was gonna stand by and let the slick son of a bitch win.

Jake gave him a strange look. "Is this thing with Lily gonna bite all of us in the ass?"

"Nope."

"It better not."

Again with the warning. Mac turned to Jake and pinned his buddy with a look that said "don't fuck with me."

"Lily's a big girl, Jake. She doesn't need you looking over her shoulder."

Jake took another sip of beer. He paused a few seconds before answering. "It's not Lily I'm concerned about."

"What the hell is that supposed to mean?"

Jake shrugged. "It means that you've never met a woman like her before, and let's move past the physical aspect. I'm talking real-life stuff. Lily can take your shit and shovel it right back in your face. She's no pushover. If you think you can get involved with her and have no problem walking away from that, then good. I don't know many guys that could."

Christ. Jake was getting all philosophical on him, which irritated the hell out of Mac. Just because his buddies had found "true love" and were happy to settle down with one woman didn't mean that Mac had any of that in his future.

And it sure as hell didn't mean that he wanted it either.

"Jesus, Jake. I just wanted to come out for a drink and chill. What's with the Dr. Phil?"

"I'm just looking out for you," Jake replied, raising his mug in the air.

Mac did the same. "Thanks for the concern, but I'm good."

He took a swig of cold beer and glanced back over to the bar. Jake was right about one thing: he needed to dial it down. He needed to come up with a plan.

He needed to figure out how to get under her skin.

With a grin, Mac settled back in the booth and, for the first time in hours, relaxed.

Chapter 13

Lily wasn't exactly sure what Sal and Blair were saying. Were they still talking about the staff needed for the following weekend? Or had they moved on to decorations?

No. Sal had nothing to do with decorations—he was donating his staff for the evening. Decorations were on Lily's list, and they'd already discussed them.

Okay. Focus.

The mayor's gala was less than a week away, and with so much to think about, Lily didn't need a distraction like the one sitting across the bar from her. She'd been insane—that was it. Temporarily insane to even consider getting involved with Mackenzie Draper right now. Especially considering she had to leave for Boston in the morning. She needed her head screwed on tight for that one.

"Right, Lily? We're good to go on that issue?" Blair asked.

Lily nodded absently, eyes on the floor as she tried to process the depth of her reaction to Mackenzie Draper. She'd felt his gaze as if he had touched her. As if he had slipped his hands around her body and drawn her up close against him.

God, she could feel his heat wrapped around her—could feel his fingers deep inside her. Squirming on the barstool, she swiveled back around, heart beating faster than a drummer on crank.

"Hey, is everything alright?" Blair leaned his elbows onto the counter, and it was concern she saw in his eyes.

She nodded. "I'm fine. I just…I didn't expect to see Mackenzie is all." He'd called her earlier in the day, and when she'd told him that she had plans with Blair, he hadn't seemed concerned.

Not even one little bit.

He'd told her that he was busy with his nephew anyway and they would catch up later in the week. They're conversation had been very adult. There'd been no drama. No, "you can't go out with Blair, you're with me" kind of thing. There'd been no sexy innuendos about the hot interlude.

There. Had. Been. None. Of. That.

And maybe it was juvenile—which was funny considering she'd accused him of that very thing—but Lily was annoyed. She just figured there would be more of a reaction, considering they'd basically agreed to an exclusive, sexual relationship.

Mac had ended the call before she could tell him that she was leaving for Boston in the morning.

And that was that.

Until now.

Until his searing gaze had cut right through her jeans and settled between her legs. Holy. Hell. What was happening to her?

Blair studied her for a few moments. "We can discuss this stuff another night. I don't mind."

"No." She shook her head. "We've only got a few more details to iron out, and since I won't be back until Saturday, we need to finish it up. It's fine."

At the look in his eyes, she plastered a fake smile to her face. "I'm fine, really."

"Well, we can leave if you want. Go someplace else. Someplace more quiet, with less"—he nodded toward the general area behind her—"people."

"And miss out on wing night? Hell, no!" She grinned.

"Okay, so Miranda, Janice, and Kim can help out Saturday night along with everyone else. Is that all you needed from me?" Sal asked as he handed Lily a glass of red wine, a delicious cabernet/merlot blend he'd started to stock, specifically for her. He really was a sweetheart.

Lily glanced to Blair, and he nodded, shaking the bar owner's hand. "Sounds good, Sal. Thanks for helping out. We appreciate it."

Sal winked at Lily. "Well, when a beautiful woman asks." He shrugged. "It's hard to say no."

Lily took a sip of wine, hypersensitive to the general area behind her. Or rather, the general area being the booth in the back corner where Mac was. She set her glass on the counter and reached for a chicken wing from the basket between her and Blair.

"Okay, so I just need to touch base with Mrs. Avery about the flower arrangements for the tables, and your secretary has the caterer in hand." She tore at a piece of chicken, savoring the extra spicy sauce, and then frowned. "Did we ever confirm the DJ? I know the Las Vegas Revue was confirmed but…"

Blair helped himself to a chicken wing and nodded. "Yep. It's all done."

"So we're good?"

"We're good. I gotta say, this idea of yours, for a Vegas-themed gala, should raise a lot of money to fund some of our local projects. The silent auction items are impressive, but have you seen the list of items to be bid on?"

She nodded. The list was extensive, and the locals had been more than generous.

"I'm glad I listened to you."

"I didn't do anything special," she replied. "We did something similar for my family's foundation a few years back, and it was a huge success."

Blair tossed the remains of his wing onto a plate beside the basket. He turned around, facing the room behind her, and leaned back.

"So," Blair said slowly. "Mac Draper? Really?"

Oh God. Not him too? She'd had a pretty blunt discussion with Jake about the idea of Mac and her together, and was surprised at how strongly Jake had advised her against getting involved with him. Especially considering Mac was one of his best friends.

A soft smile touched her mouth and she shrugged. "He's...I don't know. I find him interesting."

"Interesting." The word was spoken dryly and Blair frowned. "Man, if I knew what kind of secret ingredient that guy has stuffed up his sleeve, you bet I'd be all over it."

Blair chuckled and slid a little closer to her. The bar was noisy—half-priced wing night always brought out a big crowd—and he leaned in. "I got tell ya though, Mackenzie Draper is a loose cannon. His temper is as bad as his father's, and his reputation with the ladies rivals Cain Black's...big time. He's no saint, that's for sure."

"Well, Mr. Hubber," she teased, "I suppose that stuff would matter if I were interested in anything permanent with Mac, but I'm not. You don't need to worry about me, Blair. Whatever it is between us isn't serious."

"Really?" Blair said dryly. "And the fact that he looks

like he wants to tear my arms off and shove them down my throat says what exactly?"

"It says that he's dragging his knuckles across the floor like a Neanderthal." She couldn't quite hide her grin. "It's kind of cute, don't you think?"

"I don't know if I'd call it cute," Blair murmured. "Insane maybe. Fucked up for sure. But cute? Hell no."

Lily glanced up at her friend. His warm brown hair brushed the top of his forehead, and his eyes glittered beneath the dim glow in the bar. Blair was a good-looking man, tall and broad shouldered, with long, athletic legs. He was smart, focused, took good care of himself…he was sweet, kindhearted—really the perfect catch for some lucky lady.

It just wasn't Lily St. Clare.

"Here he comes."

Wait. What?

The hair on the back of Lily's neck coiled, as did the pulsing heat that sat low in her belly.

She inhaled sharply as that unique scent all his own fell over her like a second skin, and she looked up, catching Mac's gaze in the mirror behind the bar.

His golden hair waved crazily around his head, just touching the tops of his shoulders, as if he'd been in the wind or out on a boat. His eyes were dark and intense, and her heart skipped a beat when he bent forward because she felt the heat of him right beside her.

"Fancy running into you here, Boston."

She licked her lips and hoped like hell she didn't sound like the fourteen-year-old girl she felt kicking around inside her.

"It's wing night. Where else would I be?" she said lightly.

Still watching him through the mirror, she held her breath when his eyes dropped to her mouth.

"I can see that."

He leaned forward even more, and honest to God, it felt as if they were the only two people in the entire place. Sal's distinct and husky voice was gone. Blair, who stood on the other side of her, was gone. The crowd, the music, and the noise—all of it was gone.

There was only Mackenzie.

His warm fingers were on her chin, and he slowly turned her until she faced him. She was aware of her heart beating, of the way her breathing was erratic. She saw the pulse at the base of Mac's neck and—holy Christ, but did he have so smell do damn good?

He leaned down, his warm breath now on her cheeks, spreading goose bumps along her skin like a rash. When his tongue darted out and licked at the corner of her mouth, Lily jerked, her body coiled so tight she thought that maybe she'd just had a baby orgasm.

Here. In public. In a bar.

How the hell could he do this to her?

Mackenzie slowly straightened, his eyes never leaving hers. "Spicy," he said softly. "Somehow I knew you'd be all about the spice."

She cleared her throat. "Actually, I prefer honey garlic. Blair's the one who likes his wings hot."

Mac's eyebrow rose, and he looked over her shoulder. "Does he now?"

She nodded. "He does."

It was kind of delicious, the way Mac was looking

at her as if he wanted to devour her right there in the bar—right in front of Blair and Sal and anyone else who wanted to watch.

She squirmed. Jesus! Again with the tingle between her legs. It wasn't fair, this power he seemed to have over her.

"I like spice too," Mac said softly. Dangerously.

"Really?" Was that her? Sounding all breathless and soft and…freaking girlie?

"Yes. Really. Except…"

She held her breath. She waited for him to finish his sentence. And she refused to squirm even though the pulsing going on between her legs was something fierce. God, maybe she was ovulating. Weren't ovulating women horny as hell?

Hadn't she read that somewhere?

"I kinda like my spice in the morning. Spicy coffee. Spicy biscuits." He lowered his voice, the timbre husky. "Spicy Lily."

That just about did it.

Right there in the middle of the Coach House, Lily St. Clare was close to losing it—her body was damn close to having a freaking explosion, and all she could do was bite her lip as Mac turned away and called Sal over.

She knew he was alluding to their hot morning together, and now, there was no way she was getting those images out of her mind.

She might have whimpered. Or moaned.

Lily glanced back at Blair—who was looking at her as if she'd lost her freaking mind. And maybe she had, but right now she didn't care about that. What she cared about was the fact that the ache inside her was so intense, she wasn't sure it would ever go away.

It had been building since this morning. Since Mackenzie had put his mouth and his hands on her. Since he'd put his fingers inside her.

Oh God, she wanted a hell of a lot more than his fingers. And she wanted it now.

"I need another jug for me and the boys."

Wait. What?

"You're staying here?" she asked carefully, tugging her hair from her neck where it was sticking to the sheen of sweat on her skin.

Mac nodded. "Well, darlin', there's not much else to do in Crystal Lake on a Monday night, and since you're busy here with the mayor, I thought I'd catch up with the boys."

"Oh but—"

Blair and I are done. We can go back to my place and finish what we started earlier.

She stopped herself from making a complete and utter ass of herself just in time and grabbed her wineglass instead of spilling more words.

"But..." Mackenzie prompted.

She swallowed her wine and took a moment, hoping the breathless thing she had going on earlier was gone. "You should probably order the wings."

"The wings."

She nodded. "Yes. They're half-price, but Sal usually runs out by ten so..."

Mac grabbed the jug and smiled. "Good to know. I'll get the extra spicy." He winked and lowered his voice. "And by the way, I'm totally up for coffee tomorrow morning."

"Oh," she said softly. "I'm leaving for Boston before the sun comes up. It's a family thing, and I only found out today, and I can't get out of it because my father is, he's being difficult about it, and well, I just can't not go and…" She was rambling and needed to stop. Like now.

Something stirred in his eyes, something heavy and fierce, and it touched her. Whatever it was touched her deeply. Lily's chest tightened and she felt as if she was on the verge of tears and that was crazy.

What the hell was wrong with her?

"Is everything alright?" His voice was gentle.

No.

Shit. She was going to lose it if she didn't pull herself together. Lily counted to ten before she spoke. "It's just some stuff. You know. Family stuff."

He studied her for a few seconds, the jug of beer in one hand, his other shoved into the front pocket of his jeans.

"When are you back?"

"Saturday."

"Saturday," he said with a slow, sexy grin.

"You can be my date," she replied, holding her breath as she waited for him to answer.

"Date?"

Lily nodded. "For the mayor's gala."

Wow. She sounded like a desperate fifteen-year-old.

Mac's eyes moved from Lily to Blair. "Sounds good. See you then, Boston."

He turned and she watched him ease through the crowd, noticing that she wasn't the only one to do that either. Several women were focused on his fine butt, long legs, wide shoulders, and thick, blond hair. The woman

Lily had seen rubbing herself all over Mackenzie earlier looked as if she wanted to eat every single inch of him.

Lily finished her wine. The woman could look all she liked because Mac wanted Lily, and when she returned from Boston, Lily planned on letting Mac have all the spice he wanted.

Too bad she had Boston and four days to get through before any spice would be had.

It was going to be a long, long week.

Chapter 14

MACKENZIE SPENT THE MAJORITY OF THE WEEK OUT AT the development site with Jake. The plans for the project dubbed Crystal Lake View Estates were intensive—condos, single-family homes, and an eighteen-hole golf course that overlooked the water. The idea was to service both middle-income families and those on the higher end of the spectrum, to marry them together in a development that could meet both of their needs.

It was win-win and would bring a substantial tax base to the community, though keeping the small-town charm of Crystal Lake was a bit of a challenge and had been a bone of contention with some of the townsfolk. But Jake and his father had managed to convince them all that they'd do whatever it took to keep the integrity and simplicity of Crystal Lake intact.

They were in talks with several designers for the golf course; both Jake and Mac liked a guy from Dublin, Ian O'Reilly. O'Reilly was flying in the following week, and Mac was hoping they'd be able to tie up that bit of business sooner than later, so he could move forward with his designs for the clubhouse and the condos that would surround the golf course. He had an idea of what he wanted—to keep the beauty of the lake and woods and bring them right into the homes they were building.

He visualized soaring ceilings, rooms filled with light and glass, and materials that were modern, but ones that also took from the natural surroundings—slate, granite, steel, oak, and cedar.

This planning stage was always one that he enjoyed, the one where his artistic side could have some wings, and he was as excited about the development as Jake was. It was a different gig from a lot of the projects he'd worked on lately and a welcome change of pace.

Overall, the week had been successful. He'd managed to get the fence done at his mother's, the eves cleaned out, and one of Jake's contractors had given him a good quote on new windows.

He'd made it through his first game coaching the Crystal Lake Comets, and though his nephew's attitude still needed adjustment—there was anger there and a healthy dose of confusion—Mackenzie was content to let him ride it out. Mac could take it, and if the kid needed a punching bag, it might as well be him.

The game had started out a little bumpy until Liam found his groove somewhere between the fourth and fifth inning. They came back from behind by five runs and managed to sneak out a win against the visiting team. Jake and Cain had taken the kids for ice cream afterward, and lo and behold, his nephew had even managed a few smiles.

So, all in all, a good week.

And it was about to get a whole lot better.

Mac pulled into Lily's driveway and parked beside her BMW. He hadn't spoken to Lily since Monday, but she'd sent him a text the night before. A text that had pretty much kept him awake most of the night.

Awake and horny as hell.

Pick me up at 5. I'll be spending the night.

Mac cut the engine and glanced at his watch as he climbed out of the truck and started for the house—4:59, right on time. He was just about to knock when the door flew open and his eyes landed on a woman who bore a striking resemblance to Lily.

Barefoot, with hot pink toenails, the woman slowly smiled up at him. Mac couldn't tell if she was older or younger because she looked a little ragged around the edges—the heavy, dark eye makeup didn't help—but it had more to do with her attitude and the look in her eyes.

Skin tanned to a deep, almost unnatural shade of gold, she was dressed in skimpy shorts, boasted a stud and ring in her belly button, and her generous rack nearly spilled out of the bright fuchsia halter top. With long blond hair in disarray, a pouty mouth, and knowing eyes, the woman oozed sex and other, darker things.

He caught the sweet smell of rye whiskey and coupled with the stale scent of cigarettes, he figured the lady had been going hard for a good, long while now. She was bad news.

He didn't have to take a wild guess to know that this was Lily's notorious sister, Maddison St. Clare—reality-show sensation and not in the good way.

"Well, aren't you just delicious," she purred, leaning against the door frame. She was all kinds of sex kitten and hard edges. He knew the type and he wasn't interested.

"You must be Maddison."

"And you must be the man who's got Lily's panties all bunched up in knots."

Mac shrugged, his tone light, but he was immediately on alert. The girl was fishing. "The name's Mac."

"I know." She didn't skip a beat. "I peeked at her cell when she was in the shower. Saw your text." She licked her glossy mouth. "So tell me…does Mac have a brother?"

"Nope." Mac didn't like the predatory gleam in her eye. In fact, there wasn't much about the woman that he liked. She was so far from who Lily was, it was hard to believe they belonged in the same gene pool.

She chewed on her bottom lip, eyebrows raised slightly as she studied him for a few more seconds before she must have decided that he wasn't worth the bother. She moved to the side and motioned him in. "She's never on time."

Good to know. He'd have to file that one away.

Mac stepped inside the cottage and moved past Maddison into the kitchen. Music played softly somewhere down the hall, an old Stones song if he was hearing right.

Angie.

Ah, seems as if Lily's ear was bent to the classics. He liked that.

Fresh flowers were in a glass bowl on the counter, big blue-purple things that reminded him of his mother's lilacs, but they were round and much larger. Arranged to float on top of the water, they added a classy touch.

He liked that too.

"Maddison, have you seen my purse? I need my tickets—"

Mac's head whipped up and he damn near choked when Lily came around the corner because she stopped him cold.

She was stunning. There was no other word for it.

Stunning and sexy and mine.

Her deep blue eyes glistened, enhanced by smoky gray liner and silver shadow, giving them a dramatic look. She must have put on a bit of mascara because her lashes went on for miles. Clear gloss made him want to lick her lips, and save for a pair of classic diamond studs in her ears, she wore no other jewelry.

Her hair was secured to the side, a loose golden knot that sat near her right shoulder—a shoulder that was bare. A shoulder that was creamy and soft and so damn mouthwatering, it was hard for Mac to tear his gaze away. He wanted to lick the spot where her neck met her collarbone and then he wanted to work his way up to that delicious indent just under her ear. And then he wanted to…

Mac took a step toward her.

He wanted to take her back to his place and rip the ice-blue dress from her. Inch by inch. With his teeth.

It clung to her curves, a soft sheen of silk that invited the eye to study…the hand to touch, and the mouth to taste. It was a hot, sexy piece of material that was meant to entice, and it had done the job. Holy hell had it done the job because he wanted Lily naked. God, he wanted her naked right now.

"Mackenzie," she said softly. "I didn't hear the doorbell."

"Screw the gala. Let's head straight to my place." Nothing like getting right to the point, but it was all he had right now. He'd been waiting to see her again since Monday night, and now that he had her within his grasp, he sure as hell didn't want to share her with anyone.

Surprise lit her eyes, but only for a moment. It was

replaced with something that smoldered—he knew she was very much aware of the affect she had on him.

A soft smile touched her lips. "But then no one would see my dress."

"Good."

Her eyes darkened and that delectable tongue darted out to lick lips that he needed to kiss.

He took another step toward her.

"I bought this dress specifically for the gala."

"No you didn't."

He took two more strides until he was close enough to smell that fresh, exotic scent of hers. His eyes pinned her and he knew that she saw his need because he saw the same thing reflected in her eyes. It was some kind of power.

"You're so sure of yourself," she said throatily, her voice a sexy whisper.

"You bought the dress for me."

"And why would I do that?"

"You knew it would drive me crazy."

She laughed, a soft, sexy sound. "That wouldn't be very nice of me now, would it?"

"I don't think you're a very nice lady."

She pouted. "I'm hurt, Mackenzie."

"Don't be hurt." His mouth was close to hers now. "I'm good with you not being nice." He breathed in her scent. "In fact I'm more than good with it."

Mac brushed his lips across Lily's mouth and smiled when she shuddered.

So. Goddamn. Hot.

The way she reacted to him.

He rested his forehead against hers and took a moment

to collect himself. How the hell were they going to make it through this night? Already his dick was hard and the visuals in his mind weren't exactly making things easy.

"I'm still here in case either of you cared." Maddison's voice came from somewhere behind them, but Mac didn't give a flying fuck about her sister.

"I see you've met Maddison," Lily said, her hands against his chest, the tips of her fingers pushing into him. He didn't move at first, and when she applied a bit more pressure, Mac reluctantly let her go.

"She's staying with me." Lily's eyes moved behind him, settling on her sister. "For the next little while."

He could tell there was stuff going on—saw it in Lily's eyes. Maddison St. Clare was a mess, and it looked as if her sister was on cleanup duty.

"We should go," Lily said. She grabbed her purse off the counter and pulled out two cream-colored tickets, embossed with heavy gold script. "Can you hold on to these?"

Mac tucked the tickets into the inside pocket of his suit jacket, and then pointed to the overnight bag that was set on the chair. He raised his eyebrows in question, and when she gave him a small nod, he grabbed it.

"So you're really not coming back?" Maddison asked, her expression sullen.

Lily shook her head and started for the front door. "No. I'll see you tomorrow."

"I doubt I'll be here," Maddison shot back.

Lily paused and the look she shot her sister was somewhere north of frosty. "The closest house is nearly three miles away, and I've got the keys to the car. So, unless you're feeling energetic or stupid, I'll see you tomorrow."

"Whatever," Maddison muttered.

"And no smoking in the house. I mean it, Maddison. If I so much as smell a wisp of cigarette—"

"Who says I'd be smoking cigarettes?"

"—or anything illegal, you are done. And don't for one second think that I'll do anything to stop Dad from sending you away for six months if you don't behave and follow my rules. Not this time."

She took a deep breath and glanced at Mac. "Let's go."

He tossed her bag into the backseat and helped her up into the truck. He supposed her BMW was more in line with his tux and her dress, but Lily didn't seem to mind.

"Sorry about that," she said.

Mac shrugged. "Don't worry about it. I'm used to family drama." He nodded out into the night. "So we're really going to go to this thing?" he asked. "Go to the gala?"

"We're really going to go to this thing," she repeated softly. "A lot of people will be disappointed if I don't show. I can't do that to them."

"You mean, Hubber."

"He's just a friend, Mackenzie, and I promised him I'd be there."

He didn't like it, but he sure as hell respected the fact that she needed to see this thing out to the end. He reversed out of the driveway and headed toward town.

Mac shot a quick glance her way and swallowed hard when he found her eyes on him. They were soft and glittery, as if a fever lit her up from inside. Her mouth was parted and damn if her nipples weren't visible through the thin material of her dress.

He stifled a groan and tore his gaze away because it would be real inconvenient for them to get into an accident.

"How long?" he asked roughly, maneuvering the truck onto the main highway that led back toward town. The mayor's gala was being held in one of the banquet rooms at the new sports complex on the outskirts of town.

"Dinner runs until around eight, and before the band hits the stage, there's a live auction I need to help out with."

Mackenzie didn't know if he could wait that long to get her alone.

"How long?" he asked again, fingers gripping the steering wheel tightly. He tossed her a dark look.

"Midnight? Maybe?"

No. Fucking. Way.

Mackenzie signaled his turn and shook his head. There were things he was willing to compromise on—letting her cozy up to Hubber was one of them—but damn if he was going to wait until midnight to get her alone.

"Too late."

"But—"

He shot her a look that stopped her cold. "Try again."

She licked her lips and cleared her throat. "Eleven? I can't leave earlier than that. I promised Blair that I'd make sure the silent auction was wrapped up and—"

"Blair Hubber can find someone else to help him out. Ten o'clock and we're out of there."

"Ten? But—"

He nailed her with a hot look as they pulled into the large sports complex. "Ten."

He pulled into a parking spot and cut the engine.

"But what will people think?"

"Do you think I give a shit what anyone thinks?"

Mackenzie tugged off his seat belt and slid across the seat until he was close enough to reach down and press his mouth against hers. God, she was so soft and warm and feminine.

He slid his mouth over hers, his tongue delving inside to tease and taste while his hands cupped her face to hold her steady. He kissed her gently, his mouth coaxing and soft, but when she whimpered and leaned into him, he went deeper. Harder. He branded her with his mouth and tongue, and when he finally let her go, Lily's face was flushed and her lips were swollen.

Good. Every guy that looked her way would know she was taken.

He pulled away, his eyes eating her up, his thumb rubbing the mouth that he'd just tasted.

"Ten o'clock," he said again. "Not one minute later."

Lily closed her eyes, and he knew she was struggling with her need and desire and want, as badly as he was.

She nodded, a quick, jerky movement, and whispered against his finger.

"Let's make it nine thirty."

Mac was good with that, and she didn't have to ask twice.

Chapter 15

By nine o'clock, Lily knew the evening was a bona fide success. Heck, it was going down in history as the single greatest fundraiser the town had ever seen, and it made her feel wonderful to know she'd been such a big part of it all. The money was earmarked for social services that helped out the elderly and would fund programs like Meals on Wheels, taxis for appointments, and anything else that was needed.

The meal had been to die for—succulent steak and lobster, roasted potatoes, fresh grilled vegetables, and a strawberry delight for dessert. The live auction had also been a rousing success, with many businesses and local citizens donating generous items—and some of them had caused rollicking bidding wars.

The fishing trip to Alaska had gone to four women from the neighboring county who'd outbid their spouses in a nitty-gritty battle of dollars and cents. There had been golf weekend getaways, time-shares in Hawaii and Costa Rica, a year's worth of haircuts from A Cut Above, and the chance to appear with Cain Black in BlackRock's next music video.

The Vegas-type acts who'd entertained between courses were fabulous and Cain had come through—he'd managed to get a couple of his bandmates to fly in and they were hitting the stage for an acoustical set in a half hour.

She chuckled to herself. Dax, the eccentric British guy who played bass guitar in Cain's band, was an outrageous flirt who had charmed half of Crystal Lake—the female half—and had managed to piss off most of the men. He was a sexy-as-hell smooth operator with a quick wit, a keen eye for the ladies, and, well, he did have the whole rock-star thing going for him.

Lily was pleased—hell, she was more than pleased—but it was hard to take pleasure in her accomplishment when the sexual buzz burning through her blood was making her crazy. She blew out a long breath, seeking the shadows near the margarita bar at the back of the room. It was cooler there, and she needed to focus.

She leaned against the wall and closed her eyes. Never had she felt so alive, so hot and electric—as if every single cell in her body was on fire. It was an exhilarating feeling.

But it was also scary as hell. This was new territory for her, and she wasn't quite sure how to deal with it.

"Great job," Raine Edwards said as she sidled up alongside Lily.

Startled, Lily took a few seconds, and when she thought that maybe she could talk without sounding like a bumbling idiot, she opened her eyes and smiled.

"Thanks, though I can't take all the credit. Blair's staff did a great job pulling everything together considering he decided to change things up about five weeks ago."

Raine's eyebrows shot up. "Hon, parties aren't exactly Blair's strong suit. He might be the mayor, but he's no different from Jake or Cain or even Mac for that matter. Like the rest of them, he thinks a couple cases of beer and chicken wings will do the job. Trust me, the gala would have been a dud if you hadn't taken charge and ran with it, especially after last year."

"Last year?" Lily was almost afraid to ask.

"Blair didn't tell you?"

Lily shook her head. "No."

"Last year's big fundraiser or gala, or whatever the heck you want to call it, was a rodeo-themed event held at the fairgrounds. It was hot and smelly, and there were way too many animals which meant there was a lot of… cleanup if you know what I mean."

"Oh," Lily said, trying to hide her disgust.

"I know, right? And then there was the pig thing."

"The pig thing?"

"Yep. Someone thought it would be a great idea to have a pig riding race. Can you imagine?"

"A pig riding race." Lily couldn't help but smile.

Raine shook her head enthusiastically. "Pigs don't like to be ridden, at least the ones Mr. Fisher brought, so it got real messy, real quick."

"Wow." Lily didn't quite know what to say.

"And when old man Lawrence's pig crashed into the bingo tables—"

Lily's mouth dropped open. "Mr. Lawrence rode a pig? Isn't he pushing ninety?"

"Uh-huh." Raine drained her wineglass. "And then Mrs. Shelton chased them both all the way to the river. She was pissed because she was just about to call bingo and the pot was something like two grand."

Raine tucked an errant strand of silky dark hair behind her ear and leaned against the wall beside Lily, giggling so badly that it took a few moments for her to recover. After a while, Raine nudged Lily.

"So you and Mac seem to be getting along really well."

Just the sound of Mac's name was enough to get those damn butterflies in Lily's stomach moving like crazy. And she couldn't help herself—her gaze found him immediately. He was at the blackjack tables along the other side of the room with Jake and his father, Steven. He'd undone the top buttons of his dress shirt, loosened his tie, and shucked his tux jacket.

He really was beautiful.

And he took her breath away.

His smile was easy, his posture relaxed, but she knew what simmered beneath the surface because it fed the fire inside her—and she knew he was anything but relaxed.

The blond from the week before at the Coach House, the one who'd been all over Mac, was chatting him up, her svelte body looking sexy in a hot little red number that barely covered her butt. He was looking down at the woman, nodding to whatever she was saying, but then he casually cocked his head to the side and checked his watch.

He immediately raised his head and glanced Lily's way, her breath catching as he pointed to his watch. He held up all ten fingers, closed his fists, and then flashed them again. Twenty.

And the look he gave her was hot enough to melt her panties—if, in fact, she had been wearing panties. Which she wasn't.

Her stomach rolled over and the heat inside her curled hard and fast. Twenty minutes to go.

"What's the sign language for?" Raine asked.

Lily shrugged, playing dumb.

Raine studied her for a few moments, and Lily looked

away, not comfortable with the sly smile on her friend's face. Raine held her empty wineglass aloft. "You want a refill?"

Lily shook her head. "I'm good for now." Truthfully, she was afraid to drink any more, because she was afraid of losing control. The only way she could do this with Mackenzie was if she kept the control.

Control was key.

"Huh." Raine glanced from Lily over to Jake and then back to Lily. She set both empty wineglasses on the table beside the margarita bar. "I'm going to assume that you and Mac are heading out early."

Lily didn't take her eyes from Mac. "Why would you say that?"

"Because there is no way either one of you can hold out much longer. Jesus, Lily, I'm getting horny just watching the two of you watch each other."

Lily's cheeks burned, and she finally dragged her eyes from Mac. "Is it that obvious?"

"Yes," Raine replied with a giggle. "It is."

Great.

"I guess we'll be at the top of the gossip food chain by tomorrow morning." Lily glanced around, and when she caught the Lancasters looking her way, she averted her gaze. Was Lily ready for that kind of speculation?

"Nah."

Lily looked at Raine in surprise. "Excuse me?"

"You two are already the topic of most conversations," Raine said with a grin. "That's why Shelli pulled out the big guns."

"Shelli?"

"The blond who's doing everything she can to get

Mac to take her home. Though it's not working." A pause. "Not this time, anyway."

The two women were quiet for a few moments, and then Raine spoke, her tone serious.

"He's a good guy, Lily. Not many people know the real Mackenzie because he doesn't want them to. I like that he's opening up with you. I like that a lot."

Lily didn't know what to say to that, so she said nothing.

"Maybe you're the one who will get through to him, the one who will finally make him see that he doesn't have to be alone. He deserves love and happiness as much as anyone else. Maybe more so considering the shit card he's been dealt."

Panic settled in Lily's gut. How had this flirtation and experiment suddenly become something so much bigger?

"Raine," Lily said urgently, "it's not like that."

Raine's eyebrows shot up.

"Whatever this is…this thing that Mac and I are exploring, it's not like that."

"Like what?" Raine asked.

"It's not a permanent thing, and we're both fine with that. Really, this is just two adults…two consenting adults hanging out and getting to know each other."

"And having lots of hot monkey sex?"

Lily blushed but refused to look away. "Isn't that what consenting adults who hang out together do?"

"Well, I know you're not going to spend the night playing Scrabble."

"No." Lily shook her head. Oh God, there went the butterflies again. "No, we're not going to play Scrabble, but that doesn't make whatever this is a serious thing. We're just hanging out."

Raine snorted—she actually snorted—which kinda offended Lily.

"You can think that all you want, but you're both fooling yourselves. I've never seen Mac act this way with a woman before. *Never*. He's been undressing you with his eyes all night, and every time Blair or any other guy comes near, I expect him to pound his chest and roar like King Kong. This might not be a permanent thing in your minds, but it isn't something light or casual either. You guys aren't kids planning a covert sleepover."

Lily's eyes found their way back to Mac. He was smiling at something Jake said, his arm around his buddy as the two of them chatted with Steven Edwards. Something tightened inside Lily, something hot and a little painful. He looked relaxed and happy, and, man, did she like that look on him.

Could Raine be right?

"Just promise me you won't close yourself off from the possibility of something more with Mac, because I know that he will. He doesn't think that he wants what Jake and I have. He doesn't think he needs what Cain and Maggie have. But he does. Hell, Mac needs it more than anyone I know, and I think that maybe…I think that maybe you do too."

Lily tore her gaze from Mac, but Raine had already slipped away, her lithe body lost among the burgeoning crowd in line for the margarita bar.

With a sigh she rolled her shoulders, trying to ease the tension that sat there, but it was no use. She was wound too tight and suddenly nervous as hell. She shook out her hands and wiped damp palms across the tops of her thighs.

God, this is going to be a disaster. She couldn't remember the last time she'd been with anyone. The baseball player in Texas? Maybe?

Lily's cheeks burned as she remembered that night. Jake had already left for Crystal Lake, and she was alone in Texas. Her brother had taken a turn for the worse, and she'd drowned her sorrows in a bar around the corner from the hospital. She'd ingested way too much tequila and had allowed a jock to take her back to his hotel room.

She didn't remember much other than the walk of shame the next morning and him calling her a dead fuck.

Frigid. That's what her ex-fiancé had called her just before he'd told her that her sister, Maddison, was a better lay. All this time, Lily had thought she was just bad at sex, that her body wasn't made right. That she wasn't quite right…but Mackenzie had blown that theory out of the water.

Turned out, she was just waiting for the right man to come along, the right man who could push all the right buttons.

Warm breath caressed the back of her neck as two large hands slid around her waist and she was pulled back against a hard body, effectively pushing away all thoughts of Raine and commitment and anything else that might have been knocking around the back of Lily's mind.

"Five minutes, Boston. Say your good-byes now."

Mackenzie's voice slid over her as she melted into him, and she shuddered when his right hand splayed over her rib cage, resting just beneath the curve of her breast.

"I don't..."

His mouth brushed across the sensitive area beneath her ear and she shuddered.

"Let's just go," she said hoarsely. She wanted to erase all the memories and pain inside her, and Mackenzie was the key.

Mac's hand slid to hers, and he led them through the crush of people at the silent auction table before cutting across the dance floor to the other side of the room.

Lily nodded to the few people she knew personally, and they paused as Mackenzie scooped up his tux jacket from their table and nodded to a few men she didn't know. A couple of guys tried to waylay him, but he sidestepped them like a pro, and before Lily knew it, they were at the exit.

The air was heavy with humidity, and in the distance, she could see the last bits of daylight dropping below the horizon. An owl hooted nearby and she shivered—an omen?

"No turning back now, Boston."

Lily glanced down at their hands, still linked together intimately. His skin was golden next to her paleness, the fingers long and masculine. Even though Mackenzie had an office job in the city at some big architectural firm, she knew he still got his hands dirty. The pads of his fingers were rough.

She breathed in the hot, heavy air that was full of Mackenzie, and the ache in her lower belly grew stronger by the second.

Her heart was racing. Her cells were buzzing. Her body was alive.

Lily St. Clare had never wanted anything or anyone

as badly as she wanted Mackenzie Draper. If she lived to be a hundred years old, she was pretty damn sure she'd never feel this way again.

"Are you going to talk all night or take me back to your place?"

Mackenzie's eyes bored into her as he tugged her behind him, into the dark, toward the parking lot. He gave her one searing-hot kiss before securing the seat belt across her lap, and then he hopped into the truck, the key in the ignition and the motor turning over within seconds.

He pulled out of the parking lot and pointed his truck toward the lake.

And he didn't say one more word.

Chapter 16

Mac pulled his truck up the driveway of the cottage and cut the engine. It was pretty dark out here with the barest hint of a moon—he'd left in such a rush that he'd forgotten to leave the outside lights on—and it took a bit for his eyes to adjust.

He turned to Lily. Her hands were clasped in her lap, the long elegant fingers working each other—a nervous gesture. He got that.

Hell, he was more worked up—and maybe more nervous—than when he'd lost his virginity to Dawn Marcoux in the tenth grade after the annual homecoming football game. She was two years older than him and she'd dragged his ass into the boathouse out at the Edwards twins' after-party. She'd taken off all her clothes—it had been the first time he'd seen a woman naked—and she'd proceeded to teach him things he'd only read about in his older brother's *Penthouse Forums*.

Since that first time, he'd been with a lot of women. It wasn't something he boasted about; it just was. He'd been blessed with the Draper good looks and charm, and like bees to honey, once the girls started hanging around, they'd never left. They'd made it almost too easy for him, and he was used to getting what he wanted, whenever he wanted.

He was always in control.

But with Lily he didn't feel in control. Not one bit.

Christ, his body felt like it was on fire, and like an animal, his only thought was to rip her clothes off and possess her. He didn't want tonight to be like that, like New Year's Eve. There hadn't been much room for talking or tasting and touching that night. It had been about connecting on a physical level. It had been about release.

And now, if he didn't slow things down, he was going to blow early and there was no way he was going to let that happen.

Not with Boston.

Not tonight.

Mac took a moment to get his shit together because he wasn't entirely sure that he could speak. His body was coiled so tightly that he was afraid every damn muscle he owned was frozen, including his vocal chords.

"Hey," he managed to say.

Her head jerked up, and when her eyes met his, he felt as if he'd just been knocked on his ass. Maybe he should have taken that as a warning because no one had ever affected him like that with a look.

But he didn't.

"Hey," she answered softly.

Christ, even the sound of her voice was doing all kinds of weird things to him.

"I'm not going to lie, Lily, if I could take you right here in the truck, I would."

She swallowed. Hard. And his eyes moved down to where her breasts strained against the top of her dress. Those delectable nipples pushed against her top and he fought the urge to open his mouth and taste them.

Jesus, but she was perfect.

"There's enough room in here," he whispered. "I

could make it work. I could position us against the window. I could push up your dress. I could slide inside you, and I'm guessing it would be hot as hell."

Her chest rose and fell rapidly, and he loved that she was as affected by all of this as he was.

Mac slowly undid his seat belt and moved across the seat until he was so close to her, that even in the dim light from the dashboard, he could count the freckles across the bridge of her nose.

They looked like little bits of pale gold.

He bent forward and licked them, feeling like he was going to come apart when he heard her gasp.

His mouth hovered above hers, hands slowly slipping into the back of her hair, working the knot that laid against her shoulder until he was able to free the silky strands.

She strained against him, and it took everything that he had to hold still as she moaned and reached for him. Mac let her slide her mouth across his. He let her put her tongue inside his mouth.

Hell, he even let her tug on his bottom lip and press against him—though he paid the price with a sharp tug between his legs. Already he ached with need and his dick was hard. He was going to have to slow this down because he wanted tonight to last.

Every. Single. Minute.

That thought alone had fueled him and got him through the week.

She made this noise at the back of her throat that damn near did him in, and he had no idea how he was able to resist her—but he did.

He nipped at the valley between her breasts and then, eyes locked to hers, slowly reached across her chest and opened the truck door. His knuckles brushed over her nipples as he did so, and she inhaled sharply, her eyes widening, her lips parting.

"Get out," he said.

She licked her lips and exhaled. "What if I don't want to? What if I want to do it—"

"It?" he interrupted. He couldn't help himself and swooped in for a tug at her lips. He breathed against her. "Do you mean sex?"

Lily squirmed against him and nodded. Her hands were on his shoulders, and she pulled herself toward him. "Yes. Right here. Right now."

"I'm not going to screw you in a truck, Boston." He paused. "Not tonight anyway."

Her eyes darkened as she swiped that hot tongue over her lips.

Mac groaned and leaned away from her, because he knew that if he didn't get his ass out of this truck, he was going to lose his shit completely.

"Out," he growled like an animal.

He didn't give her a chance to refuse or to beg or to put her mouth on him again—because he knew he'd cave. He'd collapse like a goddamn row of dominoes. Mackenzie rolled back toward his own door and slid out of the truck, a little weak in the knees, but considering what was going on between his legs, it was no surprise. He had a monster hard-on.

No shit. He glanced down. Godzilla was in his pants.

He adjusted himself and rounded the vehicle, catching Lily as she stumbled out of the truck, her long dress caught around her ankles. He scooped her into his arms and headed toward the beach, picking his way down the path with care. When he got there, he took a right and strode toward the dock.

Carefully, he let Lily slide down his body, though the little minx wiggled suggestively against his erection. He dropped a quick kiss onto her mouth and whispered, "Hold on."

The boathouse was fairly new, and when Cain had stayed there a few summers back, he'd had the entire place wired for sound. Mac slipped inside the building and flipped on the lights, which he knew would give them a bit of illumination along the dock and water. Next he turned on the stereo system, chose the CD and song that he wanted, and, after tossing his necktie, joined Lily back on the dock.

She was barefoot and looked insanely hot with her pink toes peeking out from beneath the hem of that dress.

That dress that was coming off shortly, but first…

The gentle strains of an old Chris Isaak song fell over the night, a steel guitar that was all smoke and sex. It was hot summer nights, bittersweet longing, and sensual desire.

"World was on fire and no one could save me but you."

Mac held his hand out, palm facing upward, and waited.

Lily took a hesitant step, and he knew that she was a little confused.

"I want a dance," he said. "A woman who looks like you on a night like tonight should have at least one dance, don't you think?"

Lily walked toward him and didn't stop until she was pressed up against his chest. With no shoes, she tucked under his chin, and she rested her head on his shoulder. He couldn't help himself and slid his hand down her back as they slowly began to move. He wanted to cup her butt—to hold her tight to his erection—but he didn't. He splayed his fingers across the small of her back and, with his free hand, grabbed her other hand.

They moved slowly to the sounds of "Wicked Game," a song that was sex and candy and seduction—perfect really. If Mackenzie was paying attention, he would have heard the sad lament of a broken heart. He'd have heard the warning.

But Mac wasn't paying attention to anything other than how amazing the woman in his arms felt.

He breathed in her scent, a heady combination of summer—something exotic—and if it was possible for him to harden even more, he did.

There were no words as the two of them slowly moved along the dock, Mac leading as Lily melted into him, her steps following him as if they'd danced together before.

When the song ended, he stilled, his hands moving up until he cupped her chin and tipped her face toward him. Her long lashes threw spiky shadows across her cheeks, and that mouth was open, ready for him.

"You're beautiful," he whispered before lowering his head and claiming her lips in a soft, tease of a kiss. He brushed his mouth across hers once, twice, and then licked the corners before opening up and tasting what she offered so freely.

He kissed her in a slow, sensual way, and when he dragged his mouth from hers, she moaned, nearly sending him over the edge.

But it was too soon.

A wicked smile tugged on his mouth as he carefully pulled away from her. With Lily's eyes on him, Mackenzie slowly undid the buttons of his dress shirt, tugging the hem out of his pants before slipping it off and tossing it onto the dock.

"What are you…?" She licked her lips nervously and glanced around.

Mac had his shoes and socks off and then went for his belt.

She licked her lips again.

The belt landed on top of his shoes.

She moved slightly. Maybe she moaned.

He stepped out of his pants.

When his hands went to the waistband of his boxers, she shook her head.

"Mackenzie, what the hell are you doing?"

He tugged on them. "What does it look like?"

"But—" She licked her lips again and damn if Godzilla didn't tighten even more. "Anyone can see…"

Mac pinned her with a heated look. "Boston, there's no one out here but us." He yanked his boxers down and strode toward her, grinning wickedly as she gasped.

He loved the way her eyes rolled over his body, and he knew that she liked what she saw. He loved the way she swallowed hard, the way her breathing hitched at the back of her throat. Jesus, the way her nipples poked through the ice-blue dress and that damn sexy sound she made again.

He bent down and kissed her, a soft, gentle swirl of lips and tongue, before he moved to the pulse that beat erratically at the base of her neck. He suckled her there—hard—and held onto her as she swayed in his grasp.

When she began to squirm against him, he broke away and took a step backward.

"You coming in?"

"What?" She sounded breathless.

Mac turned and walked to the end of the dock and gazed at the lake. It was as smooth as glass with only a few ripples as it lapped up against the shore in gentle waves. In the distance, he saw a few lights from boats still on the water, but the shore was pretty much in darkness.

It felt as if they were the only two people in the world. He kinda liked that thought.

"Mackenzie! You're crazy."

He glanced over his shoulder. "Haven't you ever gone skinny-dipping?"

She shook her head no.

"Well, darlin', you don't know what you're missing."

With one more hot look over his shoulder, he turned and dove into the water.

Chapter 17

Lily stared at the end of the dock in shock.

She had no idea what the hell was going on. The dance had been incredible, and her blood still buzzed with unrelenting sexual frustration.

And his striptease? Good Lord, she was pretty sure she'd had a little mini-orgasm just watching him, but this? What the hell was this all about? It was not the seduction she'd been expecting, and yet her cells were electrified. It felt as if every pleasure point in her body was on fire.

The ache between her legs was so intense that she shifted slightly, rubbing her thighs together in an effort to alleviate it, and fought the urge to press her palm against herself.

She whimpered.

The night was dark, but the beam of light from the door to the boathouse spread out enough that she could see Mac's head above the water.

"Come here, Boston."

He wasn't asking—he was telling. But something about the tone of his voice told her that he wasn't as in control as he wanted her to think.

She walked about midway down the dock and paused as Mackenzie slowly moved toward her, his look predatory as he stood up, the water lapping to just below his chest.

His hair was slicked back, his eyes dark and mysterious, and his chest…good Lord, the man looked as if he was carved from granite.

The tattoo on his left bicep drew her eye. "What does that mean?" A diversion for sure, but she was trying to calm the hell down.

Mac followed her gaze, and when he looked up at her again, he grinned wickedly. "Take your clothes off and I'll tell you."

She considered him for a moment, liking this game. "You think that I won't do it?"

His grin widened. "I think that you're afraid of the water." He glanced down and raised an eyebrow wicked. "Or of what's in it."

An image of his cock jutting straight out from his body crossed her mind and again she shifted. It felt as if she was coming apart, and they hadn't done anything but flirt and dance.

Lily glanced around once more. Mac had said no one was around, but she'd never been to the cottage before and the thought of anyone watching her…

"Pussy," he said softly.

"Pussy?" she asked.

"You like scaredy-cat better? I kinda prefer pussy myself." He paused, his voice low and reassuring. "There's no one out here but us, Boston. Trust me."

A few moments passed as she stared out at him in the dark, and she felt her inhibitions falling away, slipping from her skin until there was nothing left for it but to join him.

With a toss of her hair, Lily strode forward until she stopped in the beam of light thrown from the boathouse.

She glanced down, eyes on Mackenzie as she reached for the thin straps of her gown.

Carefully, she tugged one and then the other off her shoulders, and with his eyes settled firmly on her, she pulled them down until her breasts were exposed. Her nipples, puckered from desire, were sensitive, and she hissed as the material slipped across them.

"Jesus," Mac whispered, his eyes on her breasts.

The want in his voice empowered her, and Lily's fingers trailed across her flesh until she found her nipples, and with her eyes locked on his, she slowly massaged them. The muscles along the side of his neck strained, and a slow smile spread across her face as she reveled in her feminine power.

"You like that, Mackenzie?"

He ran his hand through his hair. "What the hell do you think?"

The feeling inside her—the one of control and power—was intoxicating, and Lily threw caution to the wind. She ran with it.

Carefully she began to peel away her dress, sliding it down her body as the material stretched and gave over her hips. She paused just before she got to the good part, the part she knew he wanted to see, and cocked her head.

"Should I continue?"

"Take it off," he spit out. "Now, Boston. Or I swear to God—"

She slipped the dress over her hips and let it fall in a pile of blue at her feet. She then kicked it to the side and spread her legs slightly, loving how hot he looked as he watched her.

"Fuck me," he said hoarsely. "If I had known you were commando the entire night, I would have—"

"What would you have done, Mac?"

She took a step forward, her toes gripping the edge of the dock as she stood directly over him. His eyes, so dark under the night sky that they looked black, slowly moved down from the top of her head, lingering over her breasts before settling on the junction between her legs.

"For starters, we wouldn't have made it to the gala."

"No?"

"Hell-the-fuck-no. I would have driven you straight here and, darlin', I would have had you in the front of the truck. Hands down. Hell, I probably would have had you at the end of your driveway."

She was aching.

"And my sister?"

Heavy with need.

"She could have watched for all I care."

God, she was so wet.

"Mackenzie, I didn't take you for an exhibitionist."

This was torture, but she was totally enjoying it. Best. Foreplay. Ever.

"I can smell how much you want me," Mac said roughly.

Lily froze, embarrassed and suddenly unsure.

Mac moved toward her. "Sit down. Right here."

Her hands slipped down her belly and then slipped lower, hovering over the thin patch of blond hair there. He was between her legs and if she sat down his head—that amazing mouth of his—would be…

Dear Lord. The fire inside Lily exploded and goose bumps rolled over her skin.

"Boston."

The way he said her nickname made her insides coil tightly, as if he was starving and she was the only thing on the menu.

His hands were on the dock now, his eyes glittering as he gazed up at her.

"Ass on the dock." He might have growled. "Now."

Carefully, Lily lowered her body, but before she hit the dock, his hands were on her hips guiding her the rest of the way. Slowly. So, incredibly slowly. Until she was nearly hanging off the edge of the dock. Her feet sank into the water and it lapped halfway up her calves.

"Do you know how beautiful you are?" he said, eyes on hers as she tried to keep calm. Her heart beat fast and hard, and she was sure that he could hear it.

Lily shook her head. No. No one had ever made her feel this special or beautiful or so incredibly hot. Sure there had been men in the past, but none like him.

There was only Mackenzie.

He spread her legs a little wider, and she gripped the edge of the dock, knuckles and fingers white from the pressure, breath held when his fingers rolled across her lower belly. His mouth followed his fingers, and she squeezed her eyes shut, trying to hold back the groan in her throat when his fingers dipped lower and found her slick opening.

"You're so wet," he said hoarsely. "For me."

God. Oh God. This feels so good.

"Look at me."

She couldn't. She couldn't move.

His fingers stopped and he growled. "Now."

Lily's eyes flew open, and she gazed down at him.

He slid two fingers inside her and slowly rotated

them, curving upward, massaging, stroking—and he never took his eyes off her. Not even when he followed his fingers and kissed his way up her thighs and settled between her legs.

When his tongue darted inside her, Lily jerked, but he held her steady, his eyes on her as he licked and suckled and stroked her. The sight of him down there, his mouth on her most private part, was something she would never forget. The look in his eyes was feral, erotic, and primal.

Pressure from deep inside began to pull. It clawed and spread out in a blanket of heat that had everything clenching.

"Mackenzie," she whimpered, gyrating her hips.

His tongue flickered over her clitoris, and she jerked again, her hands finding their way into the thick hair on top his head as she struggled to hold it together. But when he kissed her there…when he licked and then suckled the engorged nub, she lost it.

An animalistic sound erupted from inside her, and she bucked her hips, body fueled by desire as she sought release.

Her fingers gripped him, and she began to shake.

"Come for me, Boston," he said roughly.

Lily arched into him and threw her head back, crying out as the pressure inside erupted. Everything went tight and hot and electric. Her body shook with convulsions as she shattered against him. Into him. Over him.

For several moments, she stared up at the night sky, panting and feeling as if her bones had liquefied. If he let go, she would slide into the water and drift away.

And then she felt his wet hands on her thighs, tugging her toward him. He was saying things, dirty things, his voice low and thick as his hands gripped her. Lily slowly righted herself and let him pull her into the water. She wrapped her legs around his waist and clung to him, her mouth seeking his hungrily.

She kissed him. She tasted herself in him.

Holy. Hell.

She groaned when his tongue slid inside her mouth, but he had a hell of a lot more control than she did…he took his time, kissing her gently and then suckling her tongue hard.

Crushed against him, the cool water was like silk on their skin, and they kissed until her head spun. Jesus, Mackenzie Draper could kiss. Never had a man taken his time with her and fed from her mouth as if it was everything he needed.

Mackenzie held her as if she was the most precious thing in the world, his mouth taking and giving, murmuring erotic things and driving her crazy her with his hands, tongue, and mouth. They were in the water for hours it seemed, but she knew it had only been a few minutes.

And she never wanted it to end. They were skin on skin, and it was the hottest thing ever.

She loved the way his hands slid up and down her body, the way his mouth worshipped her, gliding along her collarbone. Settling against her breasts. Nestling beneath her earlobe.

When he took one turgid nipple inside his mouth and blew hot air over her before suckling her hard, she felt the pull shoot all the way down to the center between her legs.

"Mac," she whimpered, gyrating against him. She felt

the heat of his erection just below her butt, and she knew that he couldn't hold out much longer.

"Say it," he said gruffly.

"Say what?" she asked, barely able to get the words out.

"What do you want?" he asked.

"I want you inside me," she answered without hesitation.

Mac dropped another kiss onto her mouth, a slow tantalizing tease as his hands kneaded her butt cheeks. He turned and slowly walked out of the water, Lily clinging to him with her legs and her arms, their mouths fused together as he headed up the path to the cottage.

She felt his strength, the muscles in his shoulders and arms, the heat in his kiss, and by the time they reached the porch, they were both breathing heavy. Slowly she slid down the length of him, and when she would have grabbed his cock, he stopped her and shook his head.

"Don't. Babe, I'm too far gone. If you touch me now, it will be all over and, Boston, I've been dreaming of sinking inside you since New Year's Eve."

He fused his mouth to hers again, pulling her into the cottage, and they didn't stop until they were in his bedroom. They didn't stop until she was on her back, on his bed, spread out like a banquet feast. Her legs were wide open, and she didn't care at all. In fact, when his heated gaze settled there, she smiled and slipped her fingers over herself.

"Jesus, Lily. Are you trying to kill me?"

"No," she answered. "I need you very much alive and inside me."

Mackenzie grabbed a condom from somewhere behind him, and she bit her bottom lip in anticipation. She heard him rip the foil, and seconds later he was over, his arms on either side of her face, his beautiful mouth close to hers.

His long, heated length was pressed intimately into hers, and she felt the rigid strength of his cock.

"I can't wait anymore, Boston, and I'm going to apologize now because I don't think I can last much longer."

And then he was inside. His long, hard length going deep.

God, the feel of him inside her.

Her legs went around him, her nails dug into his shoulders. There were no more words. No more tender kisses or gentle caresses.

There was only the hard and intense need they felt for each other. And as Mackenzie took Lily to the summit, as he rocked into her and begged for release, her last thought before she came was that she would never get this back.

At least, not with anyone else. Never anyone else.

And for that one second, she was scared to death.

But then Mackenzie's mouth found hers, and they shattered together—and Lily let all those thoughts slide away.

Chapter 18

MACKENZIE WAS WIDE AWAKE WELL BEFORE THE FIRST rays of sun crept across the horizon. He waited for his eyes to adjust to the gloom and glanced at the clock beside the bed. It was just after 3:00 a.m., and considering that he'd had Lily more than once—hell, he'd lost count after she'd pushed him onto his back and slid on top of him—he should have been down for the count for at least a few more hours.

Mac listened to Lily's slow, easy breaths. It had been a long time since he'd woken up with a woman in his arms, and he kind of liked the way it felt. Lily was warm and soft and just...right.

Her back was to him, that delectable butt pressed into his groin where—hello—Godzilla was already stirring. He'd snaked his arm around her waist, holding her tight for hours, and now that he was awake, he bent forward, inhaling the subtle scent of apples in her hair.

Damn, but Boston smelled good. And it wasn't that perfume crap that most of the women he dated liked to use. Seriously, if they only knew how much most guys hated that stuff. Who the hell wanted a nose full of heavy perfume when you were getting busy?

But Boston? She was sexy and fresh and...

She murmured something in her sleep and moved her butt against him.

Jesus.

He clenched his teeth together in an effort to hold himself together. His cock was definitely awake—hard and ready to go—and for a moment, he considered slipping inside her from behind, but then he realized his condoms were on the other side of the bed.

Mac wasn't willing to give up the feel of her against him just yet.

He winced at the thought. Christ, Jake would tell him he was turning into a woman or would called him a pussy—which was ironic, because Jake had pretty much become a pussy the moment he'd sniffed Raine's skirts and decided to chase after the one thing he wanted more than anything else.

It sure as hell wasn't Mac's gig, but he couldn't fault their happiness. Nope. That whole forever thing wasn't in the cards for him, but that didn't mean he begrudged those who were into it, the ones who believed in true love and all that shit.

Mac lay back on his pillow and gazed at the ceiling. To each his own and all that. He might not be into the commitment thing, but neither was Lily, and right now the two of them together was just about perfect.

In fact they were better than perfect if there was such a thing.

He wasn't sure how long he lay there, staring up at the ceiling and enjoying the feel of Lily in his bed, but eventually his neck cramped up and he moved gingerly, careful not to wake her.

Mac slid out of bed and took a moment to watch Lily as she slumbered, totally unaware and vulnerable—there was something so sweet about the way she looked. She was still on her side, with one hand beneath the pillow and the other curled under her chin like a child. That long mane of hair was all over the place—tangled beyond belief—and the indent of her waist, the curve of her hip, and the gentle slope at the small of her back was something he'd like to have fucking framed.

He couldn't help himself.

Mac bent over and kissed a spot at the back of her neck just under her hairline. She shifted slightly and murmured something that he couldn't understand, but she never woke up. He pulled the covers over her and tucked them under her chin before heading out into the main room of the cottage.

He was restless and wasn't sure why, because Lord knows he had no energy left. Mac was in shape, he hit the gym hard, but after the intense workout he'd had with Lily, there were places on him that were a little sore.

He chuckled. What a problem to have.

It was a good sore.

After a quick shower, he pulled on an old pair of faded green cargos and padded out to the kitchen where he made a pot of coffee and then sat at the counter where he'd left his laptop. He booted up the thing and stared at the screen absently, leaning back in his chair as he gazed around the empty room. It was quiet—too quiet. Generally, he liked to listen to music while he worked, but he didn't want to chance waking Lily.

He thought that maybe she should sleep, because he was already planning on round two later. In the meantime, he may as well get some work done. He took a sip of strong, black coffee and got to it.

Several hours later, he slid from his chair and rolled his shoulders. With sunlight streaming into the place, there was no way to hide what his last girlfriend would have called "dumpy chic." Sure the decorators hadn't been called in since 1995, but Mac kinda liked the orange and green and cedar.

The place looked lived-in and comfortable.

He'd just cracked a few eggs into the skillet and was whistling as he did so—when the hell did he ever whistle?—when he heard a knock at the door. It was just before eight in the morning, and he wasn't expecting anyone, but Mac turned the heat down and crossed the room. He glanced out at the driveway when he passed by the large windows in the family room and paused.

It was his mother's car. Huh.

With a quick glance back at the bedroom, he opened the door with a smile, the one he saved for all those times he got caught doing something he shouldn't be doing—which was kind of ridiculous considering he was thirty-five.

"Hey, Ma..."

But the words died on his lips when he spied his sister standing there and, a few feet behind her, his nephew, Liam.

"I'm so sorry to bother you on a Sunday, Mac."

He could tell that she was nervous and he knew that didn't bode well. "It's alright. What's up?"

She looked past him. "Um, can we come in?"

Mac hesitated, but Becca didn't seem to notice, or rather, she chose not to notice, because she pushed past him and beckoned the kid to follow. "Come on, Liam."

Mac stood aside and waited for his nephew to pass

before closing the door behind them. That's when he noticed Liam's bag, and he shot a look to his sister.

"What's going on, Becca?"

She hesitated, her eyes sliding away from his, and that pretty much told him all he needed to know. Whatever was going on couldn't be good.

"I need Liam to stay here for a few days."

Liam? What? No.

Mac shook his head and only stopped himself from becoming a total asshole when he realized that his nephew's eyes were on him. The kid had his hands buried in his front pockets as if he were digging for gold, and if he pushed them down any more, he was going to lose his pants. Something about the way his shoulders were hunched got to Mac, and he glared at his sister.

It was always the kids who got the shit end of the stick.

"I'm going to ask you one more time. What the hell is going on?"

Becca licked her lips and motioned to Liam. "Why don't you go down and have a look at the dock? Maybe your uncle can take you fishing one afternoon, or—"

"Yeah," Liam said. "Cuz he's so excited to have me here."

Liam pushed past his mother and headed outside, leaving the siblings alone. Mac studied his sister for a few moments before he headed back into the kitchen. What now?

"I could use a coffee if you don't mind."

Mac grimaced as he eyed the machine. He could be a total prick and tell her he had none left, or he could be the brother that he knew she needed right now and make her a damn pot of coffee. If Lily hadn't been in his bedroom, it would have been a no-brainer, but she was and he had no desire to mix his fucked-up family business with what he had going on with Lily. No one should bear witness to the screwed-up situation that he couldn't manage to escape no matter how hard he tried.

"Sorry, I don't have cream."

"Oh," Becca said. "That's okay."

"I don't have any sugar either."

She played with the edge of his laptop and shrugged. "That's fine."

He could play this game all day but so could Becca. Mac knew when he was done for, so he walked over to his bedroom and closed the door. When he turned back around, his sister was staring at him with big eyes.

"Shit, Mackenzie. I'm sorry. I didn't know you had someone here."

"There's no one—"

Becca's eyebrow shot up. "Then why did you just close the door?"

"Don't worry about it," he said, walking over to the cupboard. He pulled out two mugs and set them aside. "It's not like it would have stopped you if you had."

Mackenzie tossed the old grains and got the machine set up before he leaned against the counter. Becca was quiet, fiddling with the cup he'd set out for her, and he knew by the way she was avoiding his eyes that he wasn't going to like what she had to say. The bruise on her cheek was now a lovely shade of yellow, but the swelling had gone down and sometime between yesterday and today she'd tossed the sling her left arm had been in.

"Are you going to tell me what's going on, Becs?"

"Promise me you won't get mad."

Okay. This wasn't good.

Mackenzie clenched his teeth together and tried to relax, but his hands fisted at his side as his thoughts turned to his asshole brother-in-law. He knew where this was going. He'd seen it all before.

"I…David called last night, and I need to go and see him."

"No," Mac shot back, pushing away from the counter as his anger began to boil. It began to boil hard, and he put some distance between himself and Becca. "Are you kidding me? Jesus Christ, Becs. I thought you had more sense than that."

"Mac. He's…it's just to talk things out."

Mackenzie rounded the corner of the countertop and glared at his sister. "Let me guess. He loves you and he's sorry that he beat your face in. He didn't mean to hurt you and he sure as hell didn't mean to almost break your arm."

Becca winced but shoved her chin up at him. "Goddammit, Mac. Keep your voice down. I don't need your bimbo of the day hearing my business."

Mac had a moment where he saw red. It was a bright-crimson sheet of anger that washed over him, and he had to physically move away from his sister because he didn't trust himself.

"What is it that you think you're going to accomplish by going back to him?"

"Mac, you don't understand. He's my husband and he's—"

"He's a fucking prick who used you as a punching bag. That's not a husband. That's not a father. That's a coward and a bully, and you deserve a hell of a lot more than someone like that."

"Mac—"

"Don't Mac me. He beat you and put you in a goddamn hospital. What the hell do you want me to say? Didn't you see enough of that when we were kids? How many times did Dad slap the shit out of Mom, and when he got tired of that, he turned to us? How many times did he say he was sorry and that it wouldn't happen again?"

Her eyes got shiny, as if they were full of tears, but Mackenzie didn't give a rat's ass.

"How many times did we go to school when it was a hundred goddamn degrees outside, wearing long-sleeve shirts because we were too embarrassed for our friends to see the bruises on our arms? Or the belt marks on our backs? Ten times? Fifty? One hundred?"

Jesus, Mac was so angry. He clenched and unclenched his fists, eyeing the punching bag he'd installed in the family room.

Becca stood. "David is not our father. He's not! And I need to see him, Mackenzie. I need to talk to him."

Mac threw his hands into the air. Gone were all the warm, fuzzy feelings he'd woken with—but he should have known. This here, this brutality was his reality, and he would never get away from it.

He thought of Liam, of the lost and angry look in the kid's eyes, and he saw himself. He saw the broken kid he'd been, and it filled him with such blinding rage that for a moment he couldn't see clearly.

He took a step toward his sister, his face black and angry. "How the hell can you do this to your kid? How can you be that goddamn selfish?"

"Mac," her voice trembled. "Please, listen to me." She blew out a long breath and wiped at her face. "I need to do this but give me some credit. I'm not Mom, and he's not Dad. We need to figure some things out and just need a few days. A week or two at the most. Just David and I. I just need to..."

He'd heard that before too.

"You know what? I don't give a shit."

And he didn't. He didn't want to get involved. What the hell was the point? He could write the ending to this story in his sleep. Mac took a step back and shook his head. If his sister wanted to be that pathetic, well, she could go right ahead. She was an adult, and it was her life.

He glanced out the windows that faced the water and spied Liam standing at the edge of the beach.

"Why's the kid here? Why can't he stay with Mom?"

Becca's bottom lip trembled a bit. "Mom is teaching Bible School all week and well, Liam's a bit old for it. He...he asked if he could stay with you. He had fun the other night, and I think that he thought you would be okay with him staying for a few days, but obviously I was wrong."

Something twisted inside Mac, something hard and painful, and he glanced out the window again. He didn't have time for a kid. Christ, he was in the middle of this big project for Jake, and there was Lily...

Liam tossed a rock out over the water, and it skipped a few times before disappearing beneath the surface. He shoved his hands into his pockets again and hunched his shoulders, head down as he stared at his feet.

It was like looking at himself when he was young.

Mackenzie dragged his eyes back to his sister. He was probably going to regret this—what the hell did he know about kids?

"He can stay," Mac said. "I'm going to be busy and probably won't have much time for him but…"

His sister launched herself at him and wrapped her arms around his chest in a hug that was hard and desperate. "Thank you, Mac. I knew I could count on you."

Everything inside him was coiled tight, but after a few seconds, that part of him that still cared loosened up a bit, and he slipped his arms around his sister, holding her, supporting her when the tears started up again.

Chapter 19

Lily waited until Mac's sister left before she ventured out of the bedroom. The cottage was empty, and for a moment, she stood in the middle of the kitchen not really sure what to do.

She was still reeling from what she'd overheard and felt awful for listening in on a private family conversation, but it's not as if she'd done it on purpose. Mac's loud voice had woken her, and at that point, there was no way she couldn't listen—not even if she'd shoved her head under the covers and slid beneath the pillows.

Dressed in an old T-shirt she'd found in the bedroom, Lily pushed her hair out of the way and peeked out the window that overlooked the lake. Mac was down there talking to a young boy who looked about nine or ten. They stood at the edge of the water, both of them with their hands shoved into their front pockets.

The boy was as blond as Mackenzie with the same build—wide shoulders, tapered waist, and long legs—and if she'd never met them before, she would think he was Mac's. She watched them for a few more minutes and decided it was time for her to go when she felt something stirring in her breast. She didn't know what the hell it was, but she sure as heck knew she needed to shut it down.

Last night had been amazing, but it was over and time for her to go. She and Mac had a sex thing—nothing more—and a relaxed morning together wasn't in the cards.

Her overnight bag was still in the truck, along with her cell phone and purse. She moved gingerly because there were a lot of parts on her body that ached, which, considering the night she'd had, was par for the course. She opened the door and slipped outside, spying a pair of Mackenzie's sandals—thank God. She slipped her feet into them, nearly falling on her ass twice as she made her way up the uneven path that led to the driveway, but it was worth it—the path and driveway was strewn with rocks.

As luck would have it, the truck was locked—when the hell he'd had time to think about locking the stupid thing she had no clue—and she stared through the window at her bag.

"Dammit."

She'd never been in this situation before. Not really. When she'd been "good-time Lily," any sex she had was at a party or in a dorm room or some back alley of a club. She had sex for the express purpose of having sex because she was a St. Clare, sister to the crazy Maddison St. Clare, and well, why not give them what they all expected? It had seemed somehow easier.

Lily never thought she deserved better anyway, and considering sex wasn't exactly something she liked, doing the nasty with a stranger didn't matter. At least not back then. It was more of a way for her to mean something to someone, even if it was only for a few hours.

So there'd been no sleepovers. No waking up in bed with someone. No awkward morning conversations...

or continuations of the previous night's activities. She'd never wanted any of that.

Which is why she was a little shocked that she'd been so disappointed to wake up alone, with no sight of Mac. Instead, he'd been arguing with his sister, and now he seemed to have forgotten all about Lily.

Carefully making her way back down the path, she slipped back inside the cottage. Mac was still down at the dock with the boy, but now they were sitting side by side, gazing out at the water.

There was something bittersweet about the two of them together, and for a second time, Lily had to mentally pull away. She walked into the kitchen and spied Mac's cell on the counter. Grabbing it up, she punched in Jake's number, and he answered on the second ring.

"Draper, what the hell? I've been trying to get hold of you for the last hour."

Lily made a face. Ten guesses as to what Jake wanted to discuss with Mackenzie. In some ways, she preferred having no one who really gave a damn about her.

"I'll make sure to pass that along."

She thought that maybe Jake fell off of something because there was a whole lot of cursing and then he must have stubbed his toe because the cursing moved to a level of epic she hadn't heard in a good, long while. And then the barking started.

Jake must have closed himself into the bathroom or something because all of a sudden there was nothing.

"Shit, Lily. Sorry. I—"

"Did you fall out of bed?"

"What?"

"Bed. Did you fall out of it?" She moved back to the window, her eyes on the two boys down near the water.

"Yeah. Stubbed my fu…my damn big toe, and it's not funny."

"I'm not laughing." She was too distracted to laugh.

Jake cleared his throat. "So you're with Mac."

"Yeah. I'm at his place."

There were a few moments of silence. "Okay," he said quietly.

"Is it weird for you?" she asked, suddenly curious.

She could picture the wheels turning in Jake's mind and leaned against the sofa, balancing her butt on the edge as she continued to watch Mac and his nephew.

"No. I mean, kinda." She heard him exhale. "Look, it's none of my business."

"You mean Raine told you that it was none of your business."

"Well, yeah, but…"

"But?"

"I can't help worrying that this is gonna go south. You both mean a hell of a lot to me, and I don't want to see either one of you hurt."

"We're not kids," she murmured.

"No," he said quietly. "You're not."

"I need a favor."

"Anything."

"I need you to come get me." Silence filled her ear. "Jake?"

"Ah, sure. I can do that, but where's Mac?"

Her eyes were still on them, and Mac had moved into the boathouse, Liam following in his wake. Her throat tightened, and she took a moment to answer.

"He's busy right now. Um, some sort of family thing, and I don't really want to get involved."

Jake didn't hesitate. "I'll be there in ten minutes."

Feeling a little out of sorts and not really knowing why, Lily placed Mac's cell back onto the counter and went back to the bedroom. She needed to find his keys and get her stuff, but after a quick search of the room, she realized that there weren't any clothes or keys.

God, they'd stripped down to nothing on the dock and—her head whipped up as she groaned—their clothes probably ended up in the lake. Her dress, his clothes…his *keys*. What the hell was she going to do?

Another search of the kitchen and family room turned up nothing, and she knew that she had no choice but to walk down to the boathouse and see if maybe Mac had an extra set hanging around. There was no way she was going home in nothing but a freaking T-shirt.

Which brought to mind her second problem. The whole commando thing had seemed like such a good idea at the time, but it didn't look so good now, because she had nothing between her butt cheeks and that sweet Crystal Lake air. She rummaged through Mac's drawers and found a pair of boxers that she thought might do the trick. After pulling them up over her hips, she turned the waistband several times, but she still had to hold them so they didn't end up around her ankles.

She didn't bother looking in the mirror—she knew exactly what she looked like—and as she slipped his big-ass sandals on again, she slowly started toward the water.

It was the ultimate walk of shame.

She was so preoccupied with keeping her shorts up

that she didn't see the boat or hear the voices until it was too late. She squared her shoulders, deciding that if she looked like she didn't give a shit, then he would think that she was schooled with this sort of thing and that she was totally fine walking around in his T-shirt and boxers. She stepped into the boathouse and froze.

Lily saw Mac right away. Shirtless. Cargo pants slung so low that it was obscene. He was barefoot—something she found incredibly sexy—and his hair fell to his shoulders in waves. Her eyes traveled over his muscular chest, down past his flat abs, until they rested on the indent just above the waistband of his pants.

Jesus. It was insane how hot he looked. All conscious thought fled as she gazed across the boathouse at him. He had a fishing rod in one hand, and his eyes did a slow once-over, starting from the top of her head and traveling downward. By the time he returned to her face, her nipples were standing on end and those parts of her that ached, not only ached, but they freaking throbbed too.

He didn't say a word, but then again, he didn't have to.

Lily walked toward him, cheeks flushed with need. "Hey," she said softly when she stopped. Her right hand still clutched his boxers and his eyes flickered over her, resting on the bit of skin visible at her waist.

For several long moments he said nothing, and then he bent forward, brushing a light kiss across her mouth, before moving to her ear where his warm breath tickled the side of her face.

"This is a good look for you." He paused and the goose bumps started. "The only thing better is you minus my clothes."

Lily tried to swallow, but it was damn hard with the big lump in the back of her throat. She leaned into him, suddenly weak with need.

"You don't look so bad yourself," she whispered.

"Shit," he muttered, tossing the rod onto the ground. "Darlin', your timing sucks." His arms went around her, and she melted into him. He was big and warm and solid, and she could have stayed like that forever.

Lily rested in the crook of his neck. "I know," she replied quietly, wanting her words only for him. "I heard you and your sister arguing. I'm sorry." She pulled back so she could see his face. "I know your nephew is here."

Mac stared down at her for so long that her cheeks began to burn, and she attempted to pull away.

"That's not it, Boston. Your timing sucks way worse than that and don't you dare move…not just yet. I've got all kinds of things going on between my legs and damned if I want Cain and the other guys to see how fucking horny I am."

Lily's eyes widened, and she froze as a slow grin began to spread across Mac's face. He bent forward again, his mouth near her ear. "Don't let go of those boxers. I wouldn't want these ten-year-old boys to see more than they should."

Noises she'd not heard earlier penetrated the sexual fog that seemed to envelop her whenever she was around Mackenzie—the water lapping against the dock. Shuffling feet. A cleared throat. Or two.

Giggles.

Shit, little-boy giggles.

And then one of them whispered, "Holy cow, Mac's girlfriend is hot."

Lily wanted to dive into the water and disappear forever.

But she didn't. She very carefully gathered the ends of Mac's boxers and made sure that the T-shirt covered everything that it could cover. She shot a murderous look at Mac—because he was totally enjoying the whole thing—and turned around.

She saw Cain and his son, Michael. She saw a man she didn't recognize with another boy about the same age as Michael—the man glanced away when she met his eyes, but the kid didn't.

Cheeky little dude.

She saw Mac's nephew, Liam.

Mac's nephew, who was standing off to the side, holding up what looked like the wet remnants of her dress. Mac's clothes were in a wet pile in front of them. The kid shot them both a look and then nudged Michael. Both boys immediately started snorting and giggling, and the one she didn't know pointed at Lily and then whispered something in Liam's ear, causing another round of elbow nudging and giggles.

What the hell?

Jake chose that moment to join them, and if Lily didn't think things could get worse, she was wrong. Boy was she wrong.

Jake nodded hello and walked over to them, his eyes darting over her head to Mac before he reached forward to tug up the neckline of the T-shirt. It was big on Lily and had slipped down, exposing her shoulder.

She glanced up, eyebrows raised in question, but Jake was glaring at Mackenzie. "Seriously? Hickeys? What are you, fifteen?"

Hickeys?

Oh God. An image of Mac at her neck, his mouth gliding, kissing…suckling filled her mind, and she peeked around Jake. The boys were still giggling.

Mac's hand was warm on her shoulder. "Shove it, Edwards. I couldn't help myself. She tastes too damn good."

A new round of giggling filled the boathouse, but by this time, Lily had had enough. If this is what sleeping over at a guy's place meant, then she was all for leaving in the middle of the night.

"Take me home, Jake."

"Come on, Lily, hold on. I'll take you home. Just let me get Liam set up so he can head out fishing with Cain and the boys."

"You're not going?" she asked, eyes on Liam, who was no longer paying attention to her wet dress. In fact, he'd tossed it and was staring at his uncle, expression unreadable. There was something kinda sad about the kid.

"I can catch up with them later."

"No." She stepped away from Mac. "I just need your keys so I can grab my things from your truck."

"I have no idea where the extra key is and, well…" He pointed toward their wet clothes. "The other set isn't were I left them." He tried not to grin, but it was there… hovering around the corners of his mouth. The bastard was enjoying the whole thing.

"Fine," she snapped. "You can get my stuff back to me when you find your keys." She nodded to Jake. "Let's go."

"Lily, don't be pissed," Mac said.

"I'm not, Mackenzie. Don't worry about it."

Except she was, and she had no idea why. Shit happened,

she got that, but something about the events of the morning had her all mixed up.

"Nice to see you again, Lily," Cain said with a grin.

"You too," she said, nodding at the other man before marching her butt out of the boathouse, clutching Mac's boxers so tightly around her waist that her fingers began to cramp. Talk about a walk of shame. Hell, she gave the saying a whole new meaning.

She climbed into Jake's truck, and when he got behind the wheel and turned to her, she cut him off before he could speak. "Not a word."

It was the quietest ride home she'd ever had.

Chapter 20

Mac knew when a woman was pissed, mostly because, at some point, every woman he'd ever been involved with got pissed at him. It was pretty much par for the course. By the time they reached *that* point in their "relationship," he was okay with it. Hell, he even welcomed it. Encouraged it.

Except that usually Mac knew the why of it. The reason for the attitude. The reason a woman would go home with a guy's best friend instead of waiting for Mac to take her. There were the usual suspects.

He got hung up at the office and forgot to call.

He scheduled a meeting when he was supposed to hook up with them.

He spent too much time chatting up the hostess.

He refused a drawer in his bathroom after six months of dating.

Or the one that was always good for a scene—he was spotted out at dinner with someone else. Mackenzie got that kind of stuff—he understood it, and more importantly, he could deal with it.

But Sunday morning Lily had been more than pissed, and at first he'd been a little confused. None of that usual shit had happened. There had been no discussion about exclusive drawers or missed dates, and he sure as hell hadn't been with anyone else.

In fact, Mac had been knocked on his ass when she'd

walked into the boathouse. God, to see her curves draped in his clothes, her hands clutching his boxers—it had been all he could do not to throw her over the boat and get busy. With all that wild hair, long, sexy legs, mouth still swollen from his—he could barely keep his hands off her.

So yeah, he'd been preoccupied and maybe he'd missed a few signals, but damn if he knew what they were.

Later in the afternoon, Cain had suggested he might have let Lily know that there were a bunch of guys ogling her considering she was half-naked and all.

And maybe he might have covered up the hickeys on her shoulder.

Except that Mac kind of liked the sight of them on her skin. They were his marks. *On her skin*. Marks he'd put there while he'd been inside her. And maybe that was some kind of primal animal thing, but what the hell... he was a guy. He was a hot-blooded American man who damn well liked to see that his woman had been thoroughly looked after.

And sure, he agreed that he should have taken the time to get rid of their wet clothes on the dock because by Sunday night, half the town knew that he and Lily St. Clare had done some serious skinny-dipping. By Monday morning, the other half knew.

He stopped in for his coffee at The Donut Place on his way to the site and ran into a bunch of guys who'd been at the gala. Every single one of them had some sort of comment about Lily. Again. He got it. Men were basically one rung up from the primates, and when a gorgeous woman was around, they quickly reverted back to their inner caveman. Christ, he'd been dragging his knuckles after her all night.

But still.

After the third comment about how hot she was, he wasn't so agreeable. Jesus, it wasn't as if she was a piece of meat they were talking about. It was Boston. His Boston.

Mac stopped smiling about the time Jerry Field spoke up, and it was a good thing that his coffee order took less than a minute because he was ready to knock his goddamn teeth in.

The bastard had actually asked Mac if he could take Lily out to dinner, insinuated that Mac wasn't serious about her—or anyone for that matter—and Jerry would treat her right. Mac had taken a moment and something in his eyes must have warned Jerry to back off, because the insurance salesman took two steps back and shrugged.

"Just thought I'd ask," he'd said in his defense. "You can't blame a guy for trying. Hell, every single guy in Crystal Lake would like to have a shot at her."

"She's with me," Mac replied.

Except that he wasn't so sure. He'd called her Sunday after coming back in from fishing with the boys, but she hadn't picked up. At first, he'd just shrugged it off. It's not like he'd planned on spending the entire day fishing, but Cain had showed up in the boat and Liam had finally cracked a smile. Mac couldn't say no to the kid even though the only thing he wanted to do was head back to the cottage and climb into bed with Lily.

He tried to call her again around ten in the evening and then had given up after he went straight to voice mail—for the fifth time. Jesus, that was getting damn close to stalker territory—at least for Mackenzie.

Now it was Monday morning, and he was in a shit

mood. It felt like he hadn't slept at all, he was already ten minutes late for work, and he had Liam along for the ride. Mac had no idea what he was going to do with the kid, but what the hell was he supposed to do? Leave him at the lake all day?

He'd brought up Bible camp, but one look into Liam's eyes, and he knew he couldn't do it.

Mac took a sip of coffee and maneuvered out of the parking lot, face grim as he thought of his sister. He hadn't heard anything from her other than a text message the night before that told him she'd arrived back home and that she was okay. He knew she had called her son because he'd heard Liam talking to her, but there'd been nothing more this morning.

His mother had called to tell him she was dropping off a casserole because she wouldn't be home for dinner either. She'd gone on and on about how wonderful it was that he'd taken Liam for the week. She talked about male bonding and how good it was going to be for Liam to spend some time with his uncle.

Not once did she mention the kid's father or the fact that her idiot daughter had run back to the man who'd hurt her. Not once.

His mother had always been good for that. She thought that if she didn't talk about something, it never happened. He supposed that was her way of dealing with stuff, but it was the coward's way out, and it was something Mac would never be able to understand.

He glanced at Liam. The boy's cheeks were sunburnt and so were his arms and legs. A full day on the lake would do that to a kid when the uncle was too clueless to make sure sunscreen was applied.

"Do we need to stop and get some cream or something?" he asked, turning onto Main Street. There was a pharmacy near the grocery store, and he could hit it if need be.

"Cream?" Liam turned to him.

"For your sunburn. I didn't realize it was so bad."

"I'm good."

"Well, does it hurt?"

Liam shrugged. "It's okay."

Mac gritted his teeth as a wave of anger washed over him. For Christ's sake. If he had to hear Liam say everything was "okay" one more time, he was going to lose his shit. It wasn't okay. None of this was fucking okay.

Mackenzie pulled into the pharmacy and told Liam he'd be back in a minute. He walked inside and instead of wasting time looking for God knows what, he headed for the main counter up front. Mrs. Borstrano was just applying her lipstick when he stopped at her register. The woman had manned number one for as long as Mac could remember, and surely she would know what he needed to buy for a bad sunburn.

"Good morning, Mrs. B."

Her pale face broke open into a wide grin, as she gazed up at him. She was a petite little thing, with soft brown eyes, an easy smile, and long, dark hair most women half her age would kill for. It fell down her back just the way he remembered. Heck, back in the day, every single boy in Crystal Lake had a crush on Mrs. B.

"My goodness. Mackenzie Draper. Son, you are just what every woman should see first thing in the morning."

He winked. She'd always been a flirt. "Damn, Mrs. B., I only have time to visit one woman this morning, and it happens to be you."

"Well, it sure is nice to see that pretty face of yours, Mackenzie." She leaned forward. "Though I hear you've been stepping out with Lily St. Clare."

Mac smiled. "She's a friend."

Mrs. Borstrano's eyes softened a bit. "She's a real nice girl, Mackenzie. You best treat her nice, you hear?"

Mac didn't quite know what to say to that so he got right to the point. "I need some cream for a bad sunburn."

Mrs. Borstrano gave him the once-over. "Is this for you?"

He shook his head. "Nope. It's for my nephew, Liam."

"Ah," she replied. "Follow me."

Mrs. B. led him all the way to the back of the store, and he waited patiently while she picked out a tube of cream. She shoved it into his hands, a frown on her face. "Liam, isn't that Becca's little boy?"

"Yep."

They were back at the cash register now. "I heard she's in town staying with your mother for the summer."

Mac handed over a twenty-dollar bill. "She is."

"Huh." Mrs. B. pursed her lips as she gazed up at him.

Shit, here we go.

"Just her and the boy?"

He nodded.

"I also heard she's banged up a bit. Was she in an accident or something?"

An accidental fall into her husband's fist.

Any lightness he felt disappeared, though he was able to keep his cool. "She's doing alright."

Mrs. B. held his gaze for a bit and then sighed. "She's a good girl with a good head on her shoulders. She'll figure it out."

"Let's hope so," Mac replied as he grabbed his bag. "Thanks for this."

"No problem, Mackenzie. It's so nice to have you back in town."

Mac ran into Pastor Lancaster as he headed out to his truck, but he didn't afford him anything more than a wave. At this rate, he was never going to make it to work. He checked his cell, but there were no messages, and with a grimace, he shoved it back into his jeans before hopping into the truck.

"Here's something for your burn. It should help."

Liam took the tube and muttered, "Thanks," which was good enough for now.

It took a bit of time to make it out of the downtown core—the place was already hopping with cottage folk—and as Mac gazed around, he realized just how much had changed. There were new light standards lining the sidewalks, large pots full of colorful flowers every ten feet or so. Facades on the storefronts had been changed so that everything looked new but also kind of old-school, which was part of the charm. It was a little like stepping back in time, except everything had a fresh twist to it.

It was a total revitalization, and he grudgingly thought that Hubber must be doing a decent job along with the local business association. And considering the state of Detroit and some of the communities closer to the city, it was a heck of an accomplishment.

On a whim, Mac hung a left at the last traffic light and headed back the way he'd come, taking the next right and following the treelined street until he came to a bridge.

Everything looked exactly as he remembered. Hell, even old man Lawrence's Bait and Tackle looked the same—on the verge of being condemned. Mackenzie crossed the bridge and pulled over just before the bait and tackle. The oak trees on either side of the street were still massive, their branches nearly meeting each other overhead in a canopy of green that shaded the entire street.

Liam looked at him questioningly, and Mac pointed toward the dam, just past the old saw mill. "I used to jump off that thing."

His nephew didn't seem impressed. "Mom would kill me if I did something like that."

Huh. The kid was right. And yet as young boys, Mac, the Edwards twins, and Cain would spend all day, every day down here, fishing, swimming, doing all sorts of stupid things that could have gotten them hurt.

They had disappeared inside the excitement and stupidity of their youth. How many nights had Jake and Jesse left for dinner, racing each other home on their bikes while Cain was good to linger until dark? Back then, his mom was always working and his father had been long gone.

How many nights had Mac spent out here waiting to go home until he knew his father would be passed out cold? Christ. Too many to count.

"Are we going to the site?" Liam asked, a funny look on his face.

Startled, he snapped out a "yep" and proceeded out to the site. Of course, his little detour cost him, and by the time he pulled into the dusty parking lot where the mobile office was set up, it was nearly ten. There were several vehicles parked haphazardly, and he ended up next to a beat-up and rusted Chevy.

He glanced at it in distaste. The thing was falling apart.

Jake was outside with O'Malley already and Mackenzie joined them. "Is that all you can afford, Edwards?"

Jake glanced back at the truck and grinned. "I'll drive that thing until it dies."

Mac snorted. "I think it's already half-dead."

He shook O'Malley's hand and pointed to his nephew. "This is my sister's son, Liam. He's visiting for the summer and touring around with me this week."

Liam offered his hand and stood a little straighter when the Irishman shook it vigorously.

"Do you like to golf, son?" His accent was thick but easy to understand.

Liam glanced at Mac and shrugged. "I've never tried it."

"What?" O'Malley looked aghast, his eyes wide as he glanced at Mac.

"Hey, he's not my kid."

"That's a sad thing to hear, son. A sad thing indeed. There's nothing quite like getting out on a course first thing in the morning. Nothing. We'll have to hit a driving range while I'm here, and I'll show you how to hit a golf ball. Sound good?"

Liam dug his foot in the dirt. "I guess."

Jesus. Could the kid be any less enthusiastic?

"We're heading out to scout the best location for the course. You coming?" Jake asked.

Mac hadn't talked to Jake since he'd shown up at the cottage and taken Lily home, and he was pretty sure that Jake hadn't been too keen on finding her half-dressed.

Mac nodded. "Sounds like a plan." O'Malley moved

away, dragging Liam along with him, and he lowered his voice. "We good?"

Jake lifted his shoulders. "We're good. It's none of my business."

Mac took a second. "Have you talked to her since yesterday morning?"

Jake shook his head. "Nope. You?"

"No."

Jake's eyes narrowed. "You didn't call her?"

"Of course I called her. Geez, I'm not an asshole." *Wait.* "Her landline still works, right? I mean, I called Raine's old number because I still have her cell in my truck."

Jake nodded. "Yep. It works."

At Jake's raised eyebrows, Mac frowned. "Well, I called her over and over and got the goddamn voice mail every time."

Jake clapped Mac on his shoulder a wide smile on his face. "Never thought I'd see the day when a woman had you all tied up."

Before he could reply and tell Jake it wasn't like that—he was just a little worried that he'd pissed her off—his cell buzzed and vibrated. Mac grabbed it from his pocket and damn if his heart didn't speed up when he saw Raine's name and number—except it was Lily. It had to be Lily.

"I need to take this," he murmured.

"Sure. You've got five minutes," Jake said before walking away.

Mac turned away from the men and took the call.

"Mackenzie?"

Just the sound of her voice was enough to wipe away

the tension that stretched across his shoulders, and he found himself grinning like a goddamn idiot. Good thing Jake was behind him or he'd get the wrong idea.

"Boston."

For a moment there was silence.

"I thought I might bring dinner over tonight."

He thought of the casserole his mom was dropping by and hesitated. Shit.

"That's if you want me to." Her voice had that husky tone that shot right through him, and all those muscles that had been relaxed were suddenly tense and hard.

"Of course I want you to. I tried calling you yesterday, Lily, but you didn't pick up." He took a few steps, ran his free hand through his hair, and glanced over to where Jake was grinning at Mac as if he was a fucking idiot. So much for him not getting the wrong idea.

"I know, I was…I had stuff going on, and well, I didn't mean to leave like that either."

He stopped pacing. "So we're good?"

"We're good. I'll be over around six?"

"Four." Hell, if he could swing it he'd be home by three. He was heading toward Jake in strides. "I can't wait until six. Let yourself in. The place is open."

"You left your house unlocked?" She sounded shocked.

"It's Crystal Lake, Boston."

"Well, you locked your truck the other night."

"That's because my favorite CDs were inside."

"That doesn't make any sense."

"I expect it doesn't, but to any other guy it would."

"Mackenzie?"

"Yeah?" He stopped walking, totally focused on her.

"Is Liam still with you?"

"He's staying the week. Why?"

"Oh. I thought I'd bring my overnight bag but—"

"Bring it."

"But—"

"Bring the damn bag, Lily, unless you want to go home in my boxers."

There was a pause.

"Okay," she said softly, and he could hear the grin through his phone.

Jesus Christ, it was going to be a long day.

Chapter 21

LILY PICKED UP HER SISTER'S DIRTY CLOTHES FROM THE bathroom floor and walked down the hall to the guest room at the back of the house. Maddison was flopped on the bed like a limp Raggedy Ann doll, wrapped in a towel as she flipped through a magazine. It was nearly three in the afternoon, but her sister had slept until two—not surprising, considering she'd been up tweaking until four in the morning, high on God knows what.

Lily had come back from Mac's Sunday morning to find Maddison and a friend—some loser called Thorpe who'd flown in from New York—naked, high as kites, and eating their way through her kitchen. They'd pretty much trashed Lily's living room, including three of her paintings as well as her easel.

It had been a mess, one that triggered something in Lily she hadn't felt in a very long time. Maybe it was because she was already in a mood, confused about Mac and what had just happened, or maybe she just needed to let off steam. Or maybe it was because something had snapped inside her, and instead of pushing it away, she had let it take life and then ran with it.

She had grabbed Maddison by the hair and dragged her, kicking and clawing and hissing like an animal, all the way back to the guest room. She threw her inside, grabbed a chair, and shoved it under the doorknob so Maddison couldn't escape.

Thorpe was so out of it he didn't even notice, and he didn't move until the police showed up and hauled his ass away.

It had been one stressful afternoon and the evening hadn't been any better. Maddison coming down from a high wasn't something Lily would wish on her worst enemy. She was bitchy, whiny, and mean-spirited, with a viper tongue and a right hook that you would do good to miss.

Lily had a big bruise on her arm to prove it.

Maddison glanced up from the bed as Lily leaned against the door frame. Her sister's eyes were puffy because she'd spent a good portion of the early morning sobbing like a baby. Whatever. Lily was over the emotional blackmail. God, was she over it.

"I'm leaving," Lily said, tossing Maddison's clothes onto the edge of the bed. "You've got less than an hour."

Maddison's head jerked up, and she rolled over until she was on her knees. "You can't be serious." Gone were the big eyes and pouty mouth. Maddison was all business now.

"I am."

Maddison glared at her. "What the hell is your problem anyway? It was one mistake, and I told you that I'd pay you back for any damages Thorpe caused."

"You don't have any money."

Maddison's eyes slide away. Score one for Lily.

"I'm sorry," she said, eyes on the floor.

"I don't care."

Maddison glanced up sharply.

"I mean it." Lily shrugged. She'd heard the same bullshit before. "This was a huge mistake, and I really don't care anymore. I'm done cleaning up your messes. I'm done letting you walk all over me. I'm done letting you trash my life. I'm done with all of it." Lily took a step back. "I was your last chance, Maddison. Your. Last. Chance."

"What's that supposed to mean?" Maddison's voice rose an octave.

"It means that you blew it. It means that I won't let you stay here and ruin my life again."

"I never ruined your life—"

"You slept with my fiancé, didn't you?"

"But that was a mistake. I said I was sorry for that, and I meant it. I was drunk and high, and well, he was the one who started it, not me."

Lily didn't doubt that for a second, and yet, she didn't care. The end result had been the same. Her sister had slept with the man Lily had been engaged to.

"What about the time you stole my PIN number along with most of the cash I had in my savings account?"

"But—"

"What about pretending to be me in that stupid sex tape? Did you really think people weren't going to notice that your boobs are big and fake and mine aren't?"

Silence was the answer and maybe Lily should have been surprised at how much nothing she felt for her sister, but she wasn't going to dwell on it. Not now. Not ever.

"I want you gone when I get back."

"But…Daddy said I had to stay here because if I didn't…" Maddison's eyes widened, shiny with tears. "He'll make me go to that fucking rehab place, and there's no way in hell I'll do it."

"That's your problem, not mine."

"Dad will freak."

"I'm also done letting Dad tell me what to do. If he wants someone to clean up after you, he can damn well do it himself."

Lily turned around.

"Lily! Where am I going to go?"

"Far away from here, I hope." She headed toward the kitchen. "There's five hundred in cash on the table. I've already called a cab, and it will be here in an hour. Don't miss it, and don't be here when I get back."

"But that's not even enough for a flight and…other stuff!" Maddison's voice was shrill.

"Take the bus."

Lily grabbed her overnight bag and closed the door behind her. She'd already packed a lasagna—the first she had ever attempted to make herself, and she had Maggie Black to thank for the recipe—along with greens for a salad and a loaf of garlic bread.

By the time she reached Mac's place, she was nervous, anxious, scared, and feeling a lot like her fifteen-year-old self. It was ironic really. Most people she met had this perverted idea of what she was all about—fed, in fact, by the exploits from her youth. They thought she was a sophisticated, rich, trust-fund baby who went through men as if they were candy.

Her reality was about as far away from that as she was from the moon.

Lily's heart started to pound when she spied his truck in the driveway, and it hadn't calmed down one bit by the time she parked behind him. She smoothed her shorts, a pair of faded jean cutoffs, and glanced in the mirror quickly.

Her makeup was minimal—a bit of mascara, some pale silvery shadow, and gloss on her lips. She'd left her hair down, and it fell across her bare back—bare because she'd chosen a royal-blue silk halter top. It was a bit of class paired with the casual shorts.

She took a deep breath, opened the door, and was about to reach into the backseat for her food when the hair on the back of her neck stood up. A soft crunch along the ground told her that she wasn't alone anymore, and then his scent—that clean, masculine scent—washed over her.

"Now that's a sight I'd like to see more often. A beautiful woman bent over wearing shorts that my mama just might find a little obscene." Strong arms slid around her waist, and she was pulled back against Mac's hard and—her heart skipped a beat—bare chest. He was warm and felt so good that for a moment Lily basked in the simple pleasure she felt in his arms. Honestly, she could stay like this all day.

His mouth nuzzled her neck, and she shuddered as his arms tightened. "Jesus, Lily you taste so damn good, how the hell am I going to get through the next few hours without throwing you over my shoulders and locking us in my bedroom?"

"I guess you'll have to—"

Sweet Jesus, his mouth should be patented.

"What was that?" he asked, pushing her hair out of the way so he could get to her earlobe.

"Mackenzie, if you keep—"

Holy. Mother. Of. God.

His warm tongue slid just inside her ear, and his other hand dug into her hip so that she felt his erection pressing into her butt.

"You were saying?" he whispered, blowing hot air on her now-wet earlobe. Red-hot desire forked down her body, and of course, her nipples were saying hello. Hell, they were as hard as rocks, begging for his attention. And she didn't want to think about what was going on between her legs, because the urge to squirm and press the palm of her hand into her crotch—or anything for that matter—was so strong she was sure that she whimpered.

Lily blew out a hot breath. Was it always going to be like this? Was she always going to be a slave to his delicious mouth and wonderful hands?

Or would it pass?

"Mackenzie, please stop." She pushed him, and with a chuckle, he let her go, though he sidled alongside her and reached into the car for the box of food.

"This smells great, Boston."

She smiled, a shaky sort of thing, but she'd never cooked for anyone before, and his praise made her feel... special. Special was warm and full and intimate. God, if she could bottle special, she'd be rich, wouldn't she?

She shrugged as if it wasn't a big deal even though it was huge. "I have no idea how it tastes, but—"

He bent over and pressed his mouth to hers, a quick, soft caress that nevertheless made her knees go weak.

"Darlin', if it tastes half as good as you do, I'll be one happy man." His eyes went soft, their green depths like liquid clover. "I'm glad you're here."

Four simple words.

And suddenly special took on a whole new meaning.

Her heart kinda sorta stopped. So did her breathing. A lump the size of Texas filled her throat and just when she managed to clear it and say something—anything to get her past this unfamiliar feeling—Liam stepped forward.

"Are you guys gonna suck face all night? It's kinda gross."

Lily couldn't help herself; she started to giggle and then a wide smile claimed Mac's mouth as he hefted the box into his arms and turned to his nephew.

"We're done sucking face."

Liam shoved his hands into his front pockets. "Good."

"For now," Mac continued as he led the way down the path to the cottage. Lily's eyes feasted on the sight of his wide shoulders, muscular back, and, damn, those old, faded cargo shorts were dangerously close to exposing what she knew was one hell of a butt. God, he probably wasn't wearing any—

"I know you're staring at my ass," Mac said over his shoulder.

Wait. What?

Liam snorted and shot a look her way before running ahead of his uncle and disappearing inside.

"I was not," she began and froze when he turned back to her. The man could stop traffic with that face and smile, and at the moment, he seemed to have stopped not only her heart but all rational thought.

"It's okay. You can admit it," he said with a wicked grin. "And, Boston?"

Mouth dry, she was barely able to get an answer out. "What?"

He opened the door and motioned her closer. Hesitantly, she inched forward, and when she so close that she felt his body heat right through her top, he leaned down and whispered in her ear, "Just so you know, I'm rocking the whole commando thing."

Okay. Even though her heart was beating erratically, damn near out of her chest, Lily shrugged and walked into the cottage.

"I wasn't looking."

She glanced at Liam, who was desperately trying to act as if he wasn't paying attention to any of the adult shenanigans, but his eyes slid away from hers a second too late. A blush stained his ruddy red cheeks as he flopped onto the sofa and reached for the television remote.

Mackenzie helped her get the salad prepared, and about a bottle of wine later, they had eaten, cleaned up the plates, and stowed the leftovers in the fridge. Mackenzie suggest a boat ride, which was the only thing that brought Liam to life, and the three of them had a leisurely tour of Crystal Lake.

They stopped in at the Edwardses'—Steven was fishing off the end of his dock and Marnie brought down coffee. They also stopped at the far end of the lake and Mackenzie explained Jake's vision for the development. She heard the excitement in his voice, saw it in the way he moved his hands when he talked.

She liked this relaxed Mackenzie. Maybe a little too much.

They slid past Pot-a-hock Island and Lily's entire body was near eruption status from the heat building inside her as she thought of that first kiss. Her fingers found her lips, and when she glanced up at Mac, his eyes had darkened and she knew that he was thinking about the same thing.

They didn't speak much once Mackenzie turned

the boat back toward his cottage, though his hand found the small of her back, or the crook of her neck, more than once, and by the time they got back to the boathouse, her body was thrumming with pent-up sexual need.

Liam's face was flush with a healthy glow that had nothing to do with his sunburn—it was obvious he'd enjoyed himself. He hopped off the boat and went about securing it as if he were a pro, but when he couldn't quite get the knot done properly, Mackenzie showed him how.

Lily stood back, watching the two of them, and after a few moments, she had to look away. Mackenzie had said family and kids weren't for him, but, sweet Jesus, it sure looked good on him.

She wondered then, what it was exactly that shaped a person—and she wondered if a person could ever change.

"You can call your mother after you brush your teeth. And then it's bed, Liam."

The boys had followed her up to the cottage, and Lily leaned against the kitchen counter as Liam made a face.

"But it's not that late." Liam pouted. "It's barely dark."

"It's late enough, and we're up early tomorrow. Don't forget we told O'Malley that we'd meet him at the driving range six thirty sharp. We need to be outta here by six."

Liam tugged long bangs from his face. "We're really going?" He seemed surprised and she could tell that it didn't sit well with Mackenzie.

"Why wouldn't we?" Mackenzie asked, standing a little straighter as he faced his nephew.

Liam started fidgeting with the end of his T-shirt. He shrugged. "Dad says stuff like that all the time, but it's not like we ever do anything."

Mackenzie strode toward the boy and ruffled his hair. "Well, maybe your dad forgets or he gets busy."

"He's lame," Liam muttered.

"Yeah," Mackenzie said. "He is. But I guess we can all be lame sometimes, right?"

Liam shrugged. "I guess."

He gave him a gentle shove. "Bedtime. Lily and I are just going to, uh, watch some television for a bit."

Liam gave Lily a small wave, and before he had disappeared in his room, two big strong arms slid around her. Mac pulled her in nice and close, and Lily nestled against his chest. With her head tucked under his chin, she felt his breath and heard his heart.

"Do you like playing games, Lily?"

She was content to stay where she was for the rest of the night. It felt that good.

"Huh?" Cuddling closer, she closed her eyes.

"I want to play a game with you."

She could feel his heart beating faster, and it mimicked what was going on inside Lily. That sexual frustration from before rose up and suddenly all sorts of things were going off.

"A game?" she managed to say.

She felt him nod. "Yep, but I gotta tell you, Boston, I've never lost this game."

She moved so that she could see his face, and the look in his eyes made her mouth go dry. He swooped in and slid his tongue over her lips as he slowly started to maneuver them toward his bedroom.

Her fingers dug into his shoulders, and she whispered, “What about Liam?”

“What about him?” His mouth pressed into her neck and she sighed. “He won’t know.”

“How can you be so…” God, his mouth. “Sure…”

“It’s the game.”

“What kind of game is that?” she asked breathlessly when he closed his door behind them.

Mackenzie tugged his shirt off and tossed it onto the ground, a wicked grin on his face. “For obvious reasons, we don’t want to make a whole lot of noise, so I propose we play the quiet game.”

His shorts joined his T-shirt on the ground; Mackenzie hadn’t been teasing when he said that he was going commando.

“The quiet game,” she repeated, her eyes on his taut stomach before they followed that thin line of hair downward. Damn.

Mackenzie beckoned her, and she walked toward him, desire pooling in her stomach. Her nipples were hard, her breasts aching for his touch. He slid a hand into her hair while the other found its way into the front of her shorts. Seconds later, he’d infiltrated her panties and his fingers were between her legs, gently stroking and teasing.

She opened her mouth, a soft moan escaping, and he slid his tongue inside and kissed her so sweetly, so thoroughly that her head spun.

“So this game,” he said, dragging his mouth away as he began to slowly blaze a trail down her neck. She let her head fall back—she let everything go slack, because as far as she was concerned, Mackenzie

Draper could do whatever the hell he wanted to do with her.

Even play a game if it meant his mouth and fingers were involved.

He pressed his hard cock into her.

Oh, and there was that too.

"This game," she said, eyes closed as she leaned into him.

"You can't make a noise." He nipped at the top of her breasts. "Not one little sound. No matter what I do to you, Boston, or you lose." He paused. "And I plan on doing a lot."

Her hands crept up into his hair, and she pulled on him until he was forced to look at her.

"What about you?"

"Same rules apply."

She ground her hip against him, smiled when he inhaled sharply.

"So the first one who makes a noise loses?" she asked, tongue between her teeth as she felt for his cock. When her fingers found the hard length of him, the look on his face was hot enough to make her come.

"I like that," he murmured. "You're playing dirty."

"I'm going to win," she quipped, wrapping her hand around his cock as she slowly began to work him.

Mackenzie's fingers continued their assault as they leaned back against the door. "Trust me, darlin', even if you lose…"

He slipped two fingers inside her, but she clamped her mouth shut just in time.

"You win."

He grinned, a wicked grin that disappeared soon

after. They both got busy, and it wasn't long after that Lily lost.

Holy hell, but she lost big time.

Funny enough, she was okay with that.

Chapter 22

MAC HAD ALWAYS THOUGHT THAT HE WAS CONTENT with his lot in life. Sure, he knew that he was never going to conform to the whole Hollywood chick-flick idea of happy. But all in all, things were good.

He had a job that he loved and one that he was damn good at. He had a nice brownstone in New York City, and a car that gave him a lot of pleasure to drive. He enjoyed season tickets to both the Yankees and the Rangers, and had more women than he knew what to do with.

There'd been a time when an ideal night for him was either dinner at some fancy restaurant with a beautiful woman and sex back at her place—always her place—or drinks after work with some of the guys from the firm, which could get out of hand, but what did that matter? It's not like he had anyone to answer to.

If he felt like playing a game of hockey in the men's league he'd joined or heading out of town to ski, he did it. If he wanted to do nothing but chill in his house and work on the renovations he'd started, he did that. But no matter what, the one thing that was constant in his life was that in the morning, he was alone.

That was it. All she wrote.

It was the life he'd built—the life he'd wanted—which was why he found it a little weird that having Liam around all the time kinda fit. His sister Becca had returned a well over a week ago, a little more sad, a little more broken, but at least she was officially separated from her bastard husband. And though he hadn't suggested it or thought about it really, he'd started swinging by his mom's every morning to pick up Liam and bring him to work with him.

The kid was bright, and he liked to learn. And funny enough, Liam liked math and he liked to draw.

Even funnier? Mac liked to teach him.

But Boston, well hell, Lily St. Clare had to be the most perfect woman on the planet. Hands down. He'd never met anyone like her.

Aside from the fact that her intense blue eyes, long, blond hair, and amazing ass would make any man happy, she had a great sense of humor and was quick to laugh. Her trucker mouth came out occasionally, and damn if he didn't like that too. She was independent and had her own money, so she wasn't always whining for him to buy her something.

And the sex was mind-blowing. Christ, just this morning he'd joined her in the shower and things had quickly gotten out of hand.

Mackenzie had lost control—they both had—and by the time he realized it, there was barely enough time to pull out. He'd come hard, there against the wet tiles—like a fucking teenager without any control—but Christ, she'd felt good.

Too damn good.

And for the first time since he'd come back to Crystal Lake and Lily, he was starting to think of things he probably shouldn't think about, because there was no way any of that shit would ever work out.

It was nothing permanent that he was thinking about, Christ no, but it was something more than what they had. Like maybe Lily should be spending all of her time at the cottage. The lighting was good for her painting, and he liked the thought of her there, dressed in one of his old T-shirts, when he was at work.

The problem was he didn't know how to proceed with that train of thought. This was uncharted territory for Mac, and considering the state of bliss his buddies were living in, it's not as if they'd be good for any kind of advice.

Shit, they'd have him married before the end of the year.

"Like that will ever happen," he muttered.

Yet here he was, three weeks after he'd started up with Boston, getting ready to take part in a canoe race around the lake with Lily and Liam. The Race Of A Thousand Canoes was an annual charity event put on by the church. It was a loud, bustling family event from what he could tell, which was totally different than the memories in his head.

When he was a teenager, he and Cain used to race the Edwards twins around the lake, drinking beer and smoking cigarettes once they were out of sight of Pastor Lancaster. And now, Cain was set to race with Michael because Maggie was so pregnant she was as big as a house—still gorgeous, but shit, Mac was convinced there were at least three kids in there.

And joining them in another canoe was Raine and Jake, with their hyper retriever, Gibson.

When the hell had everything changed?

"I gave Liam a cooler with snacks and stuff." Becca

stood beside him, shading her eyes as she watched Liam and Lily discuss the merits of placement. Liam was sure that he should be in the front because he was the smallest, while Lily was pretty sure he should be in the middle to even things out.

"Thanks," Mac said. "Where's Mom?"

Becca shook her head. "I don't know. She got a phone call this morning and left a note saying she had to go meet up with someone." She chuckled. "It's not like her to be so mysterious. Maybe she's got a boyfriend."

"Yeah. Because she's finally ready to move on with her life," Mac said dryly.

"Hmm," Becca replied softly.

His sister looked tired. "Are things alright with you?" They hadn't really talked since she came back from Iowa, but he knew she was looking for a job and that she'd be staying in Crystal Lake for the immediate future.

"I'm…I'm going to be alright." She paused. "So, Lily seems real nice."

Mac stared at Becca a few seconds longer, but he wasn't going to call her out on a deflection. He new she wasn't ready to talk about stuff, and this wasn't really the place either.

"She is."

"So would she be considered your girlfriend?"

Okay, he was all for letting the deflection slide, but man, he wasn't real up on discussing his personal life with his sister. Jesus, just the day before his mother had asked if he wanted to bring Lily for dinner one night. He'd politely refused because he wasn't ready to mix his family and Boston—not yet anyway.

Then why the hell am I in this canoe race with Lily and Liam?

"She's a friend," he answered tightly. He didn't want them making assumptions on stuff he wasn't even sure about.

"Liam likes her a lot. He says that she's given him a few art lessons and that she"—Becca paused—"smells real nice."

Well, Mac couldn't fault his nephew there.

"Draper, if you don't get your canoe in the water, you're never going to have a chance to win."

Mac glanced over to Jake. "Whatever, Edwards. You've never managed to beat me before."

Jake had his arm around Raine and kissed her on the nose before flipping Mackenzie the bird. "I've never had such a pretty copilot either."

"Do you want me to make something for dinner?"

"No," he said sharply, glancing at Becca. "I have no idea how long the race will take, but when it's over, I'll drop Liam off, and then Lily and I are heading back to the cottage."

She frowned. "But it's Saturday night. I just thought that maybe a barbecue would be fun. You don't need to get your damn panties in a knot." She took a step back. "What's your problem anyway?"

"My problem?" That thing that had been buzzing in his head for the last few weeks suddenly sharpened into something hot and angry. He glared at his sister. "My problem is that my private life is private. I don't need to bring Lily by for dinner or hang out with you guys in the backyard and talk about the good ol' days because we both know there weren't any. Why are you so interested in getting to know her anyway?"

"Does it really surprise you that I want to get to know the woman you're spending so much time with?"

Mac didn't care that Mrs. Avery and her husband were staring at him, or that old man Lawrence was frowning at him either. He just wanted everyone to leave him the hell alone. Was it childish? Maybe. But he didn't give a rat's ass.

"I think, *Becca*, that instead of focusing on me, you should be getting your shit together. I don't think you need to be worrying about family dinners that would suck or nice relaxed barbecues that we both know would never happen. You've got a kid and you're on your own, so maybe a job might be something to think about. That sounds like a brilliant fucking idea to me. I'm gone after Labor Day, so this thing with me and Lily St. Clare has an expiration date. Your mess of a life doesn't."

Becca's face whitened, and as soon as the words left his mouth, Mac wanted to snatch them back.

"You're an asshole, Mackenzie. A complete and utter asshole."

He stared into his sister's eyes, saw the pain he'd caused, and suddenly his anger left as quickly as it had come. What the hell was wrong with him? This was supposed to be a fun, relaxed day.

"Jesus, Becca. I know," he said roughly. "Family genetics." Her bottom lip trembled, and Mac cleared his throat. "I'm sorry."

It was barely noon and already the day was crap. Could it get any worse?

Becca glanced around, and Mac was suddenly aware that a lot of people were listening in on the Draper family drama. She gave him a hard look and then turned and left, weaving through the crowd until he couldn't see her anymore.

He glanced over to Jake who was staring at him—his expression unreadable—and then when he turned toward his canoe, big blue eyes caught him. They caught him hard.

Lily held his gaze for several seconds and then motioned for Liam to follow her into the canoe.

Shit.

It was obvious to him that she'd heard everything, and he was guessing she wasn't real happy with the exchange.

Guess his day was about to get worse.

The three of them managed to do okay considering neither Lily nor Liam were really talking to him. They navigated their way through the crowded waters until they broke through and had an expanse of blue to themselves. Mac knew that Cain and Michael were somewhere behind them, but up ahead he spied Jake and Raine—hard not to, Gibson freaking yapped at everything.

They fell into an easy rhythm, and as the afternoon wore on, he managed to coax some conversation out of Liam, but Lily was still cool. Polite. But cool.

When they reached the turnaround, he caught a smile she shot at Liam and his chest tightened when she glanced up at him. The sun painted a halo around her golden head, and with her cheeks pink from exertion, a healthy glow to her skin, and those eyes that could see into his soul, he knew the image was one he'd remember for a long, long time.

He offered a small smile and though she didn't return it, she didn't look away either. By the time they reached the shore where they'd started, the air was cooling off and it was nearly six in the evening.

Jake invited them over to the stone cottage at Wyndham Place, but Lily politely declined before Mac could answer, though after checking with Becca, Liam rode back to Jake's with Cain, Maggie, and Michael.

Lily helped him secure the canoe on top of his truck and once they were in, seat belts in place, he revved the engine and gripped the steering wheel tightly. He wasn't sure how to fix what he'd inadvertently broken, but he knew he needed to make things right.

He knew that maybe they needed to talk about some things.

"Lily," he began carefully. "About before..."

"Can you just take me back to my place, please?" Her voice was soft—not a hint of pissed off, but shit. That's it? She was gonna bail on him because he'd blurted out a bunch of shit that was basically the truth?

"Sure," he answered sharply. "Sure thing, Boston."

Her hands were gripped tightly in her lap, and she looked out her window as they pulled away from the beach. He probably shouldn't have squealed the tires on the blacktop or cranked the tunes to ten, but he was pissed.

He felt the stirrings of something dark and heavy in him, and he thought that maybe this was good. They needed a few days to chill and figure this out, and he needed a date with his good buddy Jack.

Christ, he couldn't remember the last time he'd cradled that particular bottle in his hands and the thought of getting shit-faced drunk was a good alternative to the thought of being alone at his place.

Hell, maybe he'd hit the Coach House.

Maybe he'd…

"Can you slow down please, Mackenzie?"

Again with the soft voice. He glanced at her, his heart taking off when he found her eyes on him. They were dark and intense, the blue much closer to denim than the clear, blue sky they normally resembled.

That thing inside him—whatever it was—pressed even tighter. Jesus, it didn't feel as if he could breathe.

Automatically he relaxed his foot on the gas and slowed down as they came upon the bend just before her driveway. He maneuvered it expertly and pulled up beside her car, throwing the truck into park as he finally unclenched his hands from the wheel.

He glanced up at the cottage. She needed to water her hanging baskets or they were going to die.

For a moment, heavy silence filled the cab, and then she reached for the door handle.

"Are you going to shut this thing off?" she asked and then slid from the truck, not looking at him as she started for her porch.

Mac watched her climb the steps. He watched those long, tanned legs eat up the distance in no time. He watched her reach into her back pocket and retrieve a house key.

He watched her open the front door and pause a few seconds before disappearing inside. He had no idea what was going on or what the hell they were doing. He had no idea what Lily was thinking, and he sure as hell didn't know where his head was at.

It had been a strange afternoon, but as he cut the

engine and got out of his truck, he realized that it was time to figure this out—whatever this was.

He supposed it was time to be a grown-up.

Pretty sad, considering he was thirty-five.

Chapter 23

Lily didn't realize she'd been holding her breath until she heard the front door open and then close. She exhaled in a swoosh and grabbed a tall glass which she filled with cold water from the fridge, before leaning against the counter and staring out the window.

Her heart was beating a little crazily and she felt the heat in her cheeks. She didn't have to look in the mirror to know that she looked flushed and it wasn't from the sun either.

"This thing with me and Lily St. Clare has an expiration date."

She winced and froze when she heard Mackenzie clear his throat behind her. What he had said was true. She knew that. Of course she knew that.

But it was the other things those words had dug out of her—feelings, thoughts, and maybe a dream or two—that had torn at her all day. It was those things that had made her realize that somehow, over the last few weeks, something had changed.

She had changed.

There were things that she wanted—things that she'd never dreamed of having—and they were suddenly very clear.

The only problem was that Lily had no idea what to do about them. She had no idea how to move forward knowing that she wanted more than a casual, sexual relationship. She wanted more than the exclusive dating thing they'd first discussed.

She wanted Mackenzie in a way that she knew was going to bite her in the ass because it was obvious that he was still on the other road—the road called sex with no strings. The road that was only a single lane.

Lily had passed him and was riding fast and hard toward a two-lane highway, and if she wasn't careful, she was going to crash and burn.

So now the question was, what was she going to do about it? Did she break things off with Mackenzie now? Before there was the chance she'd be hurt? Did she wait for another man like him to walk into her life?

Or did she take a leap of faith…did she take a chance that maybe things would work out between them? Did she choose to believe that the connection they had was a hell of a lot stronger than what they'd originally envisioned?

Did she even have a choice?

She cleared her throat and turned around. "Can I get you anything?"

Mac shook his head. "No." He took a few steps into the kitchen and then stopped, rubbing the stubble along his jaw. She knew him well enough now to know that it was a nervous gesture, and while she supposed it should make her feel better to know that he was nervous too, it didn't.

It just meant that they were at a crossroads, and after the morning they'd had—that hot encounter in the shower—it was one she hadn't seen coming.

"Lily, we should talk."

"Yes, we probably should."

Good. They were going to be civil about this. Adult even.

Suddenly hot, she moved past him and headed for the deck out back. The air was cooler outside, and she inhaled a great big gulp of it as she eyed the forest that lined the property.

She'd been thinking of buying it from Raine, thinking of setting down roots in Crystal Lake.

Seems as if she'd been thinking of a lot of things.

Mackenzie stopped beside her and followed her gaze. "I'm sorry if I ruined your day. I didn't mean…I didn't mean to get into it with Becca. Sometimes…" He paused, swung out his arms, and rolled his shoulders. "Hell, most of the time, when things heat up, I lose my temper and I always say something stupid."

"It's alright, Mackenzie. You didn't say anything that wasn't true. It just would have been nice if half of Crystal Lake hadn't heard it. That's all. I'm sure I'm not the only woman on the planet who would hate to be referred to as nothing more than an expiration date."

He stared down at her and then moved a little closer. He still had on his Detroit Tigers ball cap and his long, blond hair waved over his ears in a way that made him look younger.

"That's not what I meant. Jesus, Lily. You have to know that."

She bit her bottom lip. "I know."

"I'm going to be honest, Lily. I don't know where we're at exactly, but I do know it's a place I never thought I would be." He attempted a smile. "It's a nice place, you know. But I'm pretty sure, at some point, we're going to be looking at change. I'm not staying here in Crystal Lake. I have a life in New York City."

"I know," she replied. "I knew that when we started this."

"I've never been with a woman like you." He looked so earnest, so much like his nephew Liam that, that damn thing around her heart tightened again. Shit.

Lily held herself still and waited for him to continue.

"I've never been with a woman that I wanted to spend all my time with. I just..." He shrugged. "I just never have. I didn't think she existed." His voice lowered. "I didn't think I wanted her to."

Silence stretched between them, and Mackenzie rubbed the back of his neck.

"God this is hard," he said roughly before nailing her with a look that she could only describe as haunted. "Things are great, hell, they're more than just great between us, but I don't want you to get the wrong idea. I gotta be honest with you, Lily. If you're thinking of anything long-term, I don't know that I'm the right guy for you."

A small sliver of hope erupted inside her. It wasn't as if he'd said things were over. And maybe she shouldn't have read too much into it, but it was so hard not to—so hard not to follow her heart.

"I don't know that I *can* be the right guy for you. I don't know what I am, Lily, but I do know that I'm not the white-picket fence guy. Jake and Cain and other guys I know, that's them. But me? I'm just not."

She opened her mouth to ask the question *why*, but he beat her to it.

"I don't even know if I can explain why in a way

that will make sense. I only know that the family blood running through my veins isn't the kind of thing I want to pass along to anyone. The Draper's are cursed, Lily. Christ, if you knew my father and his father before him, you'd get it. I'm not an angel. I've been the bastard that my dad is. I've been there before, in that dark place, and no kid should ever see it."

He studied her for a moment, and she could see he how conflicted he was.

"About a year after I moved to New York City, I started seeing this woman. She was smart, driven, had a great job at a PR firm…and she liked to drink. The two of us together were toxic, and one night after an argument…" He closed his eyes and shoved his clenched fists into his pockets. "That night, she pushed me too far. She was flirting with some douche bag, dancing with him and behaving inappropriately. I could have been mature and walked away. Hell, I knew what she was doing. Things were cooling off between us, and she was trying to get a rise out of me. But instead of walking away, I got into it with the asshole when he followed us out of the club. I beat the shit out of him, broke his arm and put him in the hospital, and Jenna ended up with a black eye."

He paused as if searching for the right words, and Lily's heart went out to him.

"She said it was an accident, that I hadn't meant to hurt her, and she got my elbow in the face when she tried to break up the fight." He turned to her and Lily saw the anguish in his eyes. "It doesn't matter though because what I do remember is the rage—the absolute rage that I felt, and I knew then that I was totally capable of becoming my father."

For several moments there was silence, and then he spoke quietly.

"I made a decision right there and then that a wife and kids aren't for me, and it's something that I won't change, not for anyone, because if I ever hurt a child, if I ever did what my dad did to me and my siblings…what he did to my mother, I don't…" His voice broke, and he moved back, took another moment. "Lily, you've got me considering things I'd never thought of before, and I don't know what the fuck to do about them."

Lily's clenched her fists together and decided to take the plunge. What the hell. It's not as if she had any other form of attack other than the truth of what was inside her.

"When we got together, it was pretty much based on a strong physical reaction to each other. New Year's Eve was off the charts, and these last few weeks have been amazing. Mackenzie, I've never felt that way with anyone, and I might have gone a little crazy, you know? You got me to step out of my comfort zone, and that's not something anyone has been able to do before." A ghost of a smile played around her mouth. "Except for Jake maybe, but he had to use damn near an entire bottle of tequila."

Mac reached for her and tucked a long piece of hair behind her ears.

Lily inhaled deeply and then plunged forward before she chickened out. "You taught me that there is an entirely different side to me, one that I didn't know existed—a side that I had pretty much given up on."

She unclenched her hands, grateful that her chest was loosening up.

"I like that side. I like it a lot." She watched him

carefully. "I don't know where we go from here, Mackenzie, but I can't lie either."

God, her stomach roiled so hard she was afraid she was going to be sick.

"I have feelings for you and they're more complicated than what our so-called casual but exclusive sexual relationship calls for." She watched the way his eyes darkened, the way his mouth parted slightly and his nostrils flared.

She decided that since she'd come this far, she may as well take the plunge and go all the way. Heck, the only thing she had to lose was her pride…maybe her soul…

Maybe her heart.

Mouth dry, she licked her lips and jerked when he stepped forward so that he was so close only a whisper separated them.

"I think that you might feel the same."

"The same?" he asked, his voice a little rough.

Lily nodded. "I think that things aren't so casual for you either."

He was silent for a few seconds. "No." He shook his head slowly, not taking his eyes off her. "They're about as far away from casual as you can get."

The tightness inside her loosened, and for the first time since that morning, she began to relax. She began to hope.

And maybe that was dangerous territory for her to traverse, maybe it was like walking blindly down that single lane highway in the middle of oncoming traffic, but she didn't know how to *be* any other way. Lily leaned into his hand, her fingers tracing the contours of his jaw before resting against his mouth.

"So what are we going to do?" she asked softly, loving the play of shadows on his face.

"We explore each other. We enjoy each other."

His tongue darted out, and she shuddered when he licked the tips of her fingers.

"We respect each other's boundaries and see where this goes."

Boundaries. Right. His "no white-picket fence and no kids" boundary.

Could Lily live with the knowledge that she would never have those things as long as she was with Mackenzie?

What was the alternative if not? A life alone and never feeling alive again? Never knowing the joy she took by just watching him? The way he smiled and lit up her world in colors of gold? The feel of him inside her? The sound of his voice?

Could she live a life without love now that she'd experienced it?

That thought whispered through her mind, and for one scary moment, time sort of froze. She saw herself as an old, bitter woman with no babies and no husband… and no Mackenzie.

Holy. Shit.

It hit her then. She'd fallen in love with him. She didn't know the when of it or the how of it…she just knew without a doubt that, that was what the hot, hard thing pressing into her chest was. It was love. It was a scared kind of love that had no idea what it was doing.

Maybe Mackenzie loved her but didn't know it yet, or maybe there was nothing but strong feelings inside him. It didn't matter. Not really. Those were things that she couldn't control.

What she could control was how she lived her life and what choices she made. And just like she'd chosen to cut out the parasite that was her family—her father and her awful sister—she could choose to have Mackenzie in her life, even if it meant doing so on his terms.

And because Lily loved Mackenzie, she was willing to do just that.

So when he groaned and slid his mouth across hers, whispering words of apology, she gave herself up to him. When his arms slid around her waist and pulled her into his body, she melted into him as if she was his second skin.

When Mackenzie slowly lifted her into his arms and headed back into the house, she ran her fingers over his face and buried them in his hair. She kissed him, her mouth open and hot and giving. She kissed him with all the fervent emotion inside her, and when he began to undress her, she let him worship her with his hands and his eyes and his mouth.

They didn't make it to her bedroom. They barely made it inside.

He grabbed at her clothes with an urgency she hadn't felt, not even this morning when he'd surprised her in the shower. His hands were everywhere and his mouth soon followed, tongue probing, gliding—teeth nipping and scraping.

By the time Mackenzie got her shorts down, she was squirming, hot with need.

"I want you naked," she whispered hotly as she yanked on his T-shirt and pulled it over his head. Next came his shorts and, *sweet Jesus*, but her man wasn't wearing boxers. Lily pushed him onto his back. She shook her head when he would have pulled her up against him.

She settled between his legs and began to kiss her way up his thighs, first the left and then the right. She traced her fingers over his taut muscles, loving the way they stretched and tightened beneath her touch.

"Jesus Christ, Boston you're killing me," he rasped as her mouth hovered over the head of his cock. "I don't think I've ever seen anything as hot as you right now." He slowly sat up and leaned back against the wall, dragging her up so that he could kiss her. With his hands sunk into her hair, he held her prisoner, his mouth and tongue filling her with fire.

When she pulled away from him, his eyes were flat, dark with desire. And when she slowly slid down him again, when her mouth settled over the silky hardness of his cock, he swore.

"Ah, God," he groaned when she took him deep into her mouth, and when she began to suckle him, he jerked so hard she had to hold on, digging her fingers into the tops of his thighs.

They each filled a need for each other, a hot, physical need to connect, and later, as she cuddled with Mackenzie in her bed, Lily felt some sort of peace. They'd moved forward today. They'd been honest with each other, and it hadn't meant the end of the world—or the end of them.

She had no idea what the future was going to bring, but for now, what she had with this man was enough. As she rested her head on his chest and closed her eyes, she ignored the sliver of doubt.

The one that said it wouldn't be enough for much longer.

Chapter 24

"LAST CHANCE TO CHANGE YOUR MIND, BOSTON." MAC gazed at the woman beside him and felt that familiar wash of warmth roll through his body. It was something he was still getting used to—and something that still surprised the crap out of him.

He was living a chick flick, and he didn't give a damn.

It was two weeks after that afternoon out on Lily's deck.

Two weeks into this new phase of whatever the hell it was he and Lily were doing together. They were smart enough not to label it and happy enough to let it be. They were together 24/7, and for the first time in his life, Mackenzie had met a woman who was more than worthy of that elusive drawer in the bathroom, the one that seemed to be so goddamn important to every single woman he'd ever been with, but the one that he'd never offered up once.

Until now.

Hell, he even had *his* own space back at Lily's place and damned if he wasn't fine with that too. These days it seemed he was damn fine with most everything.

Yep. Mackenzie Draper was what most people would call happy. Go figure.

Mac grabbed Lily's hand and kissed the back of it before cutting the engine of his truck. It was Wednesday, which meant that it was meatloaf night in the Draper household, and on this particular Wednesday, Mackenzie Draper was bringing a girl home for dinner.

Jesus, Jake had nearly choked on his coffee when Mac had told him earlier in the day. He'd slapped Mackenzie on shoulder. "Who are you and what have you done to my buddy, Mac?"

It was a bit over the top. Seriously. It wasn't as if he'd been abducted by aliens or committed some sort of crime.

"Ready?" he asked.

Lily nodded and slid from the truck, waiting for him to exit and join her, a bottle of wine in one hand and a fresh bouquet of flowers from her garden in the other. He grabbed the bottle and nudged her forward, following her up the path and onto the porch. He opened the door, admiring the view of her backside as he waited for her to enter the house.

She was wearing simple white pants that hugged her curves like no one's business, a sleeveless, blood-red silk blouse, and her hair was loose and wavy—just the way he liked it.

"Mackenzie, is that you?" His mother appeared from down the hall, her hands enveloped in a large tea towel.

Mac glanced up and smiled, his hand on the small of Lily's back.

"Well, come on, don't be shy. I've set the table, and we're about ready to start. Liam mentioned you have ball practice, so we didn't want to run too late."

Mac and Lily followed his mother into the kitchen, and Lily smiled at her warmly. "So nice to finally meet you, Mrs. Draper."

"Please, call me Lila," his mother said, accepting the flowers with a broad smile. "These are beautiful, but you shouldn't have. Mrs. Avery's prices are a bit extravagant if you ask me."

"Oh," Lily said, darting a look at Mac. "These are actually from my back garden."

His mother looked surprised. And touched. "Oh, honey, that was real sweet of you."

Mac could tell that his mother was more than just touched, and he thought that maybe it wouldn't have hurt him to bring her flowers now and again. It wasn't as if his bastard of a father was around to do it.

"I think this one is a keeper," his mother said with a wink. "There's a vase in the dining room cabinet. Can you grab it for me?"

"Sure thing."

He left the two women chatting about irises and flax and headed to the dining room to find the vase. He wasn't gone long, and when he returned to the kitchen, he handed over the vase and leaned against the counter while Lily went about arranging the flowers while his mother pulled out the meatloaf.

Once Lily was done, she placed the vase on the table and stood back. His mom was busy at the sink, rinsing something out, and impulsively, he slipped his hands around Lily's waist. He drew her up for a kiss, a slow, thorough kind of kiss that was probably inappropriate and had his mother clearing her throat.

Liam rounded the corner from his bedroom and slid to a stop.

"Oh God. Don't you guys ever get sick of sucking face?" he said, his face screwed up. "It's all you ever do."

Mac chuckled. "I'm not that good at it, kid. I need the practice."

Lily squeezed his hand and murmured, "I'll let you practice later."

Becca joined them, and the five of them sat down to dinner. His mother said a small prayer of thanks and told everyone to dig in. There was meatloaf, mashed potatoes, fresh green beans from her garden, and a tossed salad.

It was simple stuff, but his mom was a pro, and Mac sat back, feeling a sense of pride as Lily dug in and gave a wholehearted thumbs-up when she tasted the meatloaf.

Conversation was light—they talked about the state of the Detroit Tiger's season, the fact that old man Lawrence was finally gonna sell his bait and tackle, and bets were taken on whether Liam's ball team was going to win their next game.

His sister was quiet, which kind of surprised him, but Mac didn't have time to dwell on it—he was too busy eating up the good vibes, happy smiles, and the fact that in the space of half an hour, Lily had managed to charm his mother in the same easy way she'd charmed him.

It struck him then. Lily St. Clare was a whole lot different from the woman he'd met New Year's Eve. Heck, she didn't bear any resemblance to the one he'd run into Memorial Day at the Edwardses'.

He raised his wineglass and took a sip, unable to take his eyes off her as she smiled at something his nephew said. Her entire face lit up when she smiled, and he was pretty sure it was the nicest damn thing ever. He thought that maybe he had something to do with it.

He took a sip of wine and settled back in his chair. He was good with that.

After dinner was done, he helped clear the table and wished that his mother didn't make such a big deal about it. Christ, it wasn't as if he'd never cleared a table before—at least he was pretty sure that he had.

Maybe. Back in the day.

His mom had baked an apple cobbler, and he grabbed some napkins and tossed them onto the table. There was just enough time to have dessert, maybe a cup of coffee, and then he and Liam had to take off for the ballpark.

His cell rang just then—O'Malley—so he gave a quick apology and headed outside to take the call. It was quick, just a few questions pertaining to the golf course, and Mac had just pocketed his cell when Becca joined him on the deck.

He knew something was up as soon as he caught sight of her. She was way too quiet, way too tense, and when she worried her bottom lip like that, he knew that whatever it was, he probably wasn't going to like it.

"What's going on, Becs?"

He asked the question even though he wasn't entirely sure he wanted to know. Because if she told him that she was getting back together with David—that she'd forgiven the bastard and they were going to play nice again, he just might lose it.

Becca blew out a short, harsh breath and glanced back into the kitchen, making sure the door was closed securely before she turned to him.

Okay. The covert shit? That wasn't good.

"Don't freak out," she said.

And that wasn't good either.

Mac fingered his cell in his pocket, staring at his sister and wondering where this was all going.

"Just spit it out, Becca."

She ran her hands through her hair and muttered,

"Shit," before staring up at him and Mac's blood went cold when he got a look at what was there.

Fear.

Cold. Hard. Fear.

"God, I should have waited," she said, her voice barely above a whisper.

"Becca, you're starting to piss me off. What the hell is going on?"

She took a moment, tugging on the edge of her faded blue T-shirt. She smoothed out the tops of her shorts, her fingers lingering, moving in circles, and by this time Mac's nerves were stretched tight.

Jesus. Fucking. Christ.

He shouldn't have come. He should have known that there was no way this night could have ended well.

"I heard Mom on the phone this morning."

Mackenzie arched an eyebrow. What the hell did that have to do with anything? "And?"

Becca's eyes slid from his, and he took a step forward.

"She was talking to a lawyer." Becca still couldn't meet his eyes and suddenly Mackenzie got it. He got it loud and clear.

"Son of a bitch," he muttered, eyes swinging toward the door that led to the kitchen. "He's getting out?" His tone was hard and cold.

Becca finally met his gaze and nodded. "He might already be out. I don't know. I didn't…Mom hasn't said anything to me and I…" She visibly shuddered. "I just didn't ask. Maybe I don't want to know, but if he's out and he comes back here…"

Mac turned on a dime and pushed past his sister. "You might have a problem asking her, but I sure as hell don't."

His face was a cold, hard mask when he walked into the kitchen. It must have been, because when Lily glanced up with a smile, it faltered and then left her completely.

"Mackenzie?" she asked carefully.

He didn't hear it. Just like he didn't hear his sister come in after him, begging him not to cause a scene. His mom had just placed the cobbler onto the table, and Liam was already digging in when Mac rounded on them.

"When is he getting out?"

His focus was on his mother. On the way her fingers trembled slightly as she pushed the cobbler into the middle of the table. On the way she moved back, her eyes never meeting his.

And on the way her shoulders slumped forward, as if the weight of the entire universe was on them.

"Mackenzie," she said with a hint of warning in her voice. "Now isn't the time."

"Are you kidding me?" he exploded. He glanced back at his sister. Was their mother crazy? Did she think that this wasn't a big deal?

"When the hell is Ben Draper getting out?" He barely ground the words out because his jaw was clenched together so tightly that pain shot up the side of his head.

Lila Draper squared her shoulders and faced her son. "He is your father, Mackenzie."

For a moment he was speechless. He glanced at Lily, into her clear blue eyes, and he knew that this wasn't fair to her. She shouldn't have a front-row seat to the ugliness that was his family.

But he couldn't help himself.

Because the anger that boiled inside him wasn't going away. In fact, the longer that he stared at a mother—who was looking at him as if he was the one with the problem—the more the anger inside him festered. It twisted and turned because it wanted out.

"Ben Draper is not my father."

"How can you say that?" His mother's face flushed.

"He's nothing more than a sperm donor." Mac clenched his hands together, wishing he could hit something. "He hasn't earned the right to be called a father. He's a bully who blames all of his problems on everyone else. He's a man who gets through life using his pretty face and his fists. He's a lazy bastard who can't hold a job because he doesn't want to. Shit, the only form of exercise he gets is lifting a goddamn bottle of Jack to his mouth."

"Mackenzie," his mother said again, her voice rising.

But there was no stopping him now. Something broke open inside Mac. Something dark and dangerous. Something that had been festering longer than he could remember.

"Ben Draper likes to beat the shit out of his wife. You laid down like a fucking dog and you let him beat you."

"Mackenzie!" His mother looked horrified, her eyes wide and her bottom lip trembling. All of which would normally make Mac feel like a bag of shit. But tonight? Right here, in that moment, it did nothing.

"And then you let him beat us."

His mother's lips moved, but he didn't hear anything.

Liam scrambled up from his chair and disappeared, no doubt the anger in the room brought up memories the kid would rather forget. Lily shot a glance between Becca, Mackenzie, and his mother before following Liam out of the kitchen and leaving the three of them alone.

Happy. Fucking. Family.

This had to be some kind of record, a complete one eighty in less than five minutes. Only here in this house.

"Mac, maybe we should just…calm down for a moment." Becca froze when he glared at her.

"You should be the one freaking the hell out, Becs. You live here now. You live here now because you married a man who is just like Ben, a man who beat you and put you in the hospital."

He turned back to his mother. "Is he coming back here? Are you really going to let that bastard back into this house with Becca and Liam here?"

His mother seemed to have gathered herself together, because no longer was her bottom lip trembling. No longer was her voice shrill. Nope. She was back to the even-keel woman he'd known his entire life. She was lost in a sea of denial. "This is his home, Mackenzie. What am I supposed to do?"

"Tell him to stay the hell away. Tell him that this time you're choosing Becca. Tell him that this time you're choosing your grandchild." God, why couldn't she see? "For Christ's sake, Mom, why don't you try being a mother for once instead of a goddamn doormat?"

Lila Draper's face whitened, and she took a step back. She reached for the cobbler on the table and set it on the counter, her back to Mackenzie as she started to foil the top.

"You're going to be late for Liam's ball practice," she said.

Christ, this was typical.

"So that's it? There's no discussion? You're just going to let him walk right back into this house?"

His mother stilled, her shoulders hunched forward in a way that begged him to go to her, but Mac's feet felt like they were encased in cement. His chest was so goddamn tight he could barely breathe.

His sister stood in front of him, tugging on his arm in an effort to get him to leave, and wasn't that a joke. He was trying to help her, and she wanted him gone.

"You don't live here anymore, Mackenzie. There's nothing to discuss. I think you should leave," Lila said.

That thing inside him broke apart. It shattered into a thousand pieces and left him shaking from the force of it.

It was a hundred parts rage. A hundred parts disbelief. And a hundred parts sorrow.

He turned around and left without a backward glance.

Chapter 25

LILY WOKE UP TO RAIN.

She'd gone to bed listening to the rain—alone—and she'd lain there for hours waiting for Mac to join her, but he never came. She lost count of how many times she'd grabbed her cell phone, hoping for a text, hoping for some kind of word from him, telling her that he was okay.

But there was nothing.

And now it was still raining and she felt like shit. Her stomach wasn't exactly stable and a headache poked the corners of her mind.

With a groan, she slid from her bed and padded into the kitchen, on the hunt for coffee. After brewing a small pot, she added cream and sugar, and wandered into the living room, her eyes on the easel in front of the window. It boasted a blank canvas, one she'd been excited to fill only the day before.

But now?

She dragged her eyes away and took a sip of coffee.

Now she didn't feel like doing anything.

So she didn't. She perched on the edge of the sofa and stared out into the rain. The sky was dark and the gray clouds bulbous. From what she could tell, the rain was on for the entire day and that was annoying, and it sure as hell would do nothing to improve her black mood.

She stared at her cell, her thumb rolling over the

touch screen. *Dammit, Mackenzie, why the hell did you bail on me last night?* With a curse, she tossed the cell onto the table and tried to forget about it. She would not be that pathetic girl waiting for a phone call.

She just wouldn't.

Two cups of coffee later, Lily was trying to decide whether she would get dressed or not when the doorbell rang. For a few seconds, she considered not getting it—she knew it wasn't Mackenzie because he would just walk in—but when the bell sounded again, it was joined by someone shouting her name.

Jake!

She hurried down the hallway and yanked the door open, motioning him inside. The rain was falling harder now, so hard that it bounced back up when it hit the stone pathway. "You alone?" she asked, peeking behind him.

"Yeah," Jake answered as he slipped out of his work boots. "Damn, it's nasty out there." He shook some excess water off his head and flashed a grin, but it was a grin that didn't exactly creep into his eyes. "I'm on my way to the site, but thought I'd stop in for coffee."

Coffee. Right. Jake was a two-cups-in-the-morning kind of guy, and she knew damn well that he'd had his two cups with Raine. Her stomach roiled, and for a second, Lily felt bile rise in the back of her throat. This was so not about coffee.

She really needed to get it together.

Lily pointed to the kitchen, and Jake followed her down the hall, sliding his large frame onto one of the chairs at her counter while she poured him a cup.

"So," she said as she pushed the mug to him, "what's going on?"

Jake knew her well enough to know that she wasn't into bullshit, and she appreciated when he cut to the chase.

"Mac's at my place."

"Huh," she said, her mind wandering.

After the scene at his mother's place, he'd dropped her back here and then left for the ball diamond. He hadn't said much to her other than he wasn't sure if he'd be back. She knew he was angry and confused and pissed off, but she had no idea how to deal with it and no idea how to comfort him.

She'd pressed a kiss to his cheek and told him to call her when he was ready.

But he never called.

"Sal got ahold of me at midnight, wanting me to scoop his drunk ass up from the Coach House." Jake set his cup onto the counter. "He was in bad shape. I haven't seen him that out of it since Jesse died." He paused. "Did you guys get into it?"

Lily's eyebrows shot up. "What? He told you that we got into a fight?"

"No. He didn't say much of anything. He kept muttering something about Boston, and I just figured that you and him got into it."

Lily pushed her cup away. Jesus, her stomach really wasn't feeling good. "His dad is getting out of jail, and I think that his mother is letting him move back in with her. Mackenzie didn't take it real well."

"Shit," Jake said. "That's not good."

"No," Lily replied. "It isn't." She fingered her coffee cup. "What's the story there anyway? Mackenzie's never really talked about his father, though I get that they weren't close."

Jake leaned back in his chair with a sigh.

"His father…God, where would I even start?" Jake scrubbed at his chin and sighed heavily.

"If you don't feel comfortable sharing, I understand."

"No." Jake shook his head. "It's not that. I just… when I think of what Mac went through growing up, the shit that his father did to him and his family, it makes me sick. Christ, half the stuff none of us knew about, not until years later, and usually because Mac was piss-drunk and on a rant."

Lily gripped her mug so tightly that her fingers cramped. "I overheard some things at his mom's last night, and I know his father used to beat them." She swallowed a lump in her throat. "All of them."

Jake stared down into his cup and was silent for a few moments. "My first memory of Mac is from the fifth grade. He'd transferred in from another school, and his first day, every single kid in our class was in awe of this new guy. He was the prettiest boy we'd ever seen. Hell, even the teachers were all over him like bees on honey."

Lily smiled at the thought, picturing a little version of Liam.

"It didn't go down so well with us guys though. We were a tough nut to crack. Jesse, Cain, and I were already tight, and the other boys in our class weren't real keen on making this new kid welcome, but the girls sure as hell were."

Jake paused, and Lily's heart turned over when she saw the sadness there.

"I had a crush on this particular girl. Her name was Terre Winters. We all did. She had long hair the color of dark tobacco and these big blue eyes. But more importantly, she was into sports and could kick any of our asses when it came to soccer. She took one look at Mac and stuck to him like glue, and Mackenzie, being the natural-born charmer that he was, worked it. Even at that age, he worked it like a pro, and at first recess, she wasn't interested in playing soccer with us anymore. She wanted to hang out with him."

A ghost of a smile turned up the corners of Jake's mouth, but it quickly faded as he fingered the edge of his coffee cup.

"It didn't take him long to win the guys over. Cain… Jesse…they didn't understand why I was being such a little dick when it came to Mac. He came to school one day with a shiner that was the color of rotting grapes, and after that, he was pretty much in with the guys. Cain thought it was cool. But me? I still wasn't convinced that the pretty boy belonged.

"After school one day, I got into it with him. I don't even remember what it was about exactly, but somehow he ended up with a bloody nose and a hole the size of a golf ball in his jeans. Made me feel good. He wasn't so pretty anymore, but even now I can picture the look of terror in his eyes because he knew…"

Pinpricks of cold rolled over her skin as Lily stared at Jake. "What did he know?" she whispered.

Jake struggled. Her friend—this big tough guy—struggled with his memory, and Lily wanted to be sick.

"At school the next day, we were changing for gym class. I was still on him, ya know? Still not into this new kid who only had to smile and everyone else was ready to lay down for him. I was jealous I suppose, jealous that Cain and Jesse were willing to let him in. God, I was such a little prick. I got in his face, I taunted him, and he exploded. He gave it right back to me, and in the process of giving me exactly what I deserved, I tugged his shirt off and..."

Jake's voice was raspy, full of emotion.

"He'd been beaten. Badly. With a belt. He had the nastiest bruises and welts...I can't even describe them. They crisscrossed his back. Some were yellowed, like they'd been there for a while, but there were several that were red and raw and nasty."

"Oh my God," Lily whispered, her heart breaking for this little boy that lived inside the man she loved.

"Mac got up off the floor, threw his shirt back on, and left. We never really talked about it after that—not even when he started coming over, spending the night at our place." Jake looked at Lily, his expression fierce. "What kind of man does that to his kid?"

"A monster."

"Yeah," Jake replied. "A monster."

Silence fell between the two of them, and Lily hugged her knees as she gazed out the window into the rain. There was pain in her chest, a tightening that stretched across her body and settled in her heart. She thought of Lila Draper and she got angry. And then she got sad. So, so sad.

Her heart broke for this family that was damaged—for this man who was shaped by the sins of his parents.

"I've got to get to work," Jake said abruptly.

"Okay," Lily said as she slipped out of her chair and followed him to the front door. "How is...where is he?"

Jake pulled his boots on and glanced up at her. "He's sleeping it off at my place."

"Do you think I should go to him?"

Jake shrugged. "I don't know, Lily. He's not in a good place right now, and if I've learned anything over the years when it comes to Mackenzie, it's that he lashes out when he feels cornered. He might need some space."

"Oh," she said, unable to stop her bottom lip from trembling.

"Hey," Jake murmured, pulling her into a hug. "It will be fine. Just give him a bit of time."

"I love him," she blurted and froze when she felt Jake tense up.

"What?" Jake loosened his hold and stared down at her.

"I love him," she said simply. Jesus, she'd said it out loud.

Jake was silent for a few seconds. "Does he know?"

She shook her head. "No." She paused. "Should I tell him? Should I go over to your place and tell him right now?"

Jake's dark eyes softened a bit. "I'd give him some room. At least for a day or two. Let him get this out of his system."

"Okay." It wasn't what she wanted to hear, but Jake knew Mackenzie better than anyone, and she had to trust that his advice was golden.

"It will work out, Lily. Mac is crazy about you. I've never seen him like this with a woman, but he needs to get to where you are on his own."

Lily took a step back. "I know. I'm sure it will be fine." She pushed at him. "You better get to work."

She closed the door behind Jake and leaned against it, unable to stop the flow of tears that streamed down her face. She cried for a long time—so long that her legs cramped and she sank to the floor.

She cried so long that her cheeks stung from the salt and her eyes puffed out. She cried for a little boy who'd never had a chance.

And she cried for a man who was still living in that horror.

And then, selfishly, she cried for herself, because she had a very bad feeling about things, and no matter what she did, that bad feeling wouldn't go away.

Chapter 26

It had been two days since he'd seen Lily. Two days since he'd inhaled that fresh scent that was all her. Two days since he'd felt her warmth, and two days since he'd looked into her eyes.

It was two days too long.

He needed her. God knows he needed her, and for the first time in his adult life, he was going to reach out. He was going to roll the dice and see where they landed.

He had finally called her back the night before, and just the sound of her voice calmed him. There was no judgment, no cold and frosty attitude. There was only concern.

He would have gone to see her—had wanted to—but knew it wasn't smart because A) he'd been drinking and couldn't drive so that stopped him right there, and B) he looked like shit and didn't want her to see him like that.

They didn't talk about anything that mattered—not really. He told her that his designs were coming along, told her that the golf course was set, and it looked as if the project was ahead of schedule.

Lily had asked him what that meant exactly, and since he was trying real hard to be honest, he'd told her that it meant he could go back to New York City before Labor Day—not that he was planning on that.

She'd gone real quiet, and then she told him that they needed to talk.

No shit.

He glanced in the mirror as he dragged the razor over the stubble on his chin. Christ, he looked crap, but then hugging a bottle of Jack for two nights straight would do that to you.

For a second he froze, his green eyes unfocused as the image in the mirror wavered, and he took a step back.

It was his father's face he saw, and Mac shook his head, more than a little freaked out. He leaned on the sink, breathing heavy, counting slowly in an effort to pull his shit together.

He wasn't sure how long he stood like that, alone in his bathroom, counting, breathing, and then counting again. But when he finally dragged his gaze back to the mirror, he was grateful that it was his face staring back at him and not Ben's.

"Jesus, get it together," he said roughly.

He'd worked from the cottage today, and it was nearly time for him to head into town for Liam's ball game. His sister had swung by earlier, but they hadn't talked about Ben or his mother. She just wanted to make sure that he was okay and that was enough.

Mac pulled on a pair of jeans and T-shirt before grabbing his cell and keys off the table beside his bed. For a moment, his gaze lingered there, eyes on the twisted sheets that told the story of how he'd hardly slept. How could he? The empty bed did nothing for him, and without Lily's warmth next to him, he'd moved to the couch and settled in for a long night of channel surfing.

But that was about to change.

He'd come to a few hard realizations over the last few days, one being that he couldn't shut out the people who cared for him when he himself shut down. Jake and Cain were giving him space mainly because it was their status quo whenever Mac lost it. But he was kinda over that now.

He also realized that his mother was never going to change. She was always going to choose the bastard she'd married over herself and her kids. Mac wasn't real sure where he stood with that. He loved his mother, but he was so disappointed in her choices that it hurt. But who was he to judge? She obviously loved Ben Draper, and even though it was a twisted and screwed-up kind of love, it was all she had.

She just happened to love Ben more than anyone or anything else, including herself, and if you asked Mackenzie, that was really sad.

Mackenzie also knew that he needed to stop using the bottle to escape. Shit, it's not like it fixed anything other than maybe making him forget for a little while.

But maybe he was done forgetting. Maybe he was done avoiding. Maybe he just needed to deal with his shit once and for all, and move the hell on.

Mac slid into his truck and felt lighter the closer he got to Crystal Lake. In less than ten minutes, he'd see Lily, and right now it was the only thing getting him through.

He had some things he wanted to say to her, an idea that had taken root and hadn't let go. An idea that had come to him somewhere between that last sip of Jack and that first light of dawn.

He wanted her. He wanted her badly.

He thought that maybe he even loved her. Him. Mackenzie Draper, who had never allowed himself to love another person. Not in that way. And sure, he was man enough to admit it scared the crap out of him, but after the last few days, he knew that he didn't want to go it alone, not anymore.

And he was hoping she would consider moving to New York City to be with him.

When he pulled into the ballpark the first thing he saw was her car. The second thing he saw was her.

And suddenly everything was right in his world.

Mackenzie barely cut the engine before he was out the door and striding toward her. He didn't say anything. He just scooped her into his arms and pulled her close to him. So close that he could feel her heartbeat. So close that he felt the air swoosh out of her lungs as she nestled against him.

So close that that elusive thing he'd been searching for—peace—finally washed over him.

"Boston," he said but had to take a second because that big-ass lump that was in his throat made it hard to speak. He sank his fingers into her hair, loving the way she melted into him, and when he finally had his shit together, he spoke.

"Are we good?" God, so inadequate, but it was all he had right now.

She nodded. "We're good."

"I'm sorry I was such an asshole."

"It's okay," she murmured against his chest. "Really. I know you needed your space."

He yanked his head back because he needed her to see the truth. "No, Lily. I don't need space anymore. I need you." He brushed his mouth across hers. "I need you so badly that I can't think straight."

He cupped her chin and kissed her thoroughly. He kissed her until his head spun and the chorus of catcalls and whistles penetrated his little bubble.

Reluctantly, he dragged his mouth away and rested his forehead against hers.

"I missed you."

"Me too," she said softly before nudging him. "But you have a ball game to coach." She was silent for a moment, her eyes misty. "We'll talk later."

"Damn right we will."

She walked him to the dugout, and then he watched as she made her way over to Becca, who sat alone in the stands. Mac's mother wasn't around, which surprised him—she hadn't missed any of the ball games yet, though he supposed she was still hurt and pissed at him.

The boys were tossing the ball around, and Cain clapped Mac on the shoulder. "You want to do the infield warm-up?"

He nodded. "Sure." This was good. This was normal, and normal was what he needed right then. Mac slid his hand into his ball glove before striding onto the field and calling for his infield.

He glanced back once more, his eyes on Lily, and felt that strange sensation fill his chest again. It was hot and squishy and so damn sweet that he had to look away because something hot and wet pricked the corners of his eyes.

Holy. Hell. There was no room for a pussy out on the field.

He cleared his throat, grabbed a bat, and headed to home plate.

The game was going well until about the fifth inning. Liam gave up three hits, and the team found themselves down by two runs with the bases loaded, no outs, and the opposing team's heavy hitter at the plate.

Mac could tell that his nephew was getting frustrated, so he signaled a time-out and walked over to the mound.

Liam's head was lowered, and he kept digging at the pitcher's plate with his foot.

"Hey, buddy. Are you still feeling loose? How's your arm?"

Liam shrugged. "It's okay."

Mac waited a moment before he broached the delicate subject of a replacement. "Do you think it's time to bring in Jason?"

Liam's head shot up, and he straightened his ball cap. "I don't mean to be a dick, but he sucks, Uncle Mac. We'll lose for sure."

Mac cracked his knuckles. The kid was right.

"Well, he tries and that's what counts."

"Not if we're going to lose."

"Quit babying the kid and let's get on with the game!"

Mac stilled, his hand on Liam's shoulder, fingers digging in as everything inside him froze.

Un-fucking-believable. Would he really...

"Uncle Mac, you're hurting me," Liam whispered hoarsely.

It was enough to snap Mackenzie back into focus and dropped his hand.

"Is that him?" Liam said, eyes huge as he stared up at his uncle.

"That's him."

Liam peered around Mac, one hand gripping the ball, the other shoving the brim of his cap back. He dug into the pitcher's plate once more and exhaled. "He doesn't look that mean."

"No," Mac said carefully, trying to keep his temper in check. "He doesn't."

"My dad doesn't either."

Mac stared down into his past, and that temper that was festering inside him boiled. It rolled over and shot through him in one hard thrust.

"Are you okay, Uncle Mac?"

He nodded and lied. "Yep. So, we gonna do this kid? Are you going to get this done?"

Liam gripped the ball. "I'm going to get this done for you, Uncle Mac."

"Okay." Mac squeezed his nephew's shoulder and then turned back toward the dugout. He avoided the stands because he was pretty sure that as soon as he laid eyes on his father, he was going to lose it. And he didn't want to lose it here.

Not here.

"You alright?" Cain asked.

"No, but we've got a game to get through."

And they did.

Liam managed to pull it together. He struck out the next three batters, leaving the players on base stranded. The boys rallied at their last at bat, and by the time the game was over, they'd pulled ahead by one run.

The entire time, Mackenzie felt his father's eyes on him—boring into him like a goddamn parasite—and when he finally glanced up and met his gaze, the rage that took hold of Mac was hard to describe. He'd never felt it so intensely before. It was all consuming. It was ugly and harsh, and it left him trembling.

Ben Draper thought he could waltz back into Crystal Lake and pick up where he left off.

His father stood just behind their dugout, his arm around Lila's shoulders. "Nice comeback, Liam. I see you've got some of your granddad's talent."

Liam stood beside Mackenzie and remained silent.

Ben's mouth tightened. "I'm talking to you, boy. Show some respect."

Mac recognized the look in his father's eyes and knew that Ben was looking to get into it. He clenched his hands together, envisioning his fist connecting with his father's face. Christ, that would make him feel good.

A flash of blond drew his attention and clear, blue eyes centered him. They pulled him in and calmed his soul.

The moment passed and Mac tugged on Liam's arm. "Come on, kid. You and your mother can stay with me tonight."

"He's not worth it," Cain said as he started forward.

"I know," Mac replied. "I'm good."

And he was good. He was real good up until the moment he reached his sister in the parking lot. Lily was with her, and the two of them looked worried and upset.

"Did he touch you?" Mac tried to hold his temper in check, but it was damn hard.

Becca shook her head. "No, but I don't…I don't know what to do. Mom wants us there, but I don't think I can stay at home. Not if he's back, and she just…she just refuses to understand. She thinks that this time he'll be good, that he's miraculously become this man she's always known he could be. She's so far into denial that I don't think she'll ever come back. Mac, he'll hurt her again."

"I know." He turned to Lily. "Can you take Liam to my place?"

"No!" Liam yanked on Mac's arm. "I don't want to go without Mom. Please, Uncle Mac. Don't make me."

Mackenzie recognized the fierce need to protect in his nephew's eyes and looked at his sister because he didn't know what to do. Christ, he just didn't know what to do. His first instinct was to say no, to make Lily take Liam away from all the ugliness coming down on his head, but was that the right call? Was sheltering him from reality the way to go?

As it turned out, none of it mattered anyway.

"What the hell are you all bellyaching for? Get your asses home and be quick about it. Your mother and I have some news."

Liam's eyes went as big and as round as a silver dollar. Lily reached for him, and Becca moved in front of him, her body shielding her son from the monster behind them.

Mac turned around. "Back off, Ben."

His father laughed, a cold, dry sort of thing that rattled his chest and started a coughing fit. Lila held on to his arm, and it was all Mackenzie could do not to tear her away from him.

"I see that fancy job of yours and all that city living haven't taught you an ounce of respect." Ben sneered, his eyes narrowing to twin slits of emerald as he moved from Mac to Becca. "I told you to get your ass home, girl. I don't care how old you are, if you're living with me, you're going to abide by my rules. And when I say get your butt home for a family meeting, I don't mean in a few hours or tomorrow. I mean now."

Becca shook her head and whispered, "I'm not going anywhere with you."

"Oh, Becs," Lila said softly. "Please. Things will be different now."

Ben stared at his children for the longest time and then shrugged. "That's fine, Lila. I don't want her little bastard hanging around anyway."

Lila Draper's face crumpled, and she started to cry, and if Mackenzie thought he couldn't hate his father any more than he already did, he was sadly mistaken.

As Ben tugged on his wife's arm and ordered her to the car, he paused, his hard, green eyes on Lily, a lecherous and disgusting smile stretching his lips wide.

"So, I'm guessing you're Mackenzie's new whore?"

That was all it took. Something snapped inside Mackenzie, and the roaring in his ears moved him forward. The pain in his heart pushed forward.

Nothing could have stopped him. Not Cain or Jake.

And certainly not the woman who tugged on his arm. The woman he sent flying when he took a run at his father.

Chapter 27

Lily sat on her front porch, a glass of juice in hand, though since she could barely keep anything down, she wasn't exactly sure why she'd grabbed it.

It gave her something to do she supposed, since she was nervous as hell. Nervous and worried and, she sighed, so confused it made her head spin.

Mac had spent the night in jail and so had his father. The scene at the ballpark had been awful. It had been gut-wrenching and hateful and, on many levels, eye opening. Her stomach turned over just thinking about it.

The sound of fist meeting bone was something she hoped never to hear again. Or the anguished screams that had fallen from Lila. Never again did she want to see the red-hot rage in Mac's eyes—that look would haunt her for the rest of her days. It was almost as terrifying as the pain she'd glimpsed when Jake and Cain finally pulled him off his father.

She'd stood there, holding her bleeding lip—injured by his elbow when he'd gone after his father—and the utter hopelessness in his eyes had her fearing that she'd lost him forever.

She'd spent the night tossing and turning and knowing that her world was about to change because she couldn't go on like this. Not anymore. There were too many things left unsaid that needed to be spoken. The hourglass, it seemed, had run out of sand.

Gibson ran up onto the steps, the burly retriever yipping playfully at her feet, but she didn't have the heart to play with him.

Jake and Raine had been by an hour earlier to check on her, and she'd asked them to leave the dog. She thought that she might take Gibson into the woods for a walk, to clear her head, but she had no energy.

She had nothing, and just this once, she thought that it would be nice to feel nothing.

Lily must have dozed off because when Gibson started barking, she jerked so badly her glass went flying and shattered at her feet. Gingerly, she got to her knees and picked up the broken pieces, placing them in a little pile beside her chair.

A noise made her freeze.

Mackenzie.

He stood at the end of the driveway, still dressed in the clothes he'd worn the night before—the jeans dirty, the T-shirt splattered with blood. He'd pulled on a ball cap, and she couldn't see his eyes, but she felt them.

He looked toward her for several long moments, and when he started toward the porch, her heart leaped into her chest. He crossed the lawn swiftly on his long legs until he stopped at the bottom of the steps, and he pushed the brim of his cap back.

Sweet Jesus, but his face looked rough. He had abrasions along his jaw and beneath his eye, and stitches above his brow. Such need filled her—the need to touch him, to breathe him in, and she bounded down the stairs, straight into his arms.

He held her for a long time, not saying anything, his arms wrapped around her as if she was his lifeline, and when he finally let her go, his fingers lingered along her mouth. His thumb grazed the tender skin near the one corner that had met his elbow the night before.

She wanted him to keep touching her even if it hurt, to keep their connection alive, but he moved away, and her heart turned all over again. God, she felt sick.

"Jesus Christ, I'm so sorry, Lily."

"Mackenzie, it was an accident," she said softly. "Please don't blame yourself."

"An accident?" His voice was incredulous. "An accident is tossing colors in with whites when you're doing laundry. An accident is forgetting to leave your parking brake on or forgetting to turn off the sprinkler system." He clenched and unclenched his hands. "What happened last night wasn't an accident. It was bound to happen sooner than later. It always does. I'm just so goddamn sorry…"

He shook his head. "I don't know what to say. I lost it. I thought I could handle seeing him. I thought that I could keep my shit together, but when he called you a…"

Lily flinched and reached for him, but he moved farther away.

"When he called you a whore, I saw red." Mac scrubbed at his face. "All I could think about was getting to him and shutting his rancid mouth the hell up. I didn't think about anyone else. I didn't think about you or Becca or Liam. I screwed up, like I always do."

Something in his tone got to her, and the fear that had been building inside Lily for days erupted. He was already leaving her.

She blanked for a moment, saw nothing but his pain, heard nothing but his sorry, and felt nothing but the distance he was trying to put between them. She gave herself a mental shake and desperately tried for some kind of normal.

Conversation. Yes. Keep the conversation going.

"Is your father…"

"He's out. He's with my mom, and apparently they're going to play house again."

"Oh, Mackenzie. I don't know what to say."

He shoved his hands into his front pockets and hunched his shoulders. "There's nothing to say. It is what it is. She'll always choose him over us. God, to think there was a time I thought of trying to convince her to come live with me in New York, and now she doesn't want to talk to me."

He sighed. "Liam and Becca are at the cottage. They're going to stay there until I can figure this out. I've already talked to the Bookers, and I think he'll let us rent the place year-round since it's winterized. It's an alternative for Becca if she chooses to stay here."

Hope flared and she took a step toward him. "So you're staying in Crystal Lake?"

"What?" He shook his head vigorously. "Hell no. I'd end up killing Ben if I did. I'm heading back to New York City as soon as I get my sister settled. I just can't… this place isn't good for me. Not anymore."

"Oh," she whispered, trying to ease the pain inside her and afraid to ask the next question. "So, what are we going to do about us?"

He looked away, and she knew they were done. She knew that he'd given up on them. "I don't know, Lily. I want to make this work, but I don't see how. I won't stay here and up until yesterday I thought…"

His voice drifted off and for a few moments there was nothing.

"You thought?" she prompted.

He still wouldn't look at her. "I thought of asking you to come to New York City with me, but I don't...I just think I'm better off alone for now."

But what about me? What about what I think?

"I'm pregnant."

Oh God. The words slipped out before she could snatch them back, and for what seemed like minutes, time stood still.

Lily watched Mac closely, breath squeezed so tight inside her chest that for a moment she was dizzy. Sweat broke out on her forehead, and the nausea that had settled in her stomach since early morning threatened to turn into something a hell of a lot more.

She would not be sick in front of him. *She wouldn't.*

"What did you say?"

His voice snapped her out of her funk, and she wrapped her arms around herself, shivering and trying like hell to hold it together.

"I'm pregnant."

Mac's face was like granite. Smooth. Dark. Intense. And so lovely it made her ache. She saw so much in his eyes, but it was their brutal honestly that killed her.

He didn't want them.

Lily...or their baby.

He stared at her for so long, his expression growing darker, that she finally turned away, unable to hold his gaze because the anger that sat in his eyes made her sick. She knew he would react this way. She'd prepared herself for it and yet...

And yet it still stung. And it hurt so much more worse than she'd thought it would or even could.

Several long moments passed as Lily gazed across the grass and watched Raine's dog chase something on the wind. A leaf? A bug?

Did it really matter?

When Mac spoke, she jumped, though his voice was low. He didn't raise it or infuse it with any of the anger she'd glimpsed in his eyes. It was as if nothing colored his words…they were just words—a means for more information.

"How can you be pregnant?"

A heartbeat passed as she continued to watch the dog. And then another.

When she knew she could speak without losing her mind, she moistened her lips. "I'm assuming you had the birds and the bees talk at some point in your life?"

"Don't be flippant with me. Don't you dare. Not now. Not after everything."

His voice was closer, and she knew he'd climbed the stairs and had joined her on the porch. She felt him, there at her back, so close that her skin was seared from his heat. So close that his scent washed over her. And yet she was cold.

Her teeth chattered. She was freezing cold.

Gibson jumped straight up into the air, his paws swinging at something, and with a yelp, he rolled over on the ground, his tail wagging madly as whatever it was he'd been hunting was finally within his grasp.

"Lily."

Again with the monotone. Christ, she hated that flat sound. She would rather hear his anger, feel the wrath of it…feel something, *anything*, that would show her she meant something more than the mistake inside her.

"The shower," she said softly as she closed her eyes. If she tried real hard, she was sure she could feel the warm water on her skin, his hard, wet body against hers.

"The shower," he repeated.

He waited a heartbeat, and she knew that he remembered. "But I…I stopped…I…"

She shook her head. "No, Mackenzie. You didn't. Not in time."

Another heartbeat passed and her eyes remained closed tight.

"Are you sure?" he bit out.

She nodded. "Since I'm never late, I bought a test yesterday, one that can detect pregnancy within days, and it was positive."

"But Jesus…aren't you on the pill? Christ, I thought you said you were."

"I haven't been with anyone in a long time, and there was no need for the pill, but yes, I went to see the doctor, and I was waiting to start this month."

"Fuck."

His heat vanished from her skin, and she heard him step away. Already the pain inside her was spiraling up, expanding and infiltrating her cells. She knew she couldn't hold off the onslaught of emotion much longer.

"I don't want you to have it."

Her eyes flew open, and it took a few seconds for her to collect herself, to put in place the familiar mask she hadn't needed in so long. It slipped over her skin like an old friend, and she exhaled as she slowly turned around.

Mac glared at her with something that made her gut

clench. Lily felt the wobble in her knees, but she kept her chin raised and her eyes focused. There was no way in hell she was going to let him know how much his words cut her. There would be time to fall apart later when she was alone.

"I told you." He raked his hands through his long, blond hair. "I told you when we started this…thing between us that kids…that family…none of that was going to happen. I told you that I didn't want that." He shook his head, shoulders raised. "*You* didn't want that."

I do now. The thought whispered through her mind like a secret, and it bled into every part of her.

Mac was angry, but there was something else there… something bleak and painful and dark. She thought of the scene the night before with his father. She thought of the ugliness and pain, and she knew in that moment that Mackenzie Draper was never going to change. Not for himself. Not for her.

And definitely not for a baby he didn't want.

Pain crept into her heart, and it took everything that Lily had to keep her shit together, to not lose herself to the sadness inside and fall apart in front of him. He could never know…

He could never know how much she loved him, because he could never know how painful it felt to know that she wasn't enough to fix him.

"Jesus, Lily, I'm sorry." He shook his head, that beautiful mouth of his drawn tight, his eyes tortured. "Lily, I can't…"

"I know," she answered softly. "I know." She paused, searching for the right words. Even now, hurting like she was, she still wanted to ease his pain. "But that doesn't mean that I'm going to change my mind. That doesn't mean that I don't already feel something for this baby."

Mac shoved his hands into the front pockets of his jeans and began to pace the length of the porch.

"I don't believe this," he said harshly. "In this day and age...we're two smart, responsible adults and you're pregnant. Un-fucking-real."

His tone grew more dangerous, and Lily's hackles were up when he turned on her. His eyes fell from hers, traveling down her body until he rested on her stomach, there where her hands laid in a protective manner. It was then that it hit her. He blamed her. He blamed her for everything.

Pride kept her head up. "I didn't have to tell you, you know, but I'm not ashamed of this, and I'm not going to hide so you're going to have to deal with it. I'm having this baby, and if it's the legalities that you're worried about, I'll have my lawyer draw up papers tonight. I'll absolve you of any and all involvement with this child, both legally and financially."

He stared at her for so long that her knees began to wobble again, and Lily thought she was going to crumble at his feet.

"Jesus Christ," he whispered roughly. "You make me sound like a goddamn bastard. I can't be the only man on the planet who doesn't want a wife or kids. I'd be a disaster as a father."

Again, with the punch to the gut. Tears stung the corners of her eyes, hot pricks of pain that she forced away.

"I'm sure you're not," she managed to say. "But I also think you're wrong. I think that if you wanted to, you'd be able to love a child and a woman without reservation. And I think that if you walk away from me now, one day you'll regret it."

He glanced down at the floor, shoulders hunched forward. Pain radiated off him in waves, and the bruise along his cheekbone took on a purplish hue as the sun hit him. A bruise put there by his father. God, no wonder he was so screwed up, but it didn't stop her from hoping that she would be enough. That the "thing" they had together would be enough to heal his pain.

"I get that you didn't want this," she began.

His head snapped up.

"You don't get anything, Lily. I'm not cut out for this. I don't want to be responsible for another human being. It would never work out. I'd only end up hurting you...hurting the kid." Anguish tinged his face. "I'm no good. I'm no different than Ben or his father before him. I'm selfish and arrogant. I drink too much, and my temper is off the charts. I don't deal with shit real well, and I can't..."

"You can't what?" Angry now, she took a step forward.

"I just can't do this. You. A baby. It's not going to happen. Jesus Christ, Lily, it was never going to happen."

In some secret corner of her soul, she had thought that maybe when he found out, things would be different. She'd thought that *he* would be different.

She hugged her stomach and stared at the man she loved. A man who had managed to tear down the walls she'd built up around her heart and yet he wouldn't let her do the same to him. It was tragic, really. And it was her life.

"We're all born innocent, Mac. I truly believe that. We come into this world with no direction and only the guidance of those around us. Some people get lucky and some, like us, well, we're pretty much screwed. We can't pick our parents. We can't pick our family or where we grow up. We just get what we get. We become a product of our environment." She paused and exhaled.

"I know your father is a bastard and I know that your mother broke your heart. I know their relationship molded you into the man that you are, but, Mac, you're hiding behind all that crap. I know because I was there. I hid behind a reputation I didn't deserve and a sister who used me. I hid behind a father who didn't deserve my love and a mother who didn't want it. But I got past it. My brother and Jake helped me get past it."

And so did you.

How could she make him see?

"I was broken inside and I never thought I'd be whole again. The difference between us is that you don't want to be fixed. You'd rather go through life only half-alive. I guess I was hoping that I might be reason enough for you to change but..." She glanced down at her flat stomach. "I can't hide behind my masks anymore. I won't do it. I can't afford to be that selfish anymore. I'm going to give this baby everything that I never had. He's never going to want for anything." She couldn't help the tears that slid down her face—there were too many of them.

Angrily, Lily wiped them away. "And I hope he'll never know that he wasn't enough for his father. I'll do everything in my power to keep that from him."

"Boston." She didn't care that his voice was full of anguish or that the pain in his eyes was as great as hers. Right now, she couldn't get past her own.

"Don't call me that ever again." Lily glanced back

out at Gibson. "Can you leave please? I'll have my lawyer send the papers to your New York address."

A cool breeze swept in, rolling across the lawn. It lifted up her hair, and for a second she was blinded, but by the time she yanked the long blond strands from her face, Mac was down the steps, his long legs eating up the distance to his Mercedes.

She didn't wait for him to leave.

She ran into the house and barely made it to the bathroom before she lost everything inside her stomach.

Chapter 28

It was close to midnight before Jake found him. Mackenzie had been sitting out on the Edwardses' dock, staring into a clear night sky for hours. He never went back to the cottage he'd rented—he was too ashamed to face his nephew. Too ashamed of the violence Liam had witnessed.

Dammit, he should be stronger—or at least strong enough.

So here he was. Right back where he started. The place he always went to when things went south. He'd brought a bottle of Jack along, but he hadn't touched it.

That was something at least. That was heading in the right direction.

Mackenzie watched Jake drag a chair over to him and the two men settled into a silence that was a long time in the making. It was the kind of silence that had seen things—dark things—and it was the kind of silence that he needed right now.

Overhead the night sky was lit up with a million diamonds, and as Mac leaned back and stared out at the vastness, he saw a shooting star. He followed its trajectory until it burned out, and then there was nothing.

Watching it left him feeling empty, but he supposed he was already empty to begin with.

"Lily's pregnant," he said, voice scratchy.

Jake didn't say anything for the longest time, and when

Mac finally looked his way, he found his friend's eyes on him. They were dark and intense but instead of anger or condemnation, they were filled with compassion.

"I know," Jake replied. He dug into the cooler he'd brought and offered Mac a cold beer.

Mac declined and Jake popped open his can, taking a good long drink.

The water lapped gently along the edge of the beach, small waves rolling in as the wind picked up, and even though the night was star-heavy, Mac smelled rain.

"How is she?" he asked, feeling that damn vise around his heart tighten as he sank lower into his chair and closed his eyes.

"Not good."

No. He didn't think she would be. Christ. When had everything gone to shit? Was he cursed to go through life in a pit of misery? Thinking back on things that he should have done differently?

Take Boston for instance. He knew that he was no good for her and still he went after her. He pursued her relentlessly. He took advantage of the undeniable attraction they felt for each other, and now things were as bad as he should have known they'd get.

He thought of the freckles on her nose and the way the right side of her mouth lifted when she smiled. He thought of how amazing she smelled and how soft she was to touch.

He thought of what it felt like to wake up with her in his bed and how he looked forward to arguing with her over sports or music or movies, or just about anything. He loved getting her worked up. He loved listening to her voice.

He loved listening to her breathe, and he loved watching her sleep.

"I love her," he said, voice barely above a whisper.

Jake crumpled his can and tossed it into the cooler. "I know that too."

He looked at his friend in surprise and Jake shrugged. "It's pretty damn hard not to, and, buddy, you've had it bad for her ever since you saw her on Memorial Day." Jake settled back in his chair, stretching his long legs out as he did so. "I hate to tell you this, Mac, but you didn't have a chance where Lily was concerned. I've never met two people who belonged together as much as you guys do. I gotta say I didn't see it at first, but I do now and it would be wrong for you to throw it away."

Mac didn't answer right away because he wasn't sure that he could convey what he was feeling. He listened to the water. He let it lull him into a place of peace, or at the very least, as close to peace as he was going to get.

"I'm no good for her, Jake, and I sure as hell can't raise a kid."

"Bullshit."

Mac sat a little straighter. "What?"

"I call bullshit."

"You can't call bullshit on something like that."

"Why not?"

Was Jake trying to get under his skin?

"Because this is serious. It's not a fucking game."

"I know that and I still call bullshit."

"Who's calling bullshit on what?" The voice slid out from the dark, and Mac glanced down at the end of the dock, where a figure was slowly making his way toward them.

Cain.

The rocker looked like hell with several days' worth of stubble on his chin and clothes that looked as if he'd slept in them.

"Shit, Cain, I thought I looked bad," Mac said, moving over and giving him some room.

Cain slid into a third chair and sighed. "Maggie's, uh, not exactly in a good place right now. She's ready to have this baby, but the baby doesn't want to come out and play. She thinks she's as big as a house and ugly as sin, and goddamn, but she cries at the drop of a hat. It's like walking on broken glass these days."

Cain sighed again. "I'm telling ya, having a baby is tougher on the father than the mother, that's for sure. That's something they don't put in those stupid baby books that she leaves laying all over the place. The ones that she says I don't have to read but then when she quizzes me on them and I screw up she gets a little upset."

Jake tossed Cain a beer, but Mac still wasn't in the mood to drink.

Cain opened his can and glanced between the two of them. "So who called bullshit and what's it about?"

"Mac doesn't think he's good enough for Lily," Jake said. "And that's his excuse for bailing."

Cain shrugged. "He's right. He's not."

"See?" Mackenzie interjected. "You can't call bullshit on that."

"Well, I wouldn't go that far, Draper," Cain continued. "None of us are good enough for the women in our lives, not really. You just gotta hope that they never figure that shit out."

"So my bullshit call stands," Jake said.

"Whatever," Mackenzie muttered. "It doesn't change anything. I'm no good for her and now she knows. After the show I put on at the ballpark and the way I reacted earlier today, trust me, she's already figured that one out."

Cain glanced his way. "What about the baby?"

Damn. "Does everyone know?"

"No," Jake answered. "Just us. Just the ones who count. Just the ones who know you. The ones who know that if you walk away from this woman and your child, a woman you just told me that you love, you will never forgive yourself. Sorry, Mac, but that's a bullshit move and something your father would do."

A shot of resentment ran through Mac, and it wasn't because he was feeling sorry for himself or pissed off at his situation. It was because, as much as these two men were like brothers to him, closer than his family even, they didn't *know* him. Not like they thought they did.

Jake and Jesse had grown up in a home with two loving parents, raised in luxury on the lake. And even though Cain's dad had left before Mackenzie had met him, his mom was amazing, and Cain had always known that he was loved. Neither one of them had ever faced the belt or the back of a hand, or visiting the doctor with a mother who was coaching him to lie because it was his father who'd broken his arm and not a fall down the stairs.

That kind of shit never went away, and as far as Mackenzie was concerned, it would spill over into any kind of life he built for himself. So why the hell would he drag Lily down with him? Why would he tempt fate with a kid?

God, an innocent kid.

Just like he'd been at one time.

"I appreciate that you guys are looking out for me. Christ, it's more than I deserve."

"I hate when you do that," Jake interrupted.

"What?" Mac said, sitting a little straighter.

"I hate when you talk as if you don't deserve anything good. For fuck's sake, Mac, you, more than anyone I know, deserve to be happy. You survived that house, that toxic mess that your parents created, and don't think for one second that you survived it just to go through life alone. How is that fair? How is that not letting Ben win? Don't let him win, Mac. Take what you deserve and live."

"Jake, you don't know what you're talking about."

"Yeah," he said, leaning forward. "I do. You think that you're going to turn into your father. You think that if you and Lily get together, you're going to bloody her face or put her in the hospital. You think that if you accept her and this baby, that you're going to be an asshole father like Ben was, but you're wrong. I've seen you with your nephew. I've seen you with Lily. You're not that guy, Mackenzie."

Jake heaved a sigh, his dark eyes intense. "You were never that guy."

Mac yanked on the brim of his cap, suddenly feeling exposed and wanting to disappear into the darkness.

The three of them sat together like that for a good, long while. Long enough for the dew to fall nice and heavy and soak their clothes through.

Long enough for each of them to lose themselves in their thoughts and for Mackenzie to run over the scene with Lily a hundred times.

God, he had hurt her.

With a groan, he sank his face into his hands and closed his eyes.

"Guys, I gotta go," Cain said. "It's nearly four in the morning, and if Maggie wakes up and finds me gone, she just may kick my ass. And that woman may be pregnant and all, but trust me, if she decides that she's going to kick my ass all over Crystal Lake and back, she'll do it."

"You didn't tell her you were heading out here?" Jake asked.

"Hell no. She was already asleep and right now sound-asleep Maggie is the nice Maggie. It's the Maggie I hope I see when I go home."

Cain got to his feet and offered Mac his hand. He shook it and stood to clap his buddy on the shoulders, in the way that guys did.

"Thanks for coming out, Cain."

"Just don't do anything rash, alright? Don't make a life-changing decision until you've talked to Lily again."

He nodded but thought of how he'd left things, and he knew that it was easier said than done.

Jake jumped to his feet. "I should go to. You want a ride home? You must be tired as hell."

"Nah," Mac said, sliding back into his chair. "I think I'm going to stick around for a bit. It's been a while since I saw a sunrise."

"Okay," Jake said. He paused. "You've never been alone, you know that, Mac. Even back in the day…" Jake halted and ran his hands over his chin. "Back then, you knew that you could count on us, right?"

Mackenzie tried to smile, but he knew it was lame-ass attempt and gave up. "Sure," he answered. "I knew."

He watched Jake slowly walk up the dock and settled back in the chair, cold and wet and uncaring.

Sure, he knew that he could count on his buddies, but the problem was, at the end of the day, they all went home to houses that were free of violence and hatred.

And Mac? Well, Mac wasn't so sure he'd ever really left that place.

He wasn't so sure that he ever would.

Chapter 29

He must have fallen asleep because when Mackenzie opened his eyes, the sun was shining and the smell of fresh-brewed coffee filled his nostrils.

"Sorry, hon. Didn't mean to startle you."

Mac stretched, wincing as muscles cramped and protested. He shoved his Detroit Tigers cap back and looked up into the gentle eyes of Marnie Edwards.

"I figured you could use a cup."

He took the mug and moved over a bit when she settled into the chair her son had vacated a few hours earlier. Wrapped in a large, purple blanket, with slippers on her feet and her hair pulled back in a clip, she looked…safe. And nice. And caring.

Everything that a mother should be.

"It's going to rain today," she murmured, eyes on the horizon. There wasn't a cloud in the sky.

"I know," Mackenzie said. "I can feel it."

She took a sip of coffee. "That's good. Rain is good. It changes things. Cleans things."

Mackenzie wasn't sure where she was headed so he remained silent, and the two of them slowly sipped their coffee and watched the lake slowly come alive. They were getting into the dog days of summer; Labor Day was less than a week away, and pretty soon the vacationers would leave and both the lake and the town would go into hibernation.

He used to love this time of the year. A time when he and the rest of the Bad Boys would reclaim their lake.

God, he used to love a lot of things.

"I know you're having a hard time right now, Mackenzie. And I know you've got some big decisions to make. But what you do right now will determine the fate of three people. Yourself, Lily, and this unborn child."

Mac's mouth tightened—obviously Jake had told her everything—but he remained silent. He wasn't in the mood to discuss his personal life with Jake's mom, but he knew the woman well enough to know that if she wanted to discuss this stuff, then they were going to discuss this stuff.

"Lily is a strong woman," Marnie said softly. "And if you abandon her, she'll be fine. She might not be happy, but she'll be fine."

Abandon? Suddenly angry, he turned to Marnie. "I'm not abandoning her." He wasn't. Abandoning inferred that he didn't care, and he cared. Hell, he cared a lot. It was because he cared for her...because he loved her that he was letting her go.

Marnie continued to sip her coffee in a calm manner. "Call it what you like, Mackenzie, but the cold truth is that you'll be gone. You'll be gone, out of her life and out of the life of a child you created with her. Lily is as beautiful on the inside as she is on the outside, and I'm telling you right now, she won't be alone forever."

Mac's chest tightened, and he gripped the coffee mug between his hands as he thought about that.

"Are you okay with another man raising your child?

Are you okay knowing another man will be sharing Lily's bed—"

"Okay, Marnie. I know you mean well, but fu—shit…I can't do this with you."

For a few seconds he heard nothing but the gentle lap of water against the dock.

"When Jesse died and Jake left, I didn't think he'd ever be whole again." She turned to him, and Mac winced at the pain in her eyes. "You were there. You know how broken he was. Lily helped him get through, and she helped bring him back to us—to Steven and I, and to Raine. She's like an angel put on this earth to heal and to comfort, and she needs you now more than ever."

Emotion tightened his chest some more and for a few seconds, he wasn't able to speak.

"I don't deserve her."

Marnie looked surprised at that.

"I call bullshit."

Mac's eyebrow shot up. "Excuse me?"

"I call bullshit," she repeated firmly, her eyes on him so intense, so much like Jake's, that it was eerie.

A little chunk of something loosened inside him, and for the first time in a forever, it seemed, he cracked a smile.

"You would," he said roughly.

"I'm just calling it as I see it."

Marnie glanced down into her mug and tapped her toe along the dock. "You've had a raw deal, Mackenzie, there's no two ways about it. But don't let the sins of your parents mark you like this. Just don't. Not all of us get the chance to love or live. Some people go their whole lives without experiencing real love and some…"

She took a moment and he thought of Jesse. "Well, some people have it snatched from them. Don't take that away from Lily," she said softly.

She stood abruptly and held out her hand, a gentle smile curving her mouth as she gazed down at him.

"You need to come with me," she said.

"Ah, okay." Mac got to his feet, towering over the slight woman.

"You look awful, and I'm not letting you go anywhere until you shower."

She tugged on his hand, and he hand no choice but to follow her.

"Steven is making scrambled eggs and toast, and we can sit down and have a nice breakfast together." She glanced over her shower. "Once you're clean."

He smiled. He liked bossy Marnie.

"And then you can go and fix things with Lily."

Mackenzie stepped off the dock, and as he followed the small woman up the path to their house, he felt hope for the first time. It was a warm feeling. Light and airy.

Hope was good.

He'd take it.

By late afternoon he'd called Lily several times, and each time that he did, his call went straight to voice mail.

He wasn't surprised, though he was anxious as hell to get to her place and to make things right. He'd gone there straight from the Edwardses', but she wasn't home and now he was starting to get a little worried.

"Uncle Mac." A pause. "*Hello*."

He glanced up at his nephew. "Sorry, Liam. What was that?"

"Do I take my old room?"

"Ah, sure." He glanced at Becca and pointed her in the direction of his bedroom. "Take it, Becs. I'll sleep on the sofa."

He had just arrived back at the cottage with his sister, his truck full of her shit along with a considerable amount of groceries. It amazed him, how much a kid like Liam could eat.

Their mother had called a few hours earlier. According to Lila, Ben was out looking for a job, but Mac figured his father was holed up somewhere with one of his loser buddies, making his way through a case of beer. Either way, it had freed them up to get Becca's stuff and bring it all back here.

His mother had seemed so sad—so lonely—but for the first time in his adult life, Mackenzie truly accepted that she wasn't going to change and that it was on her. He loved her—of course he loved his mother—and he thought that, maybe sometime down the road, he would be able to forgive her for choosing Ben Draper over her kids, but right now he was content to leave things be.

Baby steps and all that.

It took a good hour or so to unpack, even with Mackenzie going full tilt. His nerves were shot to hell, and he needed to see Lily in a way that hurt. Without thinking, he pulled his cell phone from his pocket and swore when he realized the goddamn battery was dead.

How long had it been like that?

Shit.

"Becca, can I borrow your cell?"

She nodded and grabbed her purse, rummaging through it for a good minute before she found the damn thing. He had no idea what the hell she had in her bag, but he was thinking it might be a good time to purge.

"It's crap and the service sucks, but you might be able to get a call out."

He snagged the cell and headed outside, punching in Lily's number along the way. Again, it rang several times until it went to voice mail.

"Dammit," he muttered, already heading back inside for his keys. He'd track her down if he had to because he couldn't wait any longer. He would charge his phone in the truck on the way into Crystal Lake, and he wasn't leaving until he found her.

"Becca, I'm heading into town."

He punched in Jake's number before handing over Becca's cell and damned if Jake didn't pick up on the first ring.

"Mac, where…hell…trying to…you."

Jake was breaking up.

"I'm trying to find Lily." He hoped Jake would hear him. "Do you know where she is?"

Static filled his ear, and pissed off, he fought the urge to toss the damn phone. Clamping down on his anger, he exhaled and got his shit together.

"Jake, did you get that? Where are you? Where's Lily?"

"Hospital…baby."

"What?"

But there was only static and the cold, hard fear in his gut churned so heavy that he buckled over, not caring that the cell phone slipped from his fingers and fell to the floor.

"Jesus, Mac. What's going on?"

"I've got to...Jesus, Becca, I think Lily's in the hospital."

His sister's face went white, and she pointed toward his truck. "Go."

He peeled out of the driveway so fast that gravel went flying everywhere, and then he broke every speed limit there was on his way to the hospital. When he got there, he screeched to a stop and didn't bother getting into it with the paramedic who tried to stand in his way. He tossed him the keys and told him to move the truck if he had to.

Racing into the hospital, he spied Tracy, a girl he knew from back in the day. She wore pink scrubs and he was assuming she was a nurse.

"Hey," he said, skidding to a stop.

"Geez, Mac. You look like you're running a race or something."

She had no fucking idea.

"Is Lily St. Clare here?"

Tracy scrunched up her face. "Who?"

"She's blond?"

Tracy shook her head. "I don't know who—"

"Jake!" he shouted. "Where's Edwards?"

"Oh, he's up in maternity."

Mac's throat tightened up so badly that he could barely speak. "Where is that?"

"Fifth floor."

He was gone before she had a chance to say anything else. The elevator was too damn slow, so Mac took the stairs, and by the time he reached the maternity wing, he was breathing heavy, his face was flushed with sweat, and when he spied Jake, he nearly lost it.

"Where is she?" he said roughly, yanking Jake by the shoulder.

"Christ, Mac. Calm down. She's with Cain."

Wait. What?

"Is she alright?" Goddamn but he could barely form a coherent thought.

Jake grinned. He actually grinned, and it was all Mackenzie could do not to throw a punch.

"More than alright. It's a girl."

The world just may have gone on turning. The sun might even have kept shining. But in that moment, everything stopped for Mac.

"I don't understand." And he didn't. He was emotionally tapped out, tired as hell, and for the first time in a long time, instead of wanting to reach for his buddy Jack, he just needed to bury his head in Lily's neck and feel her heartbeat.

"Where's Lily? What room?"

"Lily?" Jake's frown smoothed out, and he cleared his throat, pulling Mac to the side. "Draper, Lily's not here. It's Maggie. She just gave birth to a little girl. Lily's home as far as I know."

"No," Mac said. "I was there earlier, and she wasn't home, and I've been calling her and…"

"She's there," Jake said gruffly. "And she needs you."

Cain strode up to them then, a huge grin on his face and two cigars in hand, Raine in tow.

"Here you go, boys. Mother and child are doing just fine."

Mackenzie wasn't fine. Hell, he felt as if he'd just been run over by a freight train.

Raine slipped her arm around Jake, a big grin on her face. "She's beautiful, just like her mom."

Jake clapped Cain on the back, and Mackenzie shook his hand.

"Name?" Jake said.

"We're thinking Kristen." Cain glanced at Mac. "You look like shit." He shook his head. "Why are you still here? Don't you need to be somewhere?"

Mackenzie nodded and backed up.

Yeah, he needed to be somewhere…he needed to be somewhere like yesterday.

Chapter 30

Lily heard her cell ring for the tenth time.

Or maybe it was the twentieth—she'd given up counting after the fifth. She knew it was Mackenzie, but she didn't have the heart to talk to him. Not on the phone.

She didn't know what he wanted to say, but it hurt to think that she didn't at least rate a personal visit. Not after everything.

With a sigh, she got up from her chair on the back deck and stepped off, bare feet landing in the lush grass below. She'd tried to sketch earlier, but her entire world felt as if there was no color in it, and with no color, her creativity was dead.

Kind of like what she felt inside.

As she wandered in the backyard, her hand kept drifting to her stomach. She wondered about the baby in there. It was still so new, so tiny and new that it didn't seem real. None of this seemed real.

But then a slash of pain rolled through her and the reality of her situation was more than clear. This was real.

She was going to have a baby, and she was going to have a baby alone. A harsh, bitter sound fell from between her lips. Wow. Father was going to love this one. It would seem that Maddison wasn't the only screwup.

She thought of the list she'd started, the one she'd left on the counter in the kitchen. The one with *call lawyer* written in bold red ink.

Guess she should get on that.

Black-eyed Susans blew in the breeze along the far edge of the lawn, where two massive oak trees shielded a bench. A shiver rolled over her, and it didn't seem to matter that it was hot and humid.

Lily was cold, and she thought that maybe she would never get warm again.

Carefully, she picked her way across the lawn, and she was nearly to the black-eyed Susans when she felt the first splash of rain on her face. It was a big, fat, wet drop, and she turned her face to the heavens, eyes closed, as it was followed by another. And then another.

She stood there for minutes. Or it could have been hours. But she let the warm rain slide over her body until she was drenched. Until the simple white dress she wore was plastered to her body and her hair hung in wet ropes down her back.

She stood under that summer rain, she inhaled its freshness, and she prayed for an end to the pain in her heart. As the drops began to lessen and slide over her more gently, she knew the pain inside her would never go away.

How could it?

What she felt for Mackenzie Draper was a forever kind of love, and a forever kind of love wasn't something that would just fade away and disappear into the cracks like the water at her feet.

"It's okay," she murmured to herself. "It's okay to feel like this for now."

But she knew that she needed to pull herself together—she needed to do it for the speck of life growing in her womb.

Lily wasn't sure how long she stood on the edge of the property, hands at her side, face raised to the clouds above her, but she knew the minute that she was no longer alone.

Brushing water from her eyes, she turned and gazed across the lawn at a man walking through the rain. He wore a simple blue T-shirt and old, faded jeans. His blond hair was slicked back off his face, and his intense eyes found her through the gloom.

He strode toward her, a straight path from her deck, his long legs unhurried and confident, but as he got closer, she saw the pain in his eyes. The pain and the longing and…

The love?

Mackenzie didn't stop until his arms slid around her, until he hunched forward and drew her into his embrace. She felt his heart beating inside his chest. Ba-boom. Ba-boom. Ba-boom. Ba-boom.

She inhaled his scent.

And his warmth seeped into her pores, spreading throughout her body and chasing the chill away…but not the hurt. God, not the hurt. If anything, having him so close made her heart squeeze, and a sob caught in her throat.

There were no words. How could there be?

His hands slipped into her wet hair and she gazed up at him. She let his mouth slide across hers—a tender kiss that brought tears to her eyes. He moved over her lips softly, gently, and when his hand traveled down her body and settled over her flat stomach, she couldn't help herself.

She whimpered and she tried not to cry, but the tears slid from her eyes, mixing with rain.

Mackenzie dropped to his knees and rested his head against her stomach, and she held him there. She held him for as long as she could stand to, because as much as she loved him, there were things that needed done.

Things that needed to be said.

Things that she couldn't avoid any longer.

Gently, she pushed at him, and then harder when he wouldn't let go.

"Mac," she said, shaking her head, her fingers digging between his arms and her skin.

Something in her voice must have gotten to Mackenzie, and his hands slowly slid from her, to fall at his sides as he knelt on the wet ground in front of her. His shoulders sagged and he looked so damn dejected that she started to reach for him, but then she caught herself in time.

Lily cleared her throat. "We need to talk."

"Yeah." He sounded tired, and she stepped back as he slowly got to his feet. Overhead the rain still fell, but the drops were softer now, and she knew that it wouldn't last much longer.

She waited for him, there with the rain falling over her skin. She waited for him to say something because suddenly all the things inside her were twisted and screwed up, and she wasn't so sure she would be strong enough to push him away if he didn't come through for her.

Mackenzie stared down at her for so long, rain dancing on the edges of his lashes, long hair plastered to his face, that the fear inside her began grow.

Was this an official good-bye?

"I'm not going to say sorry, Lily, because sorry doesn't come close enough. It just can't, but I..." He exhaled roughly. "I can tell you some things that might explain why I am the way I am."

The rain stopped abruptly. One moment there were drops sliding across her face, running into her eyes and covering up the tears that freely fell, and in the next moment, there were no more.

There was nothing but silence, and it was the kind of silence that made grown men shift their feet and look away. The kind of silence that was big and heavy.

It took everything Lily had to hold her ground and listen to him, because she was so afraid that this was the end.

"Ben Draper is the worst kind of man you can imagine. He's a cold son of a bitch who cares about nothing and no one other than himself and his selfish needs." He paused. "And he's sadistic as all hell. He likes to hurt. He likes to break things—doors, windows, and...bones."

The pain in Mackenzie's eyes was vivid. It was haunting and dark.

And it broke Lily's heart.

"You know what you said yesterday?" Mac asked. "About how we're all products of our upbringing? Products of our environment?"

She nodded but remained quiet.

"You're right. We are, and I..." He ran his hands through the wet hair at his nape. "God, Lily, I think I'm realizing for the first time how hard it is to change. Or, no." He shook his head violently. "I'm realizing how hard it is to know that I want to change but not knowing if I'm strong enough or good enough." He paused. "I don't know if I'm good enough for you and this baby."

"Do you want to be?" she asked, breath held, hands still clenched at her sides.

"Yeah," he said slowly. "I do."

Lily let out a long breath. "Then what are you afraid of exactly?"

"I'm afraid that no matter how much I love you, I'll end up ruining everything just like my father. I'm afraid that I'll hurt you, physically and emotionally, and that I'll screw things up and any child of ours will grow up to be just like me."

"Mackenzie," she said shakily. "The fact that you're even thinking of all that stuff tells me that you're as far away from your father as we are from the moon. You're nothing like him. Nothing," she ended hoarsely.

"I drink too much."

"Yeah, you do. But do you drink because you need it? Do you drink because you need to cope?"

"No," he said after a few moments. "I drink to forget."

She watched him carefully. "You don't need to forget anymore, Mackenzie. Not unless you want to."

Mackenzie was silent for so long that the fear she'd pushed away began to pulse inside her. Maybe she'd read this all wrong. Maybe this was good-bye.

Oh God. A sob caught in her throat and her knees buckled.

But Mackenzie was there. He caught her and dragged her close, his arms around her, holding her to him as if he would never let her go.

"I want you, Lily," he whispered into her hair. "God, I thought…"

Something in his voice made her turn her head and she glanced up at him. "What? What did you think?"

Her voice was so low that she barely heard it, but he smoothed her hair back and cupped her chin.

"I thought you'd lost the baby. I went to the hospital, and I thought it was you there and..."

"Hospital?" She didn't understand.

"It was Maggie. She and Cain had a little girl, but for a second there, I thought you'd lost the baby and I nearly lost it."

"Oh, Mac."

"I was empty and I was done, and I knew I wouldn't make it without you. I knew then that without you, I would end up just like Ben." He glanced away. "If that makes sense."

"Yeah," she said slowly. "It does."

"I love you, Lily."

She blew out a long, shuddering breath. "I know."

"You have to forgive me for being such an asshole and for treating you like crap."

"I can do that."

"I promise you that I'll do whatever it takes to make you happy. Whatever it takes to make our kid happy. I can't..." His voice caught. "I can't do this alone anymore."

Mackenzie's eyes met hers. "I don't want to do this alone anymore."

Lily cupped his head between her hands. "I love you, Mackenzie. All of you. The good parts and the bad parts. All of it." She smiled a tremulous smile and kissed him gently.

"We can do this," she murmured.

Mackenzie scooped her into his arms and carried her into the house. He didn't stop until he reached the bathroom. He turned the shower on, got the water hot, and then gently took her wet clothes off. He ditched his and then joined her in the shower.

For the longest time he held her beneath the spray, their heartbeats in tandem, murmuring words of love, words that she needed to hear.

And once more, her world was filled with color.

Carefully, he soaped up every inch of her body, cleaning and massaging and touching. He washed her hair, gently working her scalp with his fingers, until she was so relaxed she fell against him.

"I love you," he whispered, his mouth at the back of her neck, his hands at her breasts. "Holy hell, but I love you."

Lily braced herself on the wet tiles and arched her back into him. "Show me," she whispered.

And he did.

Mackenzie worshiped her with his hands and his mouth. He worshiped her with words that were so sweet and gentle they brought tears to her eyes.

He slid into her, his body claiming what had always been his, and as the two of them rocked into each other, as they came together beneath the warm spray of water, Lily had never felt so loved or content or warm in her life.

Afterward, they slid into her bed, and she cuddled into his side. She knew things weren't going to be easy. God, she didn't even know where they were going to live.

But they were together.

And for now, it was enough.

Epilogue

THEY SAY THAT RAIN IS GOOD LUCK, BUT MACKENZIE Draper frowned when he glanced up and saw the dark gray clouds in the sky.

Shit. Not good for an outdoor wedding. Not good at all. He was in the Jake's old room, out at the Edwardses' place, and for a moment, he stared down at the area rug on the floor. God, how many nights had he spent on the floor, shooting the shit with the twins and trying to forget the horror back at his house?

Too many.

It's all in the past. And for the first time that he could remember, he believed it.

The door behind him opened and he turned, a wide grin on his face when Jake and Cain walked into the room.

"Jesus Christ, Mackenzie. You're prettier than most of the women out there," Jake said with a chuckle.

Mac shrugged. "Can't help it. Good genes."

"Yeah," Jake replied. "Good genes."

The two men stared at each other for a long time, long enough for Cain to chuckle. "Okay, boys. If I didn't know any better, I would think that the two of you were getting married today. Shit, is this what they call bromance? Do you want me to break it to Raine and Lily?" Cain grinned. "Cuz I'm down with that. Just say the word."

"And ruin the fantasies of every woman who looks at

our boy, Mac?" Jake shook his head. "Nah, we'll keep this on the down low."

Cain glanced at his watch and then nudged Mackenzie. "It's time."

Nervous, Mac cleared his throat and pointed to the door. "Okay. Let's get this done before she realizes this is a big mistake and leaves."

He closed the door behind him and paused. "Guys," he said, taking a moment to collect his thoughts so that he could get this right.

Cain watched him quietly while Jake's intense gaze was a bit unnerving.

"You're like family to me, and I just want to thank you for being there, for believing in me when I didn't believe in myself. I don't…I don't think I would have made it out alive without you guys."

The emotion in his voice was palpable, and the three of them drank it in. They stood together for several moments and then Jake cleared his throat. "It's time to do this, Mac."

"Yeah."

He followed his best friends outside, down the back deck and across the lawn. He walked up the aisle, glancing at the folks he loved. The Edwardses. Lauren Black, Cain's mother. Maggie and her son, Michael, and her new baby, Kristen. He nodded to Raine and smiled when Salvatore gave him the thumbs-up.

He stopped when he reached the front row and hugged his sister. He pressed a kiss to the top of his nephew's head and then kissed his mother's cheek.

He didn't stop walking until he stood beside Jake and Cain, his brothers—if not in blood, than in every way that mattered.

Pastor Lancaster nodded and a murmur went through the crowd as everyone stood.

Everything faded away, but the woman slowly walking toward him. Her arm was tucked into Steven Edwards's, but her smile, her focus, was on him.

She was everything to him. His world. His love. His life.

Mackenzie Draper knew that he was the luckiest son of a bitch on the planet because Lily St. Clare and the child growing inside her, belonged to him.

And from this day forward, he was going to do everything in his power to make her happy, because a happy and content Lily was all he wanted.

And dammit, Jake and his mother were right.

Mackenzie Draper deserved happiness after all.

Acknowledgments

This book was a bit of a challenge for me, and there are those who stepped up big time in order for me to get this book done. My editor, Leah Hultenschmidt, was amazing and worked with me right down to the wire—thanks for that, and I am so sad to see you move on! And to everyone else at Sourcebooks who had a hand in this book, the art department, publicity, thank you!

My agent, Sara Megibow, was encouraging and always there when needed. Thanks so much for the emails and phone calls. I'm in a good place right now, and she's a big part of that. Glad to be part of TEAM MEGIBOW!

Again big thanks to the Sirens, in particular Amanda and Lauren, you guys were always there when needed. My TRW mates, Eve, Michelle, Simone, Tiffany, Maureen, and Molly, so encouraging and good company too! Thanks to the "real" Blair Hubber who donated cash to our local support center so that he could "appear" in one of my books! Much appreciated!

Lastly, a big thank you to all my readers! I'm so glad you love my Bad Boys, and I look forward to creating Bad Boys for many years to come!

The Summer He Came Home

Juliana Stone

Sometimes the best place to find love is right back where you started...

Falling asleep in a different bed every night has made it easy for Cain Black to forget his past. It's been ten years since he packed his guitar and left Crystal Lake, Michigan, to chase his dreams. Now tragedy has forced him home again. And though Cain relishes the freedom of the road, one stolen moment with Maggie O'Rourke makes him wonder if he's missing out on something bigger than fame.

For Maggie—single mother and newly settled in Crystal Lake—love is a luxury she just can't afford. Sure, she appreciates the tall, dark, and handsome looks of prodigal son Cain Black. But how long can she expect the notorious hellion to stay?

The last thing either of them wants is something complicated. But sometimes love has its own plans.

"Everything I love in a book: a hot and tender romance and a bad-boy hero to die for!" —Molly O'Keefe, author of *Can't Buy Me Love*

For more Juliana Stone, visit:

www.sourcebooks.com

The Christmas He Loved Her

by Juliana Stone

His best gift this Christmas is her.

In the small town of Crystal Lake, Christmas is a time for sledding, hot chocolate, and cozying up to the fire. For Jake Edwards, it shouldn't be a time to give in to the feelings he's always had for Raine—especially since she's his brother's widow.

No one annoys Raine quite like her brother-in-law does. But when Jake brings home a tall blond thing from the city who's bad news, Raine needs to stop him from making the biggest mistake of his life. Does Raine want this woman to leave Crystal Lake because she's all wrong for Jake? Or is it because she wants him for herself...?

"A heartfelt look into pain and grief and the saving beauty of love. Achingly beautiful."—Carly Phillips, *New York Times* bestselling author

For more Juliana Stone, visit:

www.sourcebooks.com

Boys Like You

by Juliana Stone

One mistake.

And everything changes.

For Monroe Blackwell, one small mistake has torn her family apart—leaving her empty and broken. After her little brother's death, nothing matters anymore. No one matters. And a summer in Louisiana with her Grandma isn't going to change that…

Nathan Everets knows heartache firsthand when a car accident leaves his best friend in a coma. And it's his fault. He should be the one lying in the hospital. And a new job at the Blackwell B and B isn't going to change that…

Captivating and hopeful, this achingly poignant novel brings together two lost souls struggling with grief and guilt—looking for acceptance, so they can find forgiveness.

Juliana Stone's YA debut, coming May 2014 from Sourcebooks Fire

For more Juliana Stone, visit:

www.sourcebooks.com

Surrender to Sultry

by Macy Beckett

Feeling the Heat

How do you stay under the sheriff's radar in a town that prides itself on knowing everyone's business? Leah's not sure it's possible, but she's determined to avoid Colton Bea for as long as she can. Seeing him again would be too heartbreaking—and she knows from experience his bone-melting kisses are way too tempting.

Colt still hasn't forgiven Leah for her sudden disappearing act ten years ago. He may no longer be the hellion he was in high school, but he's still willing to play dirty to get what he wants. And he won't let Leah get away again. Armed with chocolate éclairs, a killer smile, and an adorable niece, he will make sure that this time the love of his life has plenty of reasons to stay.

"This heartwarming tale will pull at the heartstrings yet still leave the reader with a sense of satisfaction." —*RT Book Reviews*, 4 Stars

"Fans will appreciate Beckett's humor and the reappearance of old friends." —*Publishers Weekly*

Welcome Back to Apple Grove

by C.H. Admirand

There's no place like home

Grace Mulcahy thought she'd finally gotten Apple Grove, Ohio, out of her system. Then she's lured back for a family barbecue and spies a broad-shouldered hottie hanging out at the grill. He somehow seems utterly at ease, whether flipping burgers or horsing around with her hellion nephews. Why didn't her brother-in-law tell her he had such gorgeous friends? Suddenly her mouth is watering for more than her best friend's famous pie.

Some fires aren't meant to be fought

When firefighter Pat Garahan sees Grace, it's like a five-alarm bell goes off and he's the one ablaze. She says she wants to leave Apple Grove, but he will do whatever it takes to keep her around. The life of a firefighter isn't an easy one though, and he'll have to prove their immediate sparks can have a lasting chance at love…

"Fans of Debbie Macomber who also like some heat with their romance—along with recipes—will devour this thoughtful series."—*Booklist*

"The dialogue is quick, often funny, and perfectly fitting for a charming small town."—*RT Book Reviews*, 4.5 Stars

For more C.H. Admirand, visit:

www.sourcebooks.com

Once a SEAL

Anne Elizabeth

A hero of her own

What woman hasn't dreamed of what it would be like to marry a Navy SEAL? Dan McCullum is everything Aria has ever imagined—sweet, strong, and sexy as hell. She just never expected how tough the SEAL life would be. Dan could be gone at a moment's notice and not allowed to tell her where he's going or when he'll be back.

Dan has never backed down from a challenge in his life. But this one is his hardest yet: How does he balance his duty to his country with a soul-deep love for Aria? It's going to require patience, ingenuity, and some of the hottest homecomings he can dream up. Because of rhim, this isn't a fling; this is forever...

Praise for *A SEAL at Heart*:

"A beautiful story." —*New York Times* bestselling author Suzanne Brockmann

"An exciting and poignant read." —*Night Owl Reviews* TOP PICK

"You will not find a better storyteller with such feeling for the hearts of our military warriors." —*Coffee Time Romance*

The Bridesmaid

by Julia London

New York Times and *USA Today* Bestselling Author

Two mismatched strangers on a disastrous cross-country trek

Kate Preston just moved to New York, but she has to get back to Seattle in time for her best friend's wedding. Joe Firretti is moving to Seattle, and he has to get there in time for a life-changing job interview. But fate's got a sense of humor.

Kate goes from rubbing elbows on the plane with a gorgeous but irritating stranger (doggone arm-rest hog) to sharing one travel disaster after another with him on four wheels. Joe thought he had his future all figured out, but sometimes fate has to knock you over the head pretty hard before you see that opportunity is standing right in front of you…in a really god-awful poufy bridesmaid dress.

Praise for Julia London:

"London's ability to draw real-life characters and settings is superb…her characters cope with life's curveballs and keep on trucking." —*RT Book Reviews*

For more Julia London, visit:

www.sourcebooks.com

The Troublemaker Next Door

The McCauley Brothers—Book 1

by Marie Harte

USA Today Bestselling Author

She's sworn off men

When Maddie Gardner's boss makes a pass at her, she decides to quit her job—and men. But when the sexy, green-eyed Flynn McCauley steps into her life, she's not sure she can stay away, especially since his brother lives right next door…

He's sworn to win her over

Flynn McCauley never thought he'd be so cliche as to fall for the girl next door. But when he's called over to fix a leaky sink, he encounters the fiery Maddie, and he's a goner. Too bad she seems to want nothing to do with him.

Introducing…the McCauley brothers

Welcome to the rough-and-tumble McCauley family, a tight-knit band of four bachelor brothers who work hard, drink beer, and relentlessly tease each other. When three independent women move in next door, all hell breaks loose.

About the Author

Juliana Stone's love of the written word and '80s rock have inspired her in more ways than one. She writes dark paranormal romance as well as contemporary romance and spends her days navigating a busy life that includes a husband, kids, and rock 'n' roll! You can find more info at www.julianastone.com.